The Ravenwood

License Statement

This e-book is licensed for your personal enjoyment only. This e-book may not be re-sold or given away to other people. If you would like to share this book with another person, please purchase an additional copy for each reader. If you are reading this book and did not purchase it, or it was not purchased for your use only, then please purchase your own copy. Thank you for respecting the hard work of this author.

Other Books by Valerie Gaumont

Brownie Oxford

Brownie Oxford and the Ashland Affair

Brownie Oxford and the Idlewild Incident

Channel Rider Series

Pilot

Storm Chaser

Alliance

Haven

Skyside

Councilor

Other Books

Keeper of the Crossroads

The Perfect Recipe

Rise of the Old Blood

Roses for Juliet

Rabbit

Wildwood

For more information about this author and her works please visit www.valeriegaumont.weebly.com

Chapter 1

I concentrated on the purplish-blue, translucent well of power cupped in my hands. I liked to think of it as a soap bubble, although I knew it made others nervous when I compared the power used to shield with anything that ephemeral. The small mass gleamed with iridescent rainbows and slowly I breathed into it pushing power out with my breath in a steady stream. I expanded the mass so that it spilled past my hands, growing ever wider until the soap bubble was the size of a beach ball and hollow inside, now truly a bubble instead of a blob. Steadily it grew, for now maintaining its round shape. When it was large enough, I stepped inside, the iridescent shield parting like water around me, letting me into it and then folding back behind me, sealing the bubble as though I made no more of an impact than dipping my toe in a really big pond.

Slowly, I expanded the bubble around me making it larger and larger. As it pressed against the walls of the small building, the shape changed. No longer round, my former bubble draped the insides of the walls, clinging to support beams and exposed wiring like a shimmering, almost solid liquid. It flowed around ceiling joists and fit snuggly into every nook and cranny of the floorboards, seeping through the miniscule spaces between the boards and reforming below their surface to coat the subflooring beneath.

I felt my shield reach its intended boundaries and adhere to the surface. Satisfied, I stopped pumping power into the shield and locked it into place, my shielding becoming as much a part of the building as the footings and the roof shingles. As I let the shield go, separating myself from my creation, it pulsed for a moment settling itself. The rainbows became brighter, shimmering along its surface in shivering waves. It grew brighter and brighter until it flashed blindingly white and disappeared. Although the shield could no longer be seen in its entirety, even by me, who still felt it, I knew the others would have seen the flash and know the shield was active, my work complete. Those who lived and visited here would never know the shield was there, going in and out of the building completely unaware of its presence, however now, no shadow creature could pass into the building harming those taking refuge inside.

I sighed and felt the weariness descend into my very bones. This had been a large job, larger than my usual. I grew accustomed to working for those rich enough to live in large sprawling edifices; after all they were the ones most able to meet the fee the Commission set for my work. My only skill in the magical community may have been setting shields, something one scheduled on a construction plan somewhere after the wiring was inspected and before the insulation was installed, but I was very good at creating those shields.

Hence, the large fee.

Still this was quite a feat, even by my standards. In addition to the fifteen thousand square foot main house, there was the pool house, with pool, of course, boat house beside the man-made lake, tennis courts, dog house, what seemed like miles of winding pathways and this final piece, the guest house. I wasn't quite sure how the construction of the dog's house came to be finished first, but thought it might have been considered part of the house plans, despite its elaborate two story design, rather than a greater interest in canine comfort over houseguests.

Luckily, no matter how fancy it looked, the dog house was relatively simple, construction wise, possibly contributing to its quick build out. I still had to crawl inside on hands and knees through the doggie door and sit in the center of the space while being watched by a very curious and somewhat puzzled

Labradoodle, named Swizzle Stick, but at least the dog's relatively large size meant that I could fit through the doggie door in the first place. While I wasn't built like a linebacker, I knew that as a five-foot-four woman, I wasn't squeezing into a house designed for a tea cup poodle.

But the dog house was completed several hours previously. I shook off my exhaustion and started for the door. This was my last bit of work for this particular estate. I knew from experience, that the owners would be keen to have me gone, they always were. Not only would they be eager for construction to resume, but I made them nervous.

I was not one of the powerhouses of the hidden magical world. I couldn't conjure illusions or call lightning. I couldn't call rain storms or even a light breeze to cool me on a hot day. Casting spells of any sort was well beyond my ability. I couldn't do anything showy; I could just create shields. It disappointed me when I was younger. Knowing some of the things that lurked in the darkness waiting to feed on anyone with magic in their blood no matter how weak, I grew up with a healthy dose of fear. For the most part, I learned to accept my own limitations.

The fact that those much more powerful than me, who were capable of important and brilliant feats of magic, still had to call someone like me to layer protections on their house to keep the nasty things away so they didn't *have* to fight them, always made those I worked for somewhat uncomfortable. They compensated by thinking of me as one of the lesser trades. I had the feeling I ranked somewhere below plumber, but maybe above painter.

On a good day at least.

Sometimes, I was fairly certain I was thought of more as the smoke alarm than one of the trades. As in my normal life I worked in the family furniture business, refinishing, upholstering and, on occasion, using my degree in design to actually create new furniture pieces, I didn't mind. It meant that I got to spend my time with the construction crew instead of forced into uncomfortable small talk with the family. The small talk I left to my handler. He didn't seem to mind it, well, with them anyway. He wasn't fond of small talk with me. I wasn't important enough for the effort to pay off, so he rarely bothered. Over the years, the association with the various trades let me add assorted skills to my repertoire, even though carpentry remained my strong point. Occasionally, it came in useful and I always liked learning new skills.

I reached the door of the guest cottage and took one more look around before leaving. Here and there I caught little glimmers of rainbow, like someone was blowing bubbles in the construction site earlier and a few of the bubbles splattered on the support beams. I knew these last remnants would fade by morning and all would seem normal when the construction crews came back to begin their insulation work prior to putting up the dry wall.

The inspectors already approved all of the plumbing and electric and the contractor in charge, the only person from the crew still on site at the moment, was as much a part of the magical community as I was, though I had yet to learn what his specialty entailed. He never volunteered and I never asked. It was considered rude to pry into such things and as he was frequently the nicest on site to me, I wanted to keep on his good side. If any tell-tale residue lasted until the morning light, it would soon be buried under the spray foam they were planning to use for insulation. It was doubtful anything would be noticed.

Satisfied with my work, I opened the door and left it behind. The family was nowhere to be seen. In truth, I didn't really expect them. I rarely saw the various owners on any site except at a distance when they came to inspect the property and check on the progress. Now, they would be even less likely to put in an appearance. It was just shy of three in the morning and corralling the various trades, including me, was what they paid the contractor for in the first place.

The contractor in question was known as Davis. I was pretty sure it was a last name, but in the time I had known him, I never heard him called anything other than just plain Davis. There was never a Mister attached to the front of it or a Mike, Dave, John, Bob or what have you appended either, just Davis. It was another thing I never asked him about.

Davis was standing a few feet away from the building, wearing his habitual scarred work boots, faded jeans and t-shirt emblazoned with his construction company's logo, the company aptly named Davis Construction. In deference to the cold, he tossed an old mud brown Carhartt jacket over the t-shirt. Light spilled from the open door into the night. As my work was finished, I snapped off the light as I closed the door behind me and walked over to Davis. His breath puffed white in the light of the faux streetlights the family installed on their estate near the winding paths connecting the separate pieces of the property. The base of each of those light posts served as an anchor for the shields protecting the pathway.

Davis stood with his back to the light, his face in shadows, expression unreadable. We started the shielding when the last of the crews left for the day around five. Despite working with him before, I wasn't certain how he felt about standing around so long while I did my thing. Usually when he stayed after hours with me we were off site by ten at the latest.

"Sorry it took so long," I told him. The cold stung my cheeks and made me shiver. I realized my coat was still in the car. When the sun was still in the sky, it wasn't cold enough to need it. It certainly was now.

"You look tapped out, Alice," he responded. His arm moved and I saw he was holding out his thermos. "It's hot."

"Thanks," I said nodding. "I could use the caffeine hit." He poured the coffee into a Styrofoam cup and handed it to me. I wrapped my hands around it for warmth and took a sip, finding the brew was already doctored with cream and sugar.

"This was a bigger job than your usual ones," Davis said as we turned and started for the driveway.

I knew Tom Malak, my handler, would be waiting in the car for me there. Technically, he was there to keep me safe, after all much of the time I was moving around dark places where bad things could always leap out of the shadows and my skills generally involved shielding until someone stronger came to do away with the bad things. Malak tended to act more as a delivery man. He brought me to the site and took me home again when I was done, figuring that if I needed something in between, I'd scream loud enough to alert him to potential dangers he needed to deal with.

Not for the first time, I wondered if he'd bother coming for me or let me get eaten.

I worked on hundreds of sites at this point in my life, many with Davis as the contractor though certainly not all, and I had much more faith in him keeping me from being snacked upon by the monsters in the darkness than I did of Malak. Even if his magic turned out to be weak, I figured the contractor liked me well enough to at least hit any monsters over the head with a handy piece of scrap wood, or at least attempt to. I wasn't certain the shadow creatures could actually be hit. With the exception of their eyes, claws and teeth, they seemed only as substantial as smoke. I was fairly certain most of the contractors I worked with would do the same, even if it was just to keep their safety record clean. Most of the time, I wasn't certain Malak even liked me that much.

"It was a long day," I told Davis, nodding in agreement. He didn't seem to mind the extended silence between his question and my answer, possibly chalking it up to my exhaustion.

"I didn't even know you *could* shield tennis courts," he continued.

"I didn't either. This was the first time someone asked," I said honestly. "The chain link surround helped, although I think there may be some sort of residual effect as the shield didn't fade from view as well as the others. It might show some rainbow prisms from time to time depending on how the sun hits it, at least for a while."

"I'll let the owners know."

I took a sip of the hot coffee and felt some of the weariness ease away from behind my eyes. It didn't go far, I could still feel it lurking, waiting to pounce and suck me into the oblivion of unconsciousness.

"I'm sorry you had to be out here so late."

Davis shrugged. "Not the first time I've had to work late. Probably won't be the last." Our breath puffed and dragged behind us as though we were steam engines chugging slowly through the yard. Malak's car, or at least the car he rented, came into view. The gray sedan looked like smoke in the shadowy half-light, as insubstantial as the creatures Malak was there to protect me from. Inside was Malak. His seat was tilted back, his eyes were closed and his mouth slightly open. I was certain that if the car had not been so well insulated, we would have been able to hear him snoring.

Davis frowned and rapped loudly on the window, startling Malak from his slumber as I walked around to the passenger's side of the vehicle. Malak straightened and pressed the button to unlock the doors. Davis turned his attention back to me as I opened the door.

"Get some rest Alice; you've had a long day." Davis told me. His voice was a neutral tone, his face a blank mask that might as well have been chiseled from stone.

I nodded and he turned, walking over to where his pick-up truck was parked. I slipped into the passenger's seat and buckled my seat belt as Malak started the engine.

"Chatty as always," Malak replied, his voice surly. He wiped the sleep from his eyes and piloted the car towards the gate, Davis in his truck following us off the property so he could make certain the gate closed and locked once we were gone. I shrugged, ignoring Malak's comment. The two men rarely spoke unless it was absolutely necessary as they seemed to have an innate dislike of each other. Malak had no respect for anyone who did any sort of job even associated with manual labor and although he never said it, I knew Davis thought Malak was a bit of a tool, and not a particularly useful one.

To keep things civil, they each ignored each other as much as possible, Malak only giving vent to snarled comments when Davis was out of ear shot. For all his distain, I was certain Malak feared Davis' sheer physical strength too much to utter most of his comments where they could be overheard. While both men were the same six foot four height, Malak was thin and wiry, his luggage the heaviest item he ever picked up. Davis on the other hand, had some mass to him and muscles built from labor rather than in a gym.

I knew who my money would be on in a fight.

Knowing the work would more than likely take until the wee hours, Malak and I checked out of the hotel before reporting to the site. Our luggage was already stowed in the trunk and Malak drove straight to the airstrip where one of the Commission's private planes waited. As he drove, Malak complained about the late hour, he complained about Davis, he complained about being forced to go to a construction site in the first place. Apparently, such things were beneath him. As I heard all of the complaints before, I didn't really pay them much attention. Malak may not have bothered with small talk where I was concerned, but he was more than comfortable using me as a wailing wall.

I sipped the last of the coffee and wondered, not for the first time, how Malak came to be assigned as my handler when he clearly despised everything about it. His assignment was, however, beyond my paygrade. The Commission lined up the shielding jobs and offered the ones they thought I was suitable for to me or one of the others. I chose which ones I wanted to accept and they sent me to wherever it was I was needed, Malak at my side to keep me safe.

For this consideration they took fifteen percent of my fee.

I finished my coffee as we arrived at the air strip. The small private jet was waiting, looking as eager as Malak to be away. The rental car was parked in the small lot and we took our luggage from the trunk, Malak complaining under his breath at the lack of assistance in ferrying it to the plane. The keys to the rental car were passed to the single attendant at the small building serving as both airport and traffic control. I threw my empty cup into the trashcan and followed Malak onto the plane. The luggage was secured in its compartment and Malak headed to the back, shutting himself away in the small private space for the rest of the trip. While the private area had a larger seat and more amenities, I didn't really mind as I had the rest of the plane to myself.

"Besides, it's a short flight." I thought as I buckled myself into the seat. "And despite the coffee I'll be asleep soon anyway." The momentary buzz of caffeine was quickly wearing off and I yawned hugely, my jaw popping. I closed my eyes as the pilot's voice came over the intercom to convey the flight's particulars. I was asleep before we hit cruising altitude.

Chapter 2

In what seemed like an eye blink, I was jolted awake by the wheels of the plane making contact with the tarmac. I yawned and stretched, my back protesting having me sleep in such a position and the rest of my body upset with the fact I was awake when it clearly needed several more hours down time. I was still tired enough that my head felt as though it were stuffed with cotton, yet slightly too heavy for my neck. In addition, my belly was rumbling due to the skipped dinner and large energy output.

Outside the little window, the sun was shining brightly. Apparently, it was going to be a glorious day. The plane rolled to a stop and as the stairs were moved into place, Malak came out of his enclosure. I stood up, preparing to retrieve my bag. He gave me a quick once over glance.

"Your hair is messed up," he informed me. I reached up and found my ponytail holder slipped as I slept. I quickly took my hair down; finger combed my long brown locks and tied it back at the nape of my neck hoping I didn't look too bedraggled. We still had to check in with the Commission's local representative, James. I harbored mixed feelings about James. I didn't really like him, but on occasion when I turned jobs down, he didn't pressure me to accept them as his predecessor had, which I appreciated. Mostly, I was just used to James and rarely gave him a thought when I wasn't in his presence.

Still he was an official representative of the Commission, the organization that helped to keep anyone born with magic safe and hidden away from the population at large. I hated looking like a bedraggled mess when brought before him. Unfortunately as I usually saw him both before and after a job, half the time I was trailing some form of dust or debris from a construction site. Resigned, I rubbed my gritty eyes, slipped on my coat, picked up my bag and followed Malak off of the plane. Despite the coat, I shivered. It was colder here, even with the brightly shining sun. The wind whipped my ponytail around and I decided it could take the blame for my disarray if anyone commented. We crossed the tarmac and went into the small airport.

This airport was larger than the one we left behind, but not by much. It was a hub for the Commission to ship people to various places for various tasks, but it also served the local community, providing commuter planes to several small nearby cities. Their normal activity kept the airport from looking suspicious. At the moment, there were only a few scattered travelers sprinkled through the airport, the bulk of them having already left. As time for the next flights drew closer, I was certain the numbers would increase, passengers ebbing and flowing with the schedule. I didn't bother looking at the signs to figure out when the next incoming tide would be. For now, those here ignored us as we moved around the edges of the waiting areas.

James kept his office in one of the back corridors and I followed Malak towards one of the security doors blocking off the corridor from the main space. Malak flashed a plastic card at the electronic scanner and the door clicked open. We stepped inside and once the sound proofed exterior door was closed and locked behind us, Malak opened the second sound proofed door located two paces further down the corridor.

I winced at the sound of the loudly voiced argument echoing off of the hallway's hard surfaces and Malak and I hurried through the second door, closing it quickly behind us in case the single layer of sound proofing wasn't enough to dull the raised voices and keep them from spilling into the public space.

"Bradford's back," Malak told me unnecessarily. I nodded having already identified the voice of the person arguing with James. Like James Rutherford, Bradford Augustus Addison, IV was from one of the powerful mage families. They consistently produced strong magic users with multiple talents and each sometime in the distant past had an ancestor or two who accumulated and managed to keep a great deal of wealth so that the current generation had little to do in the work-a-day world.

Unlike James, who claimed the Commission worked tirelessly to maintain order, and rule both effectively and judiciously, Bradford disliked the Commission as a whole. He didn't like the Commission's rules and regulations; he didn't like privileges they received and most of all he didn't like the fact that he was not born to one of the families destined to inherit a seat on the Commission. 'It is time for new blood,' had become his battle call, a call which was taken up by many likeminded people of similar families who, like the Addison Clan, weren't quite established enough to boast a seat on the Commission.

That was of course the injustice they most wanted to change.

As far as I could tell it was the only difference in their policies and politics, although they frequently liked to claim otherwise. Of course, no one was asking me. The Appleton Family tended to produce people like me with only one talent each and a tendency to go into either the trades or academics. For every carpenter and electrician we boasted, we claimed an equal number of professors, usually of ancient history or linguistics. My cousin Sean and I, currently the only two remaining members of the once large Appleton Clan, learned both Latin and Ancient Greek while learning how to make dove tailed joints and rewire lamps. None of these family facets earned us either seats on the Commission or ranked just below those destined for seats and determined to change the system.

Not that I particularly liked the system.

Like James, I was mostly used to it and didn't think the other group planned on changing more than the house sigils on the Commission's roster if they did manage to take power. I was certain that any issues I or anyone like me for that matter, raised with the way things operated would be deemed too insignificant to bother addressing and the world would go on as it had before.

Malak and I approached the office, the sound of the voices getting louder the closer we came to the source. Finally, we pushed the main door open and stepped into the office's reception area. Marcie, James Rutherford's secretary, was typing at her computer and doing her best to pretend not to hear the argument issuing from her boss's inner sanctum. She looked both relieved and resigned by our arrival. Knowing why we were there, she stood up from her chair.

"I'll let him know you are here," she said. Bravely, she turned to the office door and entered into the fray, closing the inner office door behind her. The voices behind the door quieted and moments later the door was flung open as Bradford strode into the waiting area. His color was high from his argument making his pale skin actually resemble something other than uncooked bread dough. The knot in his tie had even come slightly askew, which was the most out of sorts I had ever seen Bradford. Normally he resembled a cut out from a men's clothing advertisement, albeit one that specialized in high end expertly tailored suits. He straightened his tie and looked in our direction.

Spotting me, he sneered. "Ah, the blind, imperialist dupe returns from doing the bidding of her masters," He said. "Run along so you can report in."

Normally, I simply ignored people like Bradford, letting whatever comments they spewed roll off me. Nothing I said would really change his attitude anyway. Early on I tried questioning policy with people like him and grew tired of hitting my head on that particular brick wall. Today I was tired, hungry and Bradford was delaying me getting both food and sleep. It was my only excuse for not keeping my mouth shut, even though I knew better.

"And what would you have me do if you were in charge?" I asked before I could stop myself.

"I would have you shield those who truly needed it," He declared. I watched him march to the bookshelves and pull one of the booklets listing the shielding regulations from the available stack. He tossed the regulations at me and I caught it on reflex, pleased it hadn't actually hit me in the nose. It was a close call though and I could see Bradford knew it and didn't really care. In fact he looked almost upset by the lack of collision.

"Then why aren't you yelling at the people who make the rules rather than the one who just enforces them?" I asked, irritated as I lowered my hand.

His face colored with embarrassment, crimson staining his cheeks. "Ignorant fool," he hissed at me before stalking to the main door and flinging it open, making a dramatic exit.

"I thought I was an imperialist's dupe," I called after him. The door slammed shut behind him. Beside me Malak sighed and shook his head. I really didn't need his condemnation. I knew I should have kept my mouth shut. People like Bradford could make things very unpleasant for me with very little effort.

"Because if he tried speaking to the actual Commission like that, he'd be up on charges of sedition and he knows it," James said from the doorway of his office answering the question Bradford ignored. Marcie resumed her place, clicking away on her keyboard as though the rest of us didn't exist. "I'm a much safer option for venting his spleen."

"He certainly was in a mood, Mr. Rutherford," Malak said differentially. Listening to him, I thought Bradford might have miscalculated as to which one of us was the imperialist in residence's dupe.

Even though we were both told to call him James when he took this position, neither of us ever did so to his face and he never corrected the use of his surname. At this point I had perfected the art of not actually using his name at all when in his presence referring to him as neither Mr. Rutherford nor the more familiar James. Not that I usually spoke in his presence. James beckoned us both into his office. I followed behind Malak, still holding the booklet of rules and regulations Bradford hurled at my head, even though both of us left our luggage in the waiting area. I knew we wouldn't be gone long and I doubted Marcie would let people run off with the bags.

"He certainly was," James replied as he settled himself behind his desk. Dressed in a three piece, pin striped suit, thinning brown hair still showing the teeth marks of his comb, James looked like a stereotypical banker behind his giant mahogany desk. "One of his compatriots wanted shielding, but didn't meet the requirements. The apartment he is renting may have a tony address, but it isn't owned by anyone in the magical community and most of his neighbors are regular people, wealthy of course, but not part of the magical community."

I nodded knowing ownership of the property was the first requirement the Commission had on their list. I didn't need to look at the booklet in my hand to know there was no way Bradford's friend was going to get the Commission to break it.

"Even if he had met the requirements of course," James continued. "He wasn't willing to pay the fee, apparently believing the Commission should just give shields to him because he wanted it and comes from a powerful family. Said friend complained to Bradford, Bradford came here. I'm sure you heard enough of the rest."

James slipped on a pair of reading glasses, which only increased the banker-ly image, and turned to his computer screen. He tapped a few keys, using only his two index fingers and smiled when the information he wanted came on the screen. While watching him hunt and peck, I wondered who wanted me, or others like me to not only ignore the rules, but to work for free.

"There we are, the Fausti job. Any complications?" James asked.

"None," Malak answered.

I wondered if he would have noticed if any complications had occurred as he spent most of his time in the car either listening to audio books or sleeping. Although Malak liked to say he listened to various historical treatise and books about war to pass the time, I knew from overheard snippets that he alternated between self-help books and trashy romance novels.

I tried not to judge.

Well, at least not out loud.

Personally I didn't care what he listened to, but found it absurd that he lied about it when he knew I could see the covers of his audio books as well as overhearing bits of the text from time to time. I didn't think most history books were concerned with the inner you or used words like throbbing and smoldering quite as often as Malak's books. I could be wrong of course; perhaps Alexander the Great's secret to empire building lay in the smoldering looks he favored on his generals before battle.

"Excellent," James responded, not even looking at me. He poked a couple of more keys, frowned at the screen and poked a couple more. He nodded in satisfaction. "Ah, larger job that explains it." Through the still open door I could hear the sound of a printer. Moments later Marcie walked in, handed James two sheets of paper and walked back out. James signed each and slid them across his desk to me.

"As usual, the fee was deposited into your account electronically. It is larger than usual, given the size of the job of course." I nodded and scanned the sheet, familiar with the procedure. The sheet was my receipt and my proof that the council owed me money should the fee not appear in my bank account as promised. I started taking shielding jobs for the commission at the age of twelve, saving up the early payments to pay for college, and while there were many things I could say about the commission, delinquent in payment wasn't one of them. At thirty-two, twenty full years after my first job with them, I knew the payment would be fully accredited to my bank account before I even made it home.

I signed both copies, left one on the desk and slipped the other in the back of the rules and regulations booklet I still held. When I got home, I would file it with the other similar receipts. I liked to keep my records straight.

"I see you got the updated codes," James said, gesturing to the booklet. "Good. Not much has changed, but a refresher is always useful. Glad to see you are keeping on top of it." James crossed his hands in front of him on the desk, fingers laced together, thumbs pressed against each other to form a steeple above; his signal that our time with him was over. Malak turned and walked towards the door. I followed and we reclaimed our luggage before leaving.

Instead of returning to the main terminal, we took the back exit, going through two entirely different sound proofed doors at the end of a corridor running the opposite direction from the gates. This one left us in a secured parking lot when we exited the building. I followed Malak to his black SUV and we placed our luggage in the trunk. Once again I took the passenger's seat and Malak piloted us through the security gates and onto the highway. Malak was silent as he completed his final task on the 'keep Alice safe' detail, namely dropping me off at my apartment building. From there, I was, of course on my own.

Used to his silences, I concentrated on not falling asleep in my seat. Luckily it was a short drive, Malak soon leaving me, my luggage and my new copy of the rules and regulations at the main door to my apartment building. He drove away without a word and I entered the building, happy to be out of the cold wind. Normally, I would have gone for the stairs, today I was tired enough to take the elevator. Oddly enough the elevator smelled of charcoal and barbeque sauce.

"That's new," I said as the doors dinged open, letting me out on the third floor. The elevator smelled of lemon scented cleaner when I left and it was a bit late in the season for cook outs. The pool in our complex had been covered for at least a month. As I rolled my small bag towards my apartment door, my stomach rumbled. I debated food vs. sleep as I dug out my keys and opened the door. A flurry of excited barking greeted my arrival and Winston, my overly enthusiastic dog rushed to welcome me home. Despite being half English Staffordshire and half American Pit bull, Winston believed himself to be more of the Yorkshire terrier scale and frequently bowled me over with his overly enthusiastic greetings. I braced myself as his weight plowed into my knees and although I dropped both the booklet and the handle to my luggage, I didn't fall over.

"Yes, yes I see you," I told Winston who gave up barking so he could lick instead. "I was only gone a few days not a few months. You make it sound like I was trekking the Sahara."

"Don't let him fool you," A voice said from the hallway leading to the bedrooms. I looked up to see Sean amusedly watching my homecoming extravaganza. "We went for a nice long run in the park this morning and not only has he eaten, but he managed to completely destroy that rawhide bone thing you got him last week."

I laughed and shook my head. "That didn't take long did it?" Satisfied with his greeting, Winston left me, crossing the living room and going to the edge of the kitchen. He lay down next to his empty food bowl and rolled his eyes up to look at me while letting loose a pathetic sounding whine. "I'm not falling for that trick," I told him. "I know Sean didn't abuse or starve you while I was gone."

"So how did it go?" Sean asked as I shucked off my coat and tried to force it into our overstuffed coat closet. Sean, my cousin, business partner, best friend and roommate, settled himself on the couch watching my fight. I succeeded in wrangling a hanger and forcing my coat between a large puffy coat Sean liked to wear skiing and the wool trench coat I wore when I actually had to look nice in the cold. Feeling triumphant when the closet door managed to shut again, I moved to the kitchen to make a peanut butter sandwich, figuring something in my belly before sleep would be a good plan. The suitcase and booklet I left where they were for the time being.

"You mean how was my excursion as a blind imperialistic dupe?" I opened the bread, took two slices and put the bag back on top of the fridge.

"Or maybe an ignorant fool, I'm not sure what the final call was. Bradford was in the office when we got back." I explained.

"Ah," Sean replied, not needing more of an explanation.

"The job went well though, larger than usual so I was paid more," I continued as I spread a thick layer of peanut butter on one slice of the bread. "I learned I could shield tennis courts, so if anyone is attacked during a doubles match they will be fine no matter which of the two courts they are playing on."

"Always handy," Sean replied as I decided to add strawberry jam to my sandwich, making it a PB and J instead of just a peanut butter sandwich.

"I'm also pretty sure Malak finished *becoming the Man You Always Knew You Could Be* and moved on to *Ensnared by Passion*. The woman on the cover of that one had quite impressive breasts." I returned the jam to the fridge, poured myself a glass of milk and took the milk and plate containing my sandwich back to the living room. I placed them on the coffee table while I sat down in the arm chair across from Sean.

"Heaving bosom," Sean said.

"Excuse me?" I took a bite of my sandwich and felt the rumblings in my tummy quiet.

"I don't think they are referred to as impressive breasts. That would be tacky. If they are on the cover of a romance novel, it is referred to as a heaving bosom. It's classier that way."

"Well, I would hate to be tacky," I told him with a laugh.

"That's why I'm here, to uphold the classy level of our family."

"I thought it was because this apartment is within walking distance of the shop and neither of us has ever gotten motivated enough to look at buying our own houses?" I replied.

"That's just my cover story. Oh and speaking of the shop, Gracie stopped in while you were gone because you weren't answering your phone. I told her you were personally overseeing the delivery of a special order. I left out any other details, figuring you could add your own if you wanted."

"Thanks," I replied. Gracie was a friend I made in college and while she was a close friend, she knew nothing of the magical world or my extra abilities. This was hardly the first time we used the 'supervising a delivery' line. "I appreciate the cover story."

"No sweat. She was very eager to see you though. Apparently there is some sort of auction coming up she wants you to attend. I told her you'd be back Monday if she wanted to stop by,"

"Ah," I said nodding. "I mentioned that we were running out of space here and were either going to have to do a mass clear out or start looking at houses. She decided that because I routinely build things and have conversations with various tradesmen; a foreclosure auction would be the perfect solution. I'm guessing she found one."

"A foreclosure auction?" Sean asked frowning.

"Yeah, I think she saw it on one of those home improvement shows she likes to watch and she thought it was a good idea."

"That seems overly ambitious, *especially* for her." Sean said with a laugh.

I nodded. While Gracie had a keen eye for design, mostly used for exquisitely designed marketing campaigns, handing her any sort of tool meant that in very short order you would be making a trip to the emergency room. "I think she likes the concept of making a home completely your own from the bare bones up as well as the recycling aspect and thinks I have the skills to pull it off."

"I've seen those shows," Sean said thoughtfully. "It actually might be less risky for you since you wouldn't be trying to flip it for a profit."

"Don't encourage her," I told him. "Since we are speaking of the shop though, why are you home at this time of day anyway? Shouldn't you be chatting up designers and managing the website and workforce?"

"You do realize it is Sunday and that we are closed on Sundays?"

"Is it?" I shook my head. "I always get so mixed up when the crews work weekends." I shrugged. "That does explain the lack of commuters at the airport though. Well, at least I won't feel bad taking an extended nap once this sandwich is done. I didn't get finished until about three this morning."

"Ouch, was the hunky contractor there this time?" Sean fluttered his eyelashes at me and I frowned. Once, over martinis, I confessed to having a little crush on Davis and Sean never let me forget it.

"Davis was there," I told him, finishing off my sandwich. "Didn't you have a date with a fireman while I was gone? Shouldn't that have maxed out your man candy limit?" I reached for my milk as Sean rolled his eyes and heaved a long suffering sigh.

"Jacob. It was a complete trip to Dullsville with side trip to Boring Town for good measure. We were a total mismatch and now of course my fireman fantasy is ruined. Now when I try to bring it to mind, all I hear in my head is Jacob droning on about how many pounds he can bench press and the health benefits of protein shakes."

I laughed, finished my milk and took my plate and glass to the kitchen. "Did you at least make a dirty joke about protein shakes," I asked, knowing my cousin.

"Of course. He frowned and told me nutrition was serious business and then proceeded to point out all the bad choices heaped on my plate as compared to his own. Speaking of which, we went to that new restaurant that just opened up down on fifth, *Celeste*. Really good food and the prices weren't bad. My pork chop had some sort of Calvados and ginger glaze or sauce or something that I could guzzle by the bucketful if they'd let me and even Jacob's plain-jane steamed fish with steamed veggies looked pretty good. Admittedly, it probably would have looked better if he hadn't asked them to put the sauce on the side."

"I'll have to give it a try then," I told him. I rinsed off my dishes and left them in the rack to dry. I yawned hugely. Now that my belly was full, my exhaustion was rising. I was fed and it was time for sleep. I had one final question though and while relatively unimportant I knew it would nag me if I didn't ask.

"Do you know what's up with the charcoal smell in the elevator," I asked as I rubbed my eyes and started towards my bedroom.

"Mark was trying to get one last barbeque in before the really cold weather kicked in. There was some sort of mishap as he was taking all of the elements down to the rec area. Poor guy was shivering the whole time. He looked miserable and despite the tinfoil he put over the plate, everything had to be ice cold by the time he got it back upstairs."

"Let me guess," I said, thinking of our twenty-two year old neighbor and the group of people he usually had flocking about him. "His band of cohorts refused to eat by the covered up pool?"

"You got it," Sean told me.

"Well at least I won't stay up wondering about the elevator's new scent, thanks," I told him. "See you in a few hours."

I left Sean in the living room and headed to my bedroom. I quickly stripped off my clothes, leaving them in a heap on the floor and pulled on an oversized t-shirt to sleep in. I slipped beneath the covers, pleased to be surrounded by the scent of my fabric softener instead of the industrial detergent the motel favored. As I settled, I remembered my suitcase standing next to the front door.

"I should get that," I thought. Instead, I closed my eyes and let sleep claim me.

Chapter 3

When I woke up the angle of the sun had changed. The sun fell in thick bands through the open curtains looking almost solid and for a moment, I imagined it was summertime and that outside it was warm as well as light. I knew however that bright cloudless days usually meant that the temperature outside would be downright frigid. I felt better for my sleep, but knew that with little effort, I could sink back into slumber.

"And then tomorrow would be hell when I had to get up on time," I reminded myself knowing I needed to get back into routine. We had a large order going out this week. While I knew the basic furniture the boutique hotel wanted would be ready, the bulk of it being knocked out before I left, I still had to finish the unique, stand-out piece they wanted for their lobby. The drawings had been approved, materials ordered and work begun. In fact the only reason I felt comfortable leaving for the Commission's job was because several of the pieces that comprised the lobby's showstopper needed to sit in clamps while the glue dried completely before I continued the assembly and finishing process.

"Everything should be ready to continue tomorrow morning," I told myself. I stretched and forced myself to leave the bed. A shower and clean clothes made me feel better about being awake. I headed into the living room and found Sean seated on the couch reading through the new list of regulations Bradford chucked at my head. My suitcase had been wheeled out of the way and Winston was chewing on a large rawhide bone.

"I thought he finished the bone," I said pausing to rub Winston's head before taking a seat in the living room. Winston snorted at me and then went back to his toy.

"He did, I picked up another one when I ran out," Sean said, frowning at the regulations without looking up.

"Thanks," I replied. "Something have you concerned?" I gestured to the regulations booklet.

"You know I never really read these," he told me. "I mean they were always around since you've been taking jobs since we were kids and I always thought it was cool that you could make shields to keep the monsters out, especially after seeing them first hand."

Sean absently ran a hand over the small scars on his left arm. With time they faded and merely looked like light lines drawn over his skin rather than the claw marks left behind by some shadow creature craving the taste of his blood. I knew he sometimes still had nightmares about the attack; not as many as he once did, but still they occurred. Sometimes I still had nightmares too. It wasn't something we discussed.

"And I always thought that getting people to agree with you was a nifty trick," I countered, pretending I didn't notice his subconscious attention to the scar.

"It did make my time as a trial lawyer quite profitable, but also quite boring," He said with a weak smile as he looked up from the booklet. Sean finished top of his class in law school and sailed through his bar exams. His one magical talent meant that when he argued in court, everyone agreed with him, including the opposition, jury and judge. Essentially, he was a lawyer who couldn't lose. It didn't take long for people to start to notice. He was paid quite well by those who hired him until his brief career as a star attorney was brought to a close.

The Commission pointed out that he was gaining too much notoriety and people were beginning to question his uncanny ability to win cases. Unfortunately, Sean's gift only worked on those without magical ability of their own and Sean was unable to convince them to let him continue. He switched to contract work instead and when our grandfather became sick, began putting in more time with me at the shop, eventually the two of us running it together. While Sean still maintained an office in the one story building next to the shop and occasionally worked on legal matters not related to the business, the bulk of his work was for Appleton Furniture. He claimed not to miss it, but I often wondered.

"These regulations are quite strict," he told me.

"I know," I said nodding.

"Somewhat unnecessarily strict if you want my opinion. I mean, once the shield is put up and all of the other bits are put on top of it, you can't even tell it's there. Yet the commission limits who can actually have a shield put on their domicile in the first place."

"Yeah," I said with a sigh. It was often a bone of contention, but I had long since given up arguing with James over the restrictions. He hadn't listened to my arguments of policy any more than his predecessor, Jeffrey. I pointed out that the restrictions left too many without even the possibility of shields even beyond the actual cost of paying the person installing them. In addition, since they couldn't be seen once they were installed, what did it matter who owned the property? His answers were always the same; this is the way things are, the Commission has its reasons, there is plenty of room for you to work within the confines of the law, and my personal favorite, the restrictions place no undue burden on you so let it be.

"I think it's so they can control the pay scale," I told him. "And so they can get people to move to the suburbs." The restrictions always seemed heavier for those who lived in the city, at least to me anyway.

"They control the pay scale?" he asked with a frown.

"Yup, each person capable of creating shields is tested when the Commission gets a hold of them. Essentially for our test, we had to create a shield for a room and then they had people come in to test it until the shield broke. How long it takes to break and what force it takes to break it, determine your shielding level. The Commission then assigns you a category and tells you what that category's pay scale is. I'm in the twenty dollars per square foot range."

"Oh," Sean said. He looked back at the regulations. "You do realize that according to this, the only reason our apartment has a shield is because you live here?"

I sighed and brought the specific regulations to mind. "Article two, paragraph six, section twelve point four," I began, and then remembered the regulations had just been updated. "Unless they've changed it with this new set, of course. The building in question must be the sole property of a member of the magical community, in good standing, in order to be eligible for shield placement. If the building in question is a multi-unit dwelling, each unit must be occupied by members of the magical community or be the sole property of the individual creating, not purchasing, the shielding." I nodded as part of the punctuation. "There are other sections that deal with the sale of said properties as well as non-residential properties, but I didn't memorize them."

"I'm impressed," he told me.

"The rules don't really change much. At least that one doesn't anyway, regardless of Bradford's thoughts on the matter."

"Is that why you are an imperialist's dupe?" Sean asked letting a smile slip onto his face.

"Yup," I replied. "Apparently Bradford has a friend from a *good* family who wants his current apartment shielded despite not owning it or having any of the other requirements."

"And Bradford thought yelling at James would change that?" Sean chuckled and shook his head.

"He probably thought he could get James to bend the rules just for him."

"Of course he did."

"He also didn't want to pay for the shields."

"Sadly, that doesn't actually surprise me." Sean replied shaking his head. He glanced back down at the regulations booklet and then back up at me. "You do realize that we live in a multi-unit property, not owned by a member of the magical community and that very few, if any of our neighbors are members of the magical community either?"

"I realize that," I said. There was a note in Sean's voice I couldn't quite identify. "There is also a section that removes a lot of the restrictions for anyone who can actually create shields. I can shield away to my heart's content if I or one of my family members lives here, regardless of who owns the building or whether or not they are considered to be in good standing. Admittedly, I think they put that part in because they knew they couldn't prevent us from shielding the places we lived in regardless of who actually owned them."

"Sooner or later we are both going to have to actually look at getting places of our own, either with or without Gracie's foreclosure auction. We're already older than most of the people in this building. When Mark spilled his charcoal, he apologized to me, called me Sir and promised to clean it up right away. I think he was worried I'd be the cranky older man reporting him to the super."

I smiled, even though I could see Sean was serious. As Mark and his friends routinely referred to me as either Ma'am or Miss Alice, I understood his pain. While there were many apartment buildings throughout the city where residents lived their entire adult lives, ours wasn't one of them. It tended to attract people in their twenties who only stayed a few years at best. Sean and I moved in when we were both still in university and because it suited us, never really left, watching the apartments around us frequently change occupants. "Then when we get our own places, I will make certain you have the best shielding I can provide."

Sean waved the invoice sheet I stuck in the back of the regulations booklet. "And you think I can afford *this* on top of buying a house?"

"Are you planning to buy an enormous mansion complete with pool, pool house, boat house, manmade lake, two tennis courts, a guest house, a two story dog house and practically *miles* of winding picturesque pathways connecting them all?" I countered.

"Well no," he said with a frown. "Wait, a two story dog house?"

"Of course Swizzle Stick, the Labradoodle, deserves only the best," I replied loftily.

"Now I feel bad for only getting Winston the rawhide." We both looked over to the busily chomping Winston. Sensing our attention, he lifted his head up and looked around. He wagged his stump of a tail when he saw us looking at him, but seeing no edibles in evidence, he quickly dismissed us and returned to destroying his bone.

"Look," I told Sean returning to our conversation. "When the time comes and we both get off our butts and actually look for places to permanently live, I'll get the estimate for whatever house you buy. You'll owe the Commission their fifteen percent. I'll waive my fee." Sean frowned at me. I sighed dramatically. "If you prefer we could get a giant jar and every so often you can toss a nickel into the jar until you've paid off the rest of the shielding cost. Does that make you feel better?"

"Marginally," he replied, the worry easing back from his eyes. "But what about all of the people who can't just pay you on the jarred nickel scale?"

"I don't know," I replied. "I tried arguing with James about it, but he insisted the Commission knew what it was doing." I snorted remembering the discussion. It had been less of a discussion than I wanted. Fired up with a sense of justice, my much younger self wanted an argument where I could fight for what was right or at least have my points of contention validated. Instead, I more or less got an indulgent smile, a pat on the head and a 'don't worry your pretty little head about it' attitude. After countless repetitions of the same with little to no variation in the scene, I gave up trying. I thought of Bradford and my frown deepened. Was he right about me being an imperialist's dupe after all?

"*He wanted his friends to have shields without paying for them*," I reminded myself. "*So maybe not completely right, but maybe not completely wrong.*" While I thought I deserved some compensation for the work I did, Bradford's comment about providing shields to people who really needed them stung. While I loved dogs, I knew there were a host of people more deserving of a proper shield then Swizzle Stick. I sighed, hating for a moment that I was considering siding with Bradford about anything. The thought just seemed… wrong.

"Enough of this," Sean declared, setting the regulations aside. "No more doom and gloom for tonight. What do you say to ordering pizza? We could veg out with grade B monster movies, pizza and beer and do nothing productive until morning."

"That sounds like a plan," I replied, willing to shake off any potential mental alliances with Bradford. While Sean called in our order, I took my suitcase and the regulations booklet to my room. I filed the invoice in the folder with the rest and made a determined effort to put all thoughts of shields out of my mind until a later, but unspecified, date. I emptied my clothes from the suitcase and into the hamper and pushed all thoughts of Bradford into a deep, dark, mental hole before rejoining Sean in the living room for a nice quiet, mentally uncomplicated evening.

Chapter 4

The next morning I got up, feeling more like myself. I was rested and ready to face the day. Winston likewise was ready for normality to return. I pulled on my running clothes, making sure to add thermal tights under my yoga pants, my normal running attire. Somehow I never felt comfortable in running shorts. Even in hot weather I tended to go for the pants option. While I had skirts that showed nearly as much leg, somehow the thought of exposing that much skin while barreling full tilt through the world with a very powerful dog on a leash made me uneasy. Winston had never pulled or dragged me, being quite well behaved on our morning runs, but still if I did hit the sidewalk, I wanted at least one layer of cloth between me and it. Of course with the thermals, today I had two.

Winston waited patiently while I pulled my long straight hair up into a ponytail, once again contemplating a new cut, and did my pre run stretches. Familiar with my routine, he wiggled in excitement as he saw my stretches come to a close. I clipped his leash onto his collar and the two of us headed out. My breath puffed white in the air and I could see frosted dew on the patch of grass in front of the apartment building as we exited. Low fog still snaked along the row of trees planted to conceal our building's parking lot, hovering in the lower branches.

The stretch of sidewalk between the apartment building and the park was treated as both a warm up and cool down for both me and Winston, although I'm sure the dog could do away with the warm up. On that first stretch I could always feel him raring to go, holding himself back while I, the poor bipedal on the end of the leash, got up to speed.

This morning as I stretched my limbs, I thought about the conversation Sean and I had the day before regarding the shields. I knew why Sean worried. An attack by the things in the dark, the shadow monsters, wasn't an easy thing to forget. I was eight when it happened to us. Sean, a few months older, had just turned nine. It was a hot night, the kind where you could feel the sweat gathering behind bent knees even after the sun went down and the air was alive with the sound of the summer bugs.

That night was the community center sponsored 'Movies in the Park', a weekly summer event that caused the adults in our family to haul blankets and picnic baskets to the neighborhood park next to the community center for free entertainment. Along with us, of course, was nearly the entire neighborhood. The wall of the community center, freshly painted white at the beginning of every summer, served as the giant outdoor movie screen.

I couldn't remember later what movie played, because quite frankly I never paid too much attention to the movies. That summer we were just like any of the other kids, as magical abilities generally only kicked in at the onset of puberty unless something drastic happened to give them a jolt. I remembered the cold fried chicken, which smeared grease on lips and fingers and giant bowls full of homemade potato salad. I remembered running around with the other children. Our play was mostly silent so we didn't disturb those actually watching the movie and seemed somehow illicit due to both the silence and the flickering light splashed over the area from the improvised screen.

I could even remember the sweet-tart taste of the icy homemade lemonade we packed in thermoses. The thermoses spent the day in the freezer to make the insulated liner as cold as possible and copious amounts of ice were added before the lemonade was poured in, making each sip cold enough to burn an icy trail down my throat as I swallowed.

When the movie was over, the walk home began. It was like a parade really. The mass of adults, laden with the remnants of the feast and the seating arrangements walking slowly in the evening heat, chatting and laughing softly amongst themselves as we children ran ahead still filled with sugar amped energy. That night, Sean and I fell behind the mass group of screaming children, somehow becoming separate from both the group ahead and the adults behind. We turned one corner as the other kids turned the next. The adults had yet to follow so we were, for the moment, alone on the street.

The shadows took advantage of our momentary isolation and in a heartbeat; Sean and I were surrounded by dark monstrous shapes with long claws, sharp teeth and an appetite for magic infused blood. Their eyes were a dull red in their smoky, half see-through forms, looking more substantial than the rest of their bodies. They filled the space around us, separating us from everything in a great, gray cloud. Sean and I screamed in unison as something bit into my leg and something clawed at his arm. On instinct rather than conscious thought, my ability to shield kicked in and Sean and I huddled together inside my bubble of protection, shivering and clutching each other as the shadow creatures clawed at the shield. Their claws sounded like fingernails on a chalkboard and were nearly deafening.

Although it seemed like an eternity, the attack couldn't have lasted long. The creatures fled as the adults approached. My eyes were squinched shut and the sudden silence their flight left behind seemed terrifying. The family explained it to the non-magical neighbors as an animal attack, a rabid dog running loose, while our grandfather coaxed me into lowering the shields so we could be taken home, promising me it was once again safe.

Later, much later, we sat through a detailed explanation of what was involved with rabies shots and told how we would need to spend the next thirty days complaining about the required shots and how much they hurt. The neighborhood formed a search party to look for the animal responsible.

Unsurprisingly, none was ever found.

I tried shaking the thoughts away as Winston and I ran, putting more effort into the run than usual, trying to shed the icy sheen of the memory from my bones with good honest sweat. Winston delighted in the faster speed, his powerful muscles working hard under his covering of fur and looking like the work dog he was built to be. As we had the time, I gave him an extra lap around the park before we headed back to the apartment.

"That should hold you until you have your after work playtime with Sean," I told him as we began our cool down and I was able to catch my breath. Winston waggled his body in happiness. Sean was awake and sipping coffee when we re-entered the apartment. Dressed in one of his tailored black suits, his artfully shaggy brown hair neatly styled, he looked quite lawyer-ly as he studied us.

"Good run?" he asked.

"Yup," I replied. "I always miss the morning run when I leave town." Winston barked once to remind me his bowl had yet to be filled. "Yes, yes, I hear you," I said as I picked up his bowl. I opened the cupboard and scooped out his morning ration. I placed the filled bowl back on the floor and Winston began chomping with gusto.

"Apparently you aren't the only one who missed the morning run," Sean replied.

"He is a creature of habit," I replied. More than either of us, Winston knew exactly how the world should operate and was never happy when anything interrupted his set routine. Leaving the two of them in the kitchen, I headed back to my room, took a quick shower and got dressed for the day. As I would be spending my day in the back of the shop, predominantly with sandpaper and varnish, my work clothes were significantly less spiffy than my cousin's. When he saw me emerge from my room, he poured a cup of coffee for me. I put a bagel on to toast and sipped my coffee while I waited for the chance to smear cream cheese over its surface.

"So what's your day like?" I asked, pushing aside nagging thoughts about shadow creatures and unfair rules.

"I'm meeting with a couple of designers in the morning, from Garrett Designs. I think you worked with them on a corporate remodel a few years back. Their current project is a resort. It sounds like the usual; standard variations for each room so everything is similar, but not identical, followed by some individual pieces for impact in the public areas. In addition to the lobby, they want something for their spa entrance I believe. They are bringing sketches, which I'll send back to you for final estimates. Other than that, just a few standard meetings."

I nodded. "I'll be in the back most of the day. I want to get the lobby piece for the Alpine Hotel done so it can dry properly before the deadline. I can easily take a break when you need me, although I doubt I'll be company ready." My bagel finished toasting and after giving it the cream cheese treatment I took it and my coffee to the table, settling in across from Sean.

"If they want to talk to you directly, I don't think they would mind walking back into the shop," Sean said. "It'll add that direct from the craftsman appeal to things, provided they don't get spattered with paint of course."

"I'll try to reign in my wild brush strokes," I assured him with a laugh. The two of us finished breakfast and cleared the kitchen. By the time I finished brushing my teeth and finding a suitable coat, Sean left and Winston was settling himself and his full belly in the patch of carpet illuminated by the sun streaming through the windows. I knew that throughout the day, he would gradually shift himself like a canine sundial as the sun moved. I liked to think he spent the day recharging in the sun between my run with him in the morning and Sean's playtime with him in the park. There he would not only get to run and play with Sean, but he would get a chance to play with all of his doggie friends from around the neighborhood.

Sometimes I felt bad about having him spend the day inside the apartment alone, but when we tried taking him to a doggie daycare type place he spent the entire time sitting by the door waiting for us to return. Despite being a normally sociable creature, he didn't even acknowledge the other dogs or people and by the third day, he realized where I was trying to take him after our morning run and refused to be dragged out of the apartment.

Sean and I both put our strength into trying to get him to move, but he managed to slip his neck out of his collar and shimmy himself under the bed before we could catch him. Since then we let him stay at home and he seemed content. As I watched him settle in for his sun bath I contemplated getting a second dog as a companion. Winston liked other dogs, but he never had another one in his space before and I wasn't certain how he would take to such an invasion.

"Problems for later," I told myself, giving Winston a rub on the head. "Be good," I told him as he cracked an eye open. His stumpy tail waggled and he closed his eyes again, giving every appearance of contentment.

"Maybe I'm worried over nothing," I decided as I slipped on my jacket and grabbed my keys. A short brisk walk later and I was in the Appleton Furniture Shop. I entered through the front, looking around to make certain everything was in order.

Sammy, the manager, had just begun opening the front show room. He spotted me and walked over, quickly walking me through the few pieces that sold while I was out of town and the new jobs that came in. As usual, it was a mix of reupholstering and refinishing and he let me know who each job had been doled out to. The larger jobs, Sean dealt with, Sammy only covering the individual walk-ins. I approved of his choices and told him my plans for the day.

"Sean might bring some people by," I warned the efficient manager. Sammy kept the shop running like a well-oiled machine, but didn't do well with surprises. "Gracie also might stop by," I added. "She tried to reach me while I was out of town and Sean told her I'd be back today. I should be in the workroom all day."

Sammy nodded as he took the information in. He was much more of a scheduler than a 'go with the flow' sort of person and liked to know where he could find people when things went off schedule as well as when the possible interruptions to his planned day might occur. Occasionally his need for order made things tense, but usually he worked to rein it in.

I left the showroom as Sammy penciled in the reminder of a possible client visitation onto his calendar and added a post-it-note regarding Gracie. Once in back, I shucked my coat and hung it on one of the pegs by the door. At the moment the workshop was silent. While Sammy always arrived to open the showroom early, I had a little time before the rest of my work crew arrived. For a short while, the workshop was entirely mine.

I took a brief moment to tour the other areas, checking on the progress our three full time employees were making on their work load. In addition to the three, we had a couple of part time workers who came in when we had an extra-large job to do. With the bulk of our last major job complete, their areas seemed rather bare. As everything looked to be in order, I went to my workspace.

As expected, the glue dried on the various components of my piece and I began removing the clamps to begin the process of sanding any excess glue or slight imperfections from my work, wanting a satiny smooth texture to the surface before assembling and staining my creation. As I worked, I found my mind once again drifting to the rules and regulations. In my head, Bradford's voice mocked me.

"Provide shields to those who need it," he said mockingly in my mind. Even though I knew he meant his friends who felt above paying for such things, I agreed with the essence of it. There were a host of people who either weren't in a living situation conducive to having shielding put on their homes because they didn't actually own the place where they lived or because after purchasing a home, they didn't have the funds to pay for shielding, relying instead on stout locks and insulated glass windows.

My family did the same before I grew into my abilities. I could still remember looking out of the window at night and seeing shapes moving in the darkened yard, hungry eyes occasionally catching my gaze. After I woke up one night to find one of the shadow creatures pressed against the glass watching me sleep, I made certain to tightly draw the curtains each night before bed.

No one ever had to remind me to check the locks.

Once I began to shield, I not only shielded the house, but went around the yard, lining the perimeter of the yard with hand painted rocks to use as anchors for the shield. I used Day-Glo yellow paint so I could see them in the dark, at least until the weather wore the paint off anyway. It not only kept the shadow creatures out of the house, but an entire yard's worth of distance from my window. I knew that I was in the top and most expensive category of those who could shield, but even those with lower ranked skills were still pricey.

"And it's not like you can put, 'to add a magical shield so shadow creatures don't attack in the night' to a home loan application," I thought. I didn't know if the Commission had some sort of payment system so the cost of shielding could be paid in installments as I was usually sent

to extremely well-heeled clients. I did know that the Commission provided shielding for some of the private schools attended by only children from the magical community though. I did some work for a couple of those, the Commission offering me a small stipend out of the community fund instead of my usual fee. I waived the stipend though thinking there were better uses for it.

"Still those are private schools for mage children with a hefty tuition attached to attendance," I reminded myself. Neither Sean nor I had attended such schools, in fact most children in the magical community didn't; they were filled with children from the upper echelon of our society. This meant that for us, any after-hours school event required vigilance and planning. Thinking children easier targets than adults, the shadow creatures often lurked around school yards waiting for twilight opportunities. Those in the community moved in groups, chaperoned by adults and each group contained a mix of defensive and offensive abilities. As we grew old enough to move around after dark without adults, our own abilities kicking in, the groups remained.

While Sean's abilities weren't of any use with the shadow creatures, he could talk anyone who happened to see something strange into believing they hadn't seen anything out of the ordinary at all. My abilities with shields gave our group a protective covering if anything chanced upon us, although I was useless with offence. Jimmy Lucas however could cause an electrical spark, similar to that of a Taser, although he had no shielding capabilities and a little sister named Darcy whose only skill was to make flowers grow at an accelerated pace.

Admittedly, she also had luminous blue eyes, deep dimples, an innate look of innocence and the ability to cry on demand; all of which helped when Sean had to concoct a cover story. The four of us often moved through the darkness together. We had a system. I shielded, Jimmy zapped from behind my shields and Sean and

Darcy kept people from wondering what was going on. The system remained in place until graduation sent us all in different directions.

"I wonder what happened to Jimmy," I mused. Since graduation I hadn't heard a word. Despite the arrangement, we weren't all that close, Jimmy being the school's quarterback, Darcy growing up to be head cheerleader and prom queen, while I fell into the art-geek category with Sean as my chess club partner in crime. We worked well together because we all lived on the same block, but it did mean that I attended far more athletic events than I would have chosen on my own. Once proximity was ended, our enforced comradery evaporated.

I frowned at my own thoughts, but brightened as the others began to arrive. Their presence snapped me out of my introspective mood even though I normally reveled in my alone time. Today my thoughts wouldn't quiet and I welcomed the cacophony brought on by multiple projects in progress.

I even welcomed the interruption Sean brought with him mid-morning in the form of visiting designers. Pushing my personal swirl of thoughts away, I explained what I was working on; showing the drawings I made of what would hopefully be the finished product. Luckily, the piece was more than halfway assembled and it actually was starting to resemble the drawing. I then looked at their drawings, asking a few questions and adding a few comments, discussing materials and the final appearance.

"We're looking for a more lacquered look for a contemporary pop of color rather than something more traditional," one of the designers said, looking worriedly at the piece I was working on. It was comprised of several different types of wood, fitted together. The stain I would be using later would serve more to enhance the different tones of the wood rather than cover it up.

"I know exactly what you mean," I told the nervous designer. "For those sorts of pieces we actually have a spray system that is a bit

45

more like what one would see in an auto body shop to paint vehicles." I walked them towards one of the tables that had been through the process. The piece was a solidly build wooden table with classic lines. The designer who brought it in wanted a similar pop of bright color to modernize the piece and so the wood had been sprayed a bright yellow and lacquered with a high gloss finish. The doubtful designer made goo-goo eyes at the piece and I saw Sean smile with approval at my handling of the client. Shortly thereafter he escorted the designers back to his office.

I went back to my piece, finally pulling it all together and adding the final layer of stain over the piece. Once the last layer of stain dried, the piece would be sealed. Once the sealer dried, it would be placed with the rest of the shipment and packaged for delivery. I stepped back, pleased with the overall effect of the piece as well as the fact that I finished it a few hours ahead of schedule.

"Not bad at all," I told myself as I began to rinse out my brushes and put my workspace back to rights. My thoughts once again drifted towards shields. When the time came for Sean and I to each establish separate homes, I knew I would provide Sean with the strongest shields possible, despite the Commission. I had the feeling the Commission, or more specifically James, knew it as well, but would be content as long as they received their customary fee. Sean was right though; there were plenty of others who couldn't afford the same protection.

"I can't shield them all," I reminded myself.

"From what?" A voice behind me said, causing me to jump with surprise, my brushes clattering into the sink. I turned to find Gracie staring at me amusedly.

"Are you trying to give me a heart attack?" I asked, ignoring her question as I picked up the brushes, shook the water out of them and set them to dry.

"I wouldn't have to if you ever turned your phone on," she replied with a smirk. Gracie turned to the piece I left drying and slowly walked around it, admiring the work.

"I forgot," I told her realizing I hadn't turned the phone back on since returning to town.

"Uh huh, you know your phone is off more than it is on?" She gave her glossy black curls a toss as she continued to circle my creation. With the black curls and bright blue eyes, Gracie always reminded me of a life sized china doll.

"I don't like it ringing when I'm with clients," I told her, trying to remember if I even picked up the phone from the charger when I left the apartment. Somehow I had never gotten the drive to be connected at all times to the general goings on of the world that everyone else seemed to have and typically only used the phone to call out, more often than not forgetting to carry it entirely.

"What if they are clients trying to call you?" She asked. Unlike me, Gracie couldn't imagine a moment without her phone. The only reason it wasn't out at the moment was because she promised me. Gracie tended to ignore the world around her when texting or talking on the phone and the workshop was not a good place to do such a thing. After a near disastrous accident involving a table saw, I told her the next time her phone came out in the workshop she would be banned from entry. Luckily the incident shook her enough and she found the workshop interesting enough, that she complied.

"Clients either call Sean or Sammy," I replied with a shrug. "Same for emergencies mostly." I didn't add that even the Commission had grown accustomed to calling Sean when they had a job for me. More accurately speaking, they called Sean's assistant Gina, who passed me the message to call James. While James often complained about the relay system, it was designed to give me time to think about my schedule before James presented a new job to me and to my mind worked quite well.

Gracie shook her head and sighed heavily. "Some days you cause me to despair," she said. "Did Sean tell you I stopped by?"

"He did," I replied, ignoring her comment of despair. Usually I made a crack about extended cell phone usage being responsible for the rise in brain cancer, but today I was glad enough to be distracted from my own thoughts that I let it slide. "You found an auction."

"Yes, it's being held tomorrow around two, can you make it?"

"I suppose so," I replied slowly. I had no intention of buying a house so soon, but figured it couldn't hurt to indulge Gracie's desire to attend a foreclosure auction with someone who wouldn't necessarily break her own thumb when using a hammer as Gracie had done, twice in the time I had known her.

Both times with my hammer.

"Great," Gracie replied allowing her excitement to show in the form of a little bounce. "I got the list of rules from the people running it." She told me. I watched as Gracie rummaged around in her giant purse. I was fairly certain it was larger than my overnight bag and not for the first time, I wondered what she felt it was necessary to carry at all times.

"Do you know what properties are coming up for sale," I asked figuring I might as well get into the spirit of things.

"Oh, they don't generally announce until about an hour or so before the auction what properties are being sold. I'll pick you up and bring my laptop so you can look at them on the way there if you'd like." Gracie handed me the sheet of rules as I wondered about the wisdom of purchasing a home sight unseen.

"Apparently I'll have to go to the bank first," I said as I scanned the sheet and noticed cashier's checks would be required. Mentally I re-arranged my schedule. I could easily put the sealer on my finished piece, run to the bank and then the auction. I figured the auction couldn't take that long and by the time it was finished, the sealer would be dry, the piece could be moved from my space and the next project on my list could be moved in.

"Not too bad a schedule re-arrangement," I said. I looked up at the expectant Gracie. "I'm in," I told her. She grinned. "Just don't expect me to buy something on my first auction out," I warned her.

Chapter 5

When Gracie picked me up for the auction the next day, I was beginning to have second thoughts. After going to the bank and getting the required cashier's checks I realized I was carrying more money around with me than I ever had before. While the funds I carried weren't necessary for my day to day survival, carrying so much money made me feel like a target. Not wanting to just carry the envelope with the checks in it, I grabbed an old messenger bag from my closet. To make the bag look like it was carrying more than just an envelope of checks, I added a note book, a handful of pens, my wallet, keys and a large handful of the individually packaged soft peppermints we kept by the door of the shop for patrons. My bag still looked rather empty and as Gracie appeared I was eyeing my tools, wondering if a couple of screwdrivers might provide an adequate heft to the bag.

"Ready?" Gracie asked. She bounded into the work room looking a bit like Tigger from Winnie the Pooh, a fact enhanced by her faux fur, tiger striped coat. I heard Mason chuckle and shake his head as he turned back to the sofa he was reupholstering. While everyone liked Gracie, she was often a source of amusement as all of us tended to be rather low key while she favored the dramatic. In addition, her accident prone nature made everyone almost hyperaware of her presence when she visited, keeping one eye on her at all times.

"I'm ready," I told her, still feeling a little dubious about the situation. I wasn't entirely certain I wanted a house let alone a house suffering from a potential host of unknown problems. Wanting to know what I might be in for, I spent the previous evening scanning some of the shows I knew Gracie favored and inspired the day's outing. The fact that so much could go wrong with any one house was somewhat terrifying.

"This is so much fun," she told me hooking her arm through mine and guiding me towards the door as though afraid I would bolt at the last minute. Since this was the same maneuver she used to get me to go on blind double dates in college, I guessed she sensed my desire to bow out of the proceedings. She shared none of my misgivings.

"*It can't hurt to go,*" I mentally reminded myself, oddly enough the same thing I told myself on some of those dates. No one was saying I had to buy anything. Attending would be an experience, that's it. It would be an hour or so out of my life, nothing more. A thought occurred to me as I settled myself in the passenger's seat of Gracie's electric blue Mini Cooper.

"You aren't planning on buying one of the properties today are you?" I asked nervously. I had the feeling Gracie buying a fixer-upper would be tantamount to a suicide mission. I could see a million ways in which she would be completely over her head financially, even if she didn't manage to kill or maim herself in the process.

"Possibly," she said airily. Her bright smile increased my fears.

"Are you sure you wouldn't just rather go to lunch?" I asked as she piloted us towards what I was beginning to suspect was certain doom. "My treat?"

"Oh, quit being a spoil sport, this will be fun."

The drive was a quick one and Gracie found a parking spot with ease. It made me think of the three fates, sitting on a celestial couch while they watched the human race with amusement. I was fairly certain I could hear one of them nudge the others, point to us and say 'watch this'. It was not an encouraging thought.

"*At least they'll have to fight over the one eye they pass between them so all three fates can't watch at once,*" I told myself. It was scant consolation.

Reluctantly, I followed Gracie into the building. The auction was being held in an auction house, which I suppose shouldn't have surprised me. Somehow I expected something more courthouse themed. Instead we found ourselves in a warehouse-like building surrounded by various statuary, furniture, jewelry cases and other bits and pieces of other people's lives. The entire building reminded me of when Sean and I had to clean out our grandparent's house after our grandfather died. It had the same smell to it, the scent of dust, dark corners, and forgotten memories.

Gracie confidently led us up to a plastic folding table where a woman with close cropped gray hair sat with a cash box. As Gracie stepped forward the woman picked up the glasses hanging around her neck by a beaded chain and fitted them over her nose.

"Well let's see what we have here," the woman said as Gracie handed her an envelope. The woman checked that Gracie's cashier's checks were in order.

"If you win an auction and don't have the funds to pay for it, your $10,000 check to hold your place in the auction is forfeited," she reminded Gracie who nodded enthusiastically. The woman took the check held for the reserve from the envelope and placed it in the cash box. She wrote down Gracie's name, and gave her a bright pink piece of paper to serve as a bidding paddle. In a flash, she was registered. That apparently was all that was needed. The speed and ease with which she was registered made my stomach flip. Gracie moved to the side and the same process was repeated with me. Once settled we went to join the others in the auction.

The group waiting for the auction to begin was small, maybe eight people other than the two of us. There was one other woman present and the rest were men. Most of the men wore sunglasses so their eyes were hidden. I guessed it was for the intimidation factor or something of that nature as it was nowhere near bright enough to need sunglasses in the indoor space. I wondered if they waited until they were in the auction space to put them on as walking through the auction house with the sunglasses on could cause incidents involving rather expensive breakage. The path from the door to the sign in table was fairly narrow and lined with delicate items. I knew I would find it difficult to navigate with sunglasses on and would probably ricochet like a demented pinball.

As I wondered about their visual acuity, all of those waiting looked Gracie and me over. The eyes I could see looked appraising and territorial. Gracie radiated enthusiastic good cheer at all of them, her attitude undimmed by their dispositions. The auctioneer joined us and Gracie and I were dismissed, all attention focused on the thin, gray haired man in front. He quickly went over the rules and without any more ado, the auction began.

"First property up for auction, three-bedroom, two-bath," he began giving the address and the starting required bid. He let us know the bidding would go up in one thousand dollar increments.

"Do I have a bid for one ninety," he asked. The words barely left his lips when a slip was raised and the bidding begun. The bidding was fast and furious. I found myself watching the people as the numbers escalated. Some had phones in their ears, clearly taking bids from someone not present. Some glared at the others when their bids were topped and all of them looked rather grim. They looked more like they were preparing for a death march rather than buying property.

The first property went for two eighty and the second was brought up. Again the bidding began. I cringed when I saw Gracie bid, but was relieved when she was quickly out bid and the property sold to a grim-faced man wearing mirrored sunglasses. He cracked a smile when he won the property and then dropped back into his sour demeanor as if irritated by his own brief spasm of enjoyment.

After the fifth property sold, Gracie nudged me. "Aren't you even going to bid?" she whispered, clearly wanting me to get in on the fun. She bid on every property but the first, and seemed just as enthusiastic as she was at the start, despite her bids being quickly trumped.

"Sure," I told her trying to get into the spirit of the thing. I doubted my bid would win, especially if I put it in early since everyone else seemed so determined. My ears perked up as I heard the auctioneer call the next property. It was an eight unit apartment building located on a street a few blocks from where I lived, although I couldn't bring the building to mind. For some reason the regulations popped into my mind. As someone capable of creating shields, I could, in theory, buy an apartment building, shield it and rent it out to whoever I wanted. I decided I would try my hand at bidding on this property. The attempt might at least silence the mocking voice of Bradford in my head for a little while, soothing my conscience, as well as making Gracie happy, even if my bid was immediately trumped.

The auctioneer finished his spiel and opened up the bidding. I raised my slip of paper to start the bidding. "A bid from number 138," he said reading the number off of my bidding slip and acknowledging me. He called for other bids. There were none. My heart plummeted into my stomach. Silence ruled the group. No one moved, lest a stray twitch be determined as interest.

"Going once, going twice," he paused. No one spoke. "And sold to number 138. Next we have a four-bedroom, three-bath," he continued with barely a breath between the sale of the apartment building to me and the next house up for auction. I stood dazed as the auction progressed. Beside me, Gracie nearly vibrated with excitement, her thrill encouraging her to bid more, even though she was continued to be out bid.

"*I bought an apartment building,*" I thought to myself, paying little attention to Gracie or the rest of the auction. I blinked feeling dazed. "*Dear God.*"

The auction ended, Gracie having bought nothing. She followed me over to the table where the short-haired woman congratulated me on my purchase and took my money. I signed papers, she signed papers and in less time than I thought reasonable, Gracie and I were heading out of the door, property officially mine. Gracie waited until we were in her car before her verbal explosion began.

"Oh my God, that was so exciting," she gushed. "I can't believe you got a building, and for so little," she continued.

"I can't believe no one bid against me," I said. "I wonder what's wrong with the building."

Gracie shrugged, enthusiasm undimmed. "Maybe it's just because it is an apartment building and they are house flippers," she suggested. "I'm sure nothing's wrong with it. Do you want to go over there now?"

"We might want to swing by the shop and pick up a few things first," I told her. "Like maybe a flashlight and a drill to get through the front door lock and maybe a new lock to replace the one we'll have to take out." The foreclosure auction sold the properties, but they didn't give out keys to the locks, apparently leaving it up to the new owner to figure out how to get in.

Gracie nodded. "That's really smart," she said apparently believing I knew what I was doing. "And we can tell Sean, you know he'll be super jazzed." I nodded, still feeling dazed by the entire process, worry starting to nag at my belly as I wondered why no one else bid on the property. Did they know something I didn't? What on earth had I gotten myself into? A million thoughts swirled through my brain ranging from the prosaic, like cracked foundations, to the fantastical, such as demons residing in the basement as the result of some sort of satanic rite by the previous owner.

We reached the shop and found Sean talking to Sammy. "Hey," Sean said with a grin. "We found a buyer for that Edwardian…"

His voice trailed off as he got a look at my face. His eyes immediately filled with concern. Apparently, I looked as shocked as I felt.

"We just came from the foreclosure auction," Gracie told him delightedly. "Alice bought an apartment building. Isn't that so cool?"

"An apartment building?" Sammy asked, puzzled. "What on earth for?"

"An apartment building," Sean repeated. I saw a smile tug at the corner of his mouth and I had the feeling he was thinking of the regulations. "That sounds like it could be a good investment."

"Alice wanted to get a few things before we headed over. Do you want to come?" Gracie said.

I left them to get the few things I needed from the back as Gracie gave a detailed and much more exciting replay of the auction. I picked up a large flashlight, a couple of screwdrivers, a drill and a new lock set from our supply closet. I looked around my workspace and tried to think of what else I would need.

"Possibly a therapy session to confirm that I have gone insane," I muttered to myself. "Maybe a straight-jacket." What was I thinking bidding on a property? I knew furniture, not buildings. Sure, I had picked up a few skills after spending so many years running through construction sites, but not enough for this sort of project. This was way above my skill level.

"*Why did no one else bid?*" I thought as I turned away from my work space and headed back to the front. The thought gnawed at me. Sean decided to join us in our surveying excursion and Sammy wished us well as we piled back into Gracie's car and drove the few blocks to my newly purchased building.

"Not far," Sean said as Gracie parked and we got out. "Easy enough to walk over and check on things." He nodded with approval. I nodded, but focused on the building before me. It was set back a little from the street with two giant oak trees shielding the facade from view. There was a drive to the left of the façade. It was gated off and held a sign claiming the space the gate protected as parking for The Ravenwood Arms Apartments. The gate was old chain link, but secured with a shiny new padlock. A broken concrete path led from the sidewalk, between the two trees and up to the front of the building.

I looked at Sean who maintained his half smile and Gracie who was fairly bouncing on her feet. "Here goes nothing," I said to myself leading them up the pathway to the front door. As we approached the front entrance, the building came into view. The sight was unimpressive. From the outside, it looked like a three story box covered with solidified marshmallow fluff. Regularly spaced windows had been cut into the solid fluff and over the main door was a sign bearing the name The Ravenwood Arms and some sort of coat of arms.

"I guess it comes with parking," I said to myself.

Once at the door, I handed Sean my giant flashlight and as I was given no keys, I quickly drilled out the lock so we could get inside. Unlocked, the doors opened easily and the three of us stepped into the building's lobby. The lobby was, more accurately speaking, a vestibule. The floor was some dark stone covered with dust and looked like it had been installed when the building was first erected. The walls were a yellow color that looked as though they might have started life white, and then spent a couple of decades living with a three pack a day smoker. Attached to the wall, to the left of the door, was a row of silvery mailboxes, appropriately labeled one through eight. Overhead, capped off wires dangled from the center of a plaster medallion. At some point the light fixture had been removed. The wires however looked new.

At the back of the vestibule was a second door, or at least the space for what should have been a second door. My guess was that it was a security feature. The door had however been removed. I led my small exploring party through the open doorway and into the hallway. The hallway was fairly wide. I could probably stand in the center of it with my arms outstretched and not touch either wall. Despite the fact that the lights here had been removed as well, the hallway was bright. Not only was there a large window at the far end of the hallway, but each of the doors leading to each apartment on this floor had been removed allowing light to spill in from their windows into the space providing illumination. On this floor were four openings for apartments. The fire door to the stairwell remained intact. Taking a deep breath to brace myself for whatever I was to find, be it peeling wall paper or a zombie army, I ducked into the first apartment.

I blinked in surprise as I looked around. Someone had apparently been hard at work in the recent past. The interior walls had been taken down to studs. Whatever insulation there was before was gone. White electrical wire, silver duct work and plastic plumbing pipes met my eyes. There was no plaster or drywall on either the walls or ceiling. It was as though the entire thing had been gutted and then abandoned. It felt a lot like the construction sites I visited. As I wandered through the space, I could see that even the kitchen and bathrooms had been stripped, bare pipes projecting, wire hanging and nary an appliance or fixture in sight. I shivered a little, realizing there was no heat in the building.

"Do you think someone bought it and then ran out of money?" Sean asked. "It certainly looks like someone was doing something."

"Could be," I replied, the dazed feeling staring to fade under worry. I had no idea if the plumbing and electric were done to code. I didn't know if they had been inspected or not, let alone passed. I also had no idea how to figure that out.

"This floor is kinda strange, not like the hallway at all," Gracie said frowning at the floor beneath our feet. I looked down.

"It's the sub floor," I told her, pleased I at least knew that much. "The hallway has flooring, this doesn't. The flooring goes over it."

"Oh," she replied. We left the first apartment and went into the second. It was a repeat of the first. The third and fourth apartments were likewise stripped to the bones. We finished the first floor inspection and I opened the fire door leading into the stairwell. It was heavy and felt as though it were made of solid steel.

"Up or down?" Sean asked when we stepped onto the landing.

"Up first," I decided. We went up. Windows were placed so the stairwell was fairly easy to navigate, even without electricity. I could see wires sticking out from the walls where light fixtures would have been placed to illuminate the space when the sun was not available for the task.

While the second floor was also stripped, there were only three apartments. After looking in each, I realized they were larger. The four apartments on the first floor were all one-bedroom apartments; the second floor had three two-bedroom apartments. After inspecting the second floor we went up to the third floor and found one large four bedroom apartment taking up the entire space.

"And this is the penthouse I guess," I said. I added the apartments up in my head and came up with eight. "I guess there are no apartments in the basement then."

"Maybe it is just storage," Sean suggested. The three of us headed back down. While there were a couple of small windows in the basement, over all it was a shadowy expanse and Sean turned on the flashlight I handed him at the door. By its light we looked around.

"Wow," Sean said when we arrived. "I guess we know where everything went." I nodded and looked around. While the open door marked 'Laundry' was empty, bare pipes sticking out of what looked like a fairly new concrete floor, the rest of the basement was far from bare. Against one wall was a row of bathtubs. They were older cast iron and some of them looked as though with a bit of work, they could be cleaned up and re installed above. There were a few heavy porcelain sinks as well, although there were no bases. Closer inspection found a pile of metal legs which had at one time no doubt supported the sinks. It didn't look like there were enough of them to support the number of sinks left behind.

Likewise, there were odd arrangements of cabinets, most in rather rough shape and nowhere near enough of them to furnish the number of kitchens above. No toilets or kitchen appliances were in evidence although we did find the motherlode of doors, their brass doorknobs gleaming in the light from the flashlight. I guessed that whoever was working on the building prior to going into foreclosure saved all that could be saved and hauled the rest away.

"No furnace," I said to no one in particular as I saw my breath foam white in the air.

Satisfied that we saw all there was to be seen, we headed back to the front door. I took off the drilled out lock and installed a new one to discourage trespassers. While I did so, Sean went to the end of the corridor and looked out the back window.

"It's a pretty decent parking lot back there," he reported. "About a dozen spaces with a fence around it." I nodded and finished my installation. We exited the building and I locked it up. I decided the inspection of the parking lot could wait as I hadn't brought either bolt cutters or a replacement padlock. Gracie quieted after our tour, her excitement dimming.

"It looks like a lot of work," she replied. "I think a house would be easier to fix up. Then you could buy pretty things instead of furnaces and toilets." She shrugged. "Maybe I'll get one at the next auction. Do you guys want a ride back to the shop?"

"I think I'll walk actually," I told her, wanting a few minutes to process this strange turn of events and resisting the urge to comment on the likelihood of an essentially abandoned house needing a new furnace.

"I'll walk too I think," Sean told her as well. "It's a nice day and good to be out of the office for a bit, even if it is cold. I'll get the blood flowing before I have to sit back down to the computer."

"Better you than me," Gracie said. "See you guys later and congrats on the building, even if it is a lot of work."

Gracie pulled away from the curb and Sean and I watched her drive away. Once she was out of sight, Sean turned to me and grinned. "I can't believe you actually bought an apartment building. I mean I know from the rules and regulations booklet it is pretty much the only thing you could do that would make shielded apartments available, but I can't believe you actually did it." He gave me a quick, enthusiastic hug, lifting me momentarily off of my feet and causing me to laugh despite my concerns.

There was a note of pride in his voice and I decided not to tell him it was an accident. I kind of liked the idea that someone believed I bought the place on purpose with some sort of idea in mind rather than accidentally bidding on something no one else wanted. It made me feel a bit better about the fact that I had no idea what to do next.

"So what are you going to do now," Sean asked. Like Gracie, he seemed to think I had a plan.

Our quick walk through of the building made me realize how much I didn't know about this sort of project. I decided the first thing I needed to do is call someone who did. "I was thinking about getting in touch with Davis," I told Sean. "I think he might be located somewhere in the area based on the location of the projects I've worked on with him in the past and even if he isn't willing to work with me on this, he might know someone who would be."

Sean nodded. "And you've worked with him enough that you trust him, and would trust his recommendation. I like that better than just the cold calling of contractors for estimates. Besides, he's one of us isn't he?"

I nodded. Like Sean, I didn't refer to the magical community in anything, but vague terms when in public even if there were only a few people out walking at the moment. "He'd know what other contractors were around with the same background."

"Let me guess," Sean said. "He gave you his phone number and told you to call him *anytime* you needed something?" Sean fluttered his eyelashes at me and laughed when I blushed.

"No," I told him. "I was going to call James and see if he had the contact information and if he doesn't then I would just look up Davis Construction. I've seen the logo on his and his crews' shirts enough I could probably pick out the right Davis Company from their website." I thought about it for a moment and tried to decide if the possible ease of getting his info from James was worth explaining to him about my recent purchase or if the website would be a better option.

"I'd vote website first," Sean said, echoing my thoughts. "Less questions."

I nodded. "And if by some chance Davis does show up here to look over the building, you will be nice. No innuendos or embarrassing comments," I warned him.

Sean laughed. "Would I do that?"

"In a heartbeat and without any form of guilt or remorse."

Sean laughed again. "All right, I promise if the hunky contractor comes within my sphere, I will be polite and discrete."

I sighed. "That's the best I'm going to get isn't it?"

"If you want anything better, then you need to learn to date better. If you weren't so dating-challenged I wouldn't have to resort to assisting you."

"I am not dating challenged," I replied. "And even if I were, isn't that one of those pot and kettle things? I don't recall your last few dates going so well."

"That is an entirely different matter," Sean said. The two of us argued all the way to the shop over which of us outranked the other in the world of dating. Once at the shop I made certain the large piece I was working on was completely dry and then had Mason and Cole help me move it to the back room where the rest of the order waited.

"That should be the last of it," Mason told me. He handed me the clipboard and the three of us walked through the space, counting furniture. We each came up with the same number, sure enough, every item present and accounted for.

"I'll let Sammy know," I told the others. I headed towards the front and passed the information on. Given that I knew I wouldn't be able to keep my mind on work for what little remained of the day, I told Sammy I was taking off a little early. It was time to use my internet skills to track down Davis. With any luck, he'd at least be able to point me in the right direction.

Chapter 6

It turned out, Davis Construction wasn't that hard to find. Davis was a fairly common name, but the logo was quite distinct. Their headquarters were even located in town, albeit on the other side of town, which probably explained why I never ran into him during my daily life. Unfortunately, that is where my good luck ended. Davis Construction proved to be a family company and according to their directory employed several people with the last name Davis, but added no pictures.

"And if I call the office and ask for Davis, they are going to ask me which one I want," I said to myself as I stared at the screen. "I guess I could say it was the Davis that worked on the Fausti job."

Having no better plan and figuring Davis, at least the one I knew, was probably still on site at the Fausti job since there was still a lot of work to be done once I left, I thought it might be a decent idea. As my taking off early put me home prior to five I thought I might actually be able to at least leave a message with the company receptionist before she left for the day, even if I couldn't talk to Davis directly.

"At least then I won't worry about it until morning," I told myself as I dialed the office number listed on their website.

"Davis Construction, this is Christy how may I direct your call?" Came a polite female voice.

"Actually, I am unsure," I began, already feeling foolish. "I'm trying to get in touch with a contractor that works for you. I never caught his first name as he just goes by Davis. He was or is I guess as they are probably still out there, in charge of the Fausti estate construction at the moment." I could feel my face color.

The woman laughed politely and I heard keys clicking. "That would probably be Will although in truth no one ever calls him anything but Davis." There were a couple of more keys clicking in the background. "Fausti? Ah yes there it is. And yes, that would be Will Davis. I'm afraid he is still on site at the moment. May I ask what this is in relation to?"

"Yes, this is Alice Appleton," I realized that I didn't know if she knew anything about the magical community and the Commission and found myself tripping over my words as I tried to figure out what I could say and what I couldn't. "I suppose it is in relation to a potential job. I'm not certain if it is the type of thing he would do, but I figured if he didn't do this sort of work he might have a recommendation. It's an apartment building. Anyway could I leave a number for him to call when he gets back?" I shook my head and wished I thought out my request a little bit more before picking up the phone.

"I would be happy to pass on a message," Christy told me. I figured she was either accustomed to receiving fairly tongue tied requests or she was trained to be polite no matter what nut jobs called the office. I quickly gave her my phone number and ended the call.

"And now I feel like a total spaz," I decided. Pushing the thought away, as well as the thought of what Christy would say to Davis when she actually passed on the message, I made a list of things I thought I might need to know about my property, and about owning an apartment building in general. With luck I would be able to use a slew of facts to keep any form of panic at bay.

The next morning, I awoke early and for a moment studied my ceiling. I let everything from the day before wash over me. "Clearly, I have gone insane." I said to myself. Hearing the sound of my voice, Winston padded into the room. I felt movement on the edge of the bed and rolled over to see Winston watching me, his head resting on the edge of my pillow.

"Let me guess, since I'm awake I might as well get up?" I said to him. His stump of a tail was a blur as he wagged in agreement. "Fine, I'll just worry some more if I lay here anyway." To his delight, I threw off the covers, got out of bed and began preparing for our morning run. As the slap of cold air hit me when we reached the sidewalk, I thought about the lack of furnace in the apartment building and wondered how much such a thing would cost.

"Or will I need more than one?" I mused. "Does an apartment building need more than one furnace?" I had no clue. It was yet another thing to add my growing list of questions. The night before it seemed that for every question I found an answer for, three more questions arose. I gave up my internet search the night before after finding my way onto a website that seemed to be designed for landlords. While my questions involved codes and permits, I somehow found myself following several horrifying threads involving situations with terrifying tenants and situations that sounded as though they belonged more in some sort of telenovela than real life. The scenarios danced through my nightmares as soon as I closed my eyes.

Given my early start and my attempt to outrun my own nightmares, Winston and I made several more laps through the park than usual and when we got back to the apartment he flopped down on the floor, giving the appearance of being completely spent. I filled his food bowl and after a moment of contemplation, Winston pushed to his feet to consume the offering.

"That'll teach you to leave well enough alone when I wake up early," I told him.

"Are you threatening the dog with more exercise?" Sean said as he walked into the kitchen rubbing his eyes. Sean had yet to get ready for the day and was still wearing a faded t-shirt and rumpled pajama pants as he padded over to the coffee pot.

"He's the one who wanted to go out early," I replied. I looked over to the clock thinking it was still early as Sean had yet to be dressed and pressed. To my surprise, I wasn't early, Sean was late. "You sleep through your alarm this morning?"

"While in the park with Winston last night I ran into Jake and agreed to meet him for dinner. Dinner turned into drinks and I got in late."

"Jake huh?" Of all Sean's ex-boyfriends, Jake was one of my favorites. Sean had been his happiest when they were dating. Their break-up occurred due to Jake's decision to move overseas and Sean's dislike of long distance relationships rather than personal disagreements. "So he's back in town?" I kept my tone light so I didn't look like I was prying.

"It was just dinner and drinks," Sean said dryly.

"I never said it was anything more." I replied, holding my hands up in mock self-defense.

Sean frowned at me. "Yes, he is back in town."

"Oh," I said in a non-committal tone. Sean looked at me as though daring me to add more. "I'm going to take a shower." I left him frowning at my back and Winston finishing up his morning chow. The shower was quick and I dressed for a day in the workshop. Remembering I gave Christy my cell number to pass on to Davis I turned on my phone and remembered to slip it into my back pocket after checking for missed calls. Apparently the only ones I missed were calls from Gracie, all of which came in before the auction.

Deciding I was too fidgety to sit down to breakfast, I filled a travel mug with coffee and headed into the workshop early. As I walked, I thought of Gracie. She hadn't been as enthused about the idea of the apartment building once she saw all of the work it would require. I found it a great relief.

"And buying a furnace isn't exactly sexy," I told myself. I didn't know how often foreclosure auctions were held, but I sincerely hoped that seeing the Ravenwood Arms Apartments dimmed her enthusiasm for such endeavors.

Due to my early arrival, I not only beat the rest of the crew into the workshop, but I managed to arrive before Sammy. I left the showroom in shadow, not wanting to mess with his morning routine, and headed back to the workroom. While Sammy kept the world of Appleton Furniture running smoothly and could, if pressed, sell ice to Eskimos, if anyone tried opening before he arrived he would spend the rest of the day off kilter. The last time I tried opening the front without him, he double checked each detail three times, looking wide eyed and fidgety the rest of the day and spent the next week coming in an hour early, just to make certain it didn't happen again.

I learned my lesson.

According to the roster, my next job was a simple refinishing and reupholstering of six dining room chairs. Figuring something straightforward and completely within my skill level was a good way to keep the worry about the unknown of the apartment building at bay; I brought out the first of the chairs and began my assigned task.

Uncomplicated was exactly what I needed and by the time I broke for lunch, my mood was drastically improved. Here I was on firm ground and knew exactly what I was doing. After lunch I finished the last of the chairs and moved on to a table for a different client, which required only minor repairs before sanding and staining. The day passed pleasantly and uneventfully.

As I prepared to leave, I felt the need to check on the apartment building, making certain it was still secure. I figured the last thing I needed was squatters. The website I stumbled on the night before had several rather traumatizing threads dealing with the issue. The building was still secure with no squatters, zombies or demons rising in evidence either, so I figured I was doing all right.

Wednesday passed much as Tuesday had and I managed to bang out several projects from the shop's to-do list. The focus helped me push all other thoughts away, not only making me incredibly productive, but keeping me from worrying. The only time I managed to think about the building was during my after work visits to insure everything was still locked up tightly.

On Thursday Sean stopped by to share a sandwich at lunch. "I know you are trying to clear as much off of the slate as you can before you dive into working on the apartment building," Sean began as he handed me the ham and swiss he picked up at the deli next door. He settled himself across from me and unwrapped his roast beef. "We only have the one major job coming up, with the Garrett Designers group. While you will need to oversee the standout pieces as usual, they aren't terribly complicated and all of the other pieces are standard. I was thinking we could see if any of our part-timers wanted to come on full time for a while. What do you think? It would free you up to take care of the building."

Like the accidental purchase of the apartments to begin with, I didn't correct Sean in his assumption that my bout of productivity was due to a slate clearing endeavor instead of nerves. "I know Gary could use the work and the regular hours," I told him, thinking of our part timers. Gary did good work and while he was accustomed to freelancing, he and his wife were currently expecting their first child, so I had the feeling regular pay would come in handy. A thought occurred to me as Sean nodded.

"Gary tends to specialize in cabinetry when he is working on his own," I began, thinking things through. "Even if all the cabinets in the basement can be fixed up and re-installed, there aren't enough for each apartment. If I got him to work on some of those as well as the regular items, I could pay for his hours out of my own funds rather than the shop's normal operating budget if he is interested in the work."

"I'll talk to him about it and look at setting up a separate budgeting system for the apartments," Sean told me.

"And maybe call Kyle, his work is solid and unless he's taken another job, he might be up for more hours on the shop's regular jobs," I suggested feeling better that no matter how crazed the apartment became, at least the furniture shop would be covered. After lunch Sean left to make the staff and budgeting arrangements.

After realizing that all of the pieces customers were waiting for had been dealt with, I went into the back storage area and selected an old hope chest from our stash of random unrepaired furniture. In addition to building and designing my own pieces, I tended to scour flea markets and garage sales for old furniture in desperate need of some love. Once repaired, the pieces were photographed for our website, the sale price listed next to it, and the item was added to our show room up front.

This hope chest had certainly seen better days. Most of the wood veneer was missing and what was left behind looked shredded. The inside was solid though, even if it did look as though it had fought and lost some sort of battle. Leaning in close I could still smell the scent of cedar emanating from the deeper scratches. Once there had been a tray that fit snuggly inside, providing a space for smaller items. It was long gone and would have to be rebuilt. Deciding it would do for my next project, I had Mason help me lift it onto a furniture dolly and settle it into my space.

"Getting rid of the old veneer seems like a good place to start," I told myself. I reached for my tools, as I did, my phone rang.

I frowned for a moment, wondering why I bothered to have the thing on during working hours. I pulled it from my pocket, my frown deepening when I saw an unfamiliar number on the screen. "Hello?" I asked cautiously answering it and wondering who would call me.

"Hello, Alice, this is Davis. I was told you called the office looking for me?" Davis sounded different on the phone than he did on the job site. I wondered if it was his phone voice rather than his calling orders to his crew one.

"Yes, I did actually," I told him. "You see earlier this week I sort of accidentally bought an apartment building," I confessed. There was silence for a moment followed by a soft snort of laughter. I flushed realizing Davis was laughing at me.

"You accidentally bought an apartment building," he repeated, amusement staining his voice.

"Yes," I told him. "I got talked into going to a foreclosure auction and I gave the opening bid for the property and then no one bid against me. So I got it. By accident." Davis was openly laughing at me now.

"I thought I should talk to a contractor and thought if you didn't want to look at the building then you might recommend someone," I pushed on, my cheeks burning as his laughter tapered off.

"Where is your building Alice?" He asked, clearly still amused. I gave him the address.

"It's called the Ravenwood Arms," I added.

"Local then," he replied. "Would tomorrow work for you? I could meet you there around ten to take a look at your accidental building purchase and we can go from there."

Relief flooded me despite his amusement. "That would be great," I told him. "I'll see you there." I hung up feeling much better about the situation, even if I had been laughed at.

"Face it," I told myself as I turned my attention back to the hope chest. "If it were someone else you would find it amusing as well."

Chapter 7

The next day I left the shop a little before ten and headed over to Ravenwood for my meeting with Davis. I brought along my messenger bag, stocked with a note book and assorted items I thought might come in handy, including a pair of bolt cutters and a new padlock in case he wanted to check out the parking lot. The bolt cutters stuck out from under the bag's flap and made me feel as though I were planning on committing some sort of burglary. I had the paperwork proving I owned the building with me just in case I was stopped by the police thinking I was up to something nefarious. When I added the bolt cutters to the bag, I found the peppermints I tossed in earlier in the week and as I walked I ate them compulsively trying not to worry about the possible horrors Davis might uncover.

"I really need to stop looking at that website," I told myself. No matter how disturbing I found the landlord themed website to be, somehow I kept finding myself going back to it. Last night's viewing had taken me into the world of potential sewage disasters. "Really need to stop looking." I repeated shaking my head.

Davis beat me to the property and was standing on the sidewalk, studying the half hidden building while he waited. Since he didn't see me, I let myself study him for a moment as I approached. I had to admit, he was an easy on the eyes study. He turned to me as he heard the scuff of my shoes on the sidewalk and smiled an easy grin. He looked much more relaxed than usual and I guessed it was because he wasn't knee deep in construction and bucking a deadline. I shook my head as I realized he still looked amused.

"Hi, thanks for coming," I said by way of greeting.

"Well far be it for me to resist an accidental building purchase," he replied. "No wonder your message was so vague."

"I was mid-way through the call when I realized I didn't know if your receptionist was part of the magical community or not which meant I couldn't say, I'm the Alice who the Commission sent to do the shielding and then I realized I didn't know your first name and your website listed a lot of Davis men it its registry so I sort of got a mental kink." I explained.

"I see," he replied, still looking amused.

"I hope I didn't sound like too much of a spaz," I added.

"Nope," he assured me. "Just vague."

"Good."

"Shall we see what you got yourself into?" he asked, gesturing to the front door.

"Sure," I replied turning towards the door and pulling the keys out of my pocket. The bag with the bolt cutters swung around and smacked me in the back. Davis grabbed the protruding handle and slowly extracted the tool from the bag. He looked at me quizzically. "The lock on the gate to the parking lot isn't mine," I explained. "I was going to remove it and replace it with one I have the keys to."

"Ah," he said looking like he was holding in a laugh. "I'll set them down inside the door and we can get them after we have a look around then."

"It's not that funny," I told him as I continued towards the door. "I needed bolt cutters, so I brought bolt cutters." I unlocked the front door.

"In a messenger bag," he added clearly still amused. I ignored the comment and led him inside. Once in the door, Davis let his amusement fade and I could see his eyes start to appraise the building around him. We moved through the vestibule and into the hallway, Davis studying things as we moved. He crouched down to look at the hall's floor boards and tapped the walls. One by one we went through each apartment, finally ending up back down in the basement. Davis's amusement returned as I pulled my large flashlight from my bag and handed it to him.

"Very practical," he replied still grinning at me. He moved deeper into the basement than my visiting party had as he looked at the building's foundation. Satisfied by what he saw, he poked around at the supplies left behind by whoever owned the building before me. He looked into the laundry room studying the arrangement of pipes and then led me to a door I hadn't seen before. It was large and, like the door to the stairwell, made of a heavy metal. While I didn't have keys to it any more than I did the front door, it was locked from the inside with a dead bolt rather than something requiring a key. He unlocked the door and pushed it open.

I followed him outside and found myself standing in the parking lot behind the building. As Sean mentioned, it was fenced off from the surrounding buildings. The fencing however looked as though it had seen better days. The asphalt of the lot was cracked and in a few spots around the perimeter, buckled by tree roots. Davis crossed the asphalt and looked at the fence. I had no idea what he was looking at, but he seemed satisfied by what he saw.

Together we went back into the building, Davis locking the door to the parking lot behind him. We left the basement and stepped back into the first floor hallway.

"So," Davis began. "Why don't you tell me what you have planned?"

"Planned," I repeated as though the word were foreign to me and this the first time I heard it spoken aloud. "Right, planned. I figured I would look at getting the apartments finished and then look at renting them out." I told him.

Davis laughed and shook his head. "Okay, let's start with this, are you planning to put shields in the building?"

"Yes," I replied feeling like I was on solid ground again. "That is a definite."

"Okay, who are you planning to rent these shielded apartments to?" He asked.

"People," I replied. "Mostly those who need shielded apartments." I added when I saw his lips twitch in amusement. My solid ground began to get a little soggy. "Just average people."

"I see," Davis replied. "What sort of rents were you looking at getting for these shielded apartments?" he asked.

"Oh," I said pleased I had the answer. "I looked up buildings in the area, which isn't hard since I live in the area and I know what I pay." I took out my notebook and flipped to one of my pages of notes. As I extracted the notebook a couple of still packaged mints spilled to the floor. Davis picked them up as I looked for the notes I made on rent prices.

"I always liked this kind better than the hard ones," he said. He held them out to me.

"Oh go ahead and keep them, we have a jar of them at the store." I didn't add that I put them in the bag to make it look like I was carrying more than cashier's checks on the day of the auction. I figured it would just amuse him more. He took out one of the mints and popped it in his mouth, tucking the other one in his pocket for later. I found the page with the ranges I marked down and held out the notebook to him.

He nodded as he read the notes. "You are looking at mid-range rentals then, not high end?" He seemed somewhat surprised.

"It's not a terribly high end area," I replied. He smiled at me, his eyes crinkling in the corners. "Well, I mean it's not a low end area either," I continued. "We are sort of in the middle, but definitely not swanky or very trendy."

"I see," he replied rolling the mint around in his mouth. "So you are looking at doing a mid-range remodel of these apartments."

"Yes." He flipped the page over and saw some of my other notes.

"The city should have permits on file," he told me as he read some of my notes, his lips once again twitching.

"Really?" I asked. "I suppose that makes sense." He chuckled and shook his head. "I build and restore furniture, not apartment buildings. The best I can do is rewire a lamp." I told him.

"You did pretty good when we needed an extra hand with the tiling," he reminded me.

"Well yeah, I can do some stuff like that, but I can't tell if a building is wired correctly or if the plumbing is up to code. That's an entirely different matter than just installing tile or painting a wall. Pretty stuff I can tackle, permits not so much." I thought about Greg's agreement to add cabinetry to his duties while working at the furniture shop. "We have someone to build cabinets and to see if any of the ones in the basement can be reused," I added.

"I can work with that," Davis told me. "I'll need to get a few measurements jotted down before I can get you any estimates." He unclipped a tape measure from his belt and pulled out a small notepad with a golf pencil tucked into the spiral binding. He handed me his small notebook and as he began measuring things he called the measurements out to me so I could write them down. When we were finished, he took back his notepad, made a few more notations and then tucked it away again.

"Do you mind if I ask, and I hope you aren't offended, but what do you normally charge for shielding?" Davis asked as he clipped the tape measure back onto his belt.

"I don't mind," I said with a shrug. "The Commission sets the pay scale actually. The rate they set for my shields is twenty dollars per square foot."

"I didn't realize the Commission set the rates," Davis said with a frown.

"Most people don't it seems, my cousin Sean was surprised when he found out the other day."

"Yeah, I don't think they advertise that fact. I was going to ask if you wouldn't mind trading some of your skills for some of mine. Of course if the Commission set the rates that might not be possible."

"I do have some wiggle room," I told him. "I can double check the regulations, but as long as the Commission gets it's fifteen percent I am willing to barter on the rest. I think there is a form I have to fill out regarding taking a job they didn't recommend so they know they don't have to pay my transportation fees or send Malak. Assuming you would keep the shadow creatures from attacking me while I'm putting up your shields. Unless, of course, you want Malak there. I think they might charge extra for him since an outside job wouldn't be on their schedule. I'd have to check." It had been a while since I took an outside job and I couldn't remember the exact wording of the regulations.

"I think we can do without Malak," Davis said dryly. He thought about it for a minute. "Do you have to do the shielding at night?"

"Nope," I replied. "That's just the off time when the construction crews aren't working. Unfortunately that is when the shadow creatures attack, hence Malak."

"So if you were to put up the shields during the day, there would be less likelihood of an attack, hence no need for Malak." Davis countered.

"This is true," I replied with a smile.

"So just the fifteen percent to the Commission and the possibility of bartering my skills for yours based on the rest of it? I should be able to get the estimates to you in a few days and we can discuss the details then."

"Excellent," I replied, feeling relieved that there was the possibility I was not alone and piloting a doomed ship heading straight to the bottom of the ocean. Having someone who knew what he was doing at least thinking of working with me, made me feel immensely better. "You can call since you have my number or if you want to meet in person, Appleton Furniture is just a few blocks that way. As long as you don't mind the mess, I can usually be found in the workshop."

"I think I can deal with the mess," he replied once again smiling. As we reached the door he picked up my bolt cutters and followed me out. As I locked the door, he headed to the gate across the driveway.

"Do you have a replacement lock?" he asked.

"Yup," I replied, fishing it out of my messenger bag. I walked over as Davis snapped the old lock off of the fence. He made it look easy. In the past, the few locks I had to cut took a great deal of effort on my part and generally required my body weight thrown into it as well as my hand strength. "Wow that would have taken me forever to get off and I'm pretty sure I'd accidentally cut the fence too," I told him as he slipped the cut lock off of the loops and held his hand out for my new one.

"It's all in the technique," he told me with a wink, flexing his arms a little. He handed the bolt cutters back to me and I shoved them back into the messenger bag, trying not to let the handle jab me in the ribs.

"Uh huh," I replied. "I'm pretty sure my technique is only missing muscle mass and hand strength."

"You are an itty bitty thing aren't you," he replied looking me over.

"I am not," I protested. "I'm just not…" I waved my hands around indicating his general size and mass which made him laugh.

"Well, if you were I wouldn't be able to barter for shields, so that's probably a good thing." He handed me the keys to the new gate lock. "I'll stop by the furniture store on Tuesday probably around mid-morning if that works for you. We can go over the details then."

"Great, and thanks again for even being willing to look at this. I really appreciate it." He waved off my thanks and headed to his parked truck. I shivered as the wind picked up and pulled my coat closer. I turned my steps back to the shop, more than ready to be warm again. As I walked, I realized I was smiling. At the moment, I felt really good about everything.

Back at the workshop, I threw myself into the items on my sheet and tried to push the slowly surfacing doubts away. Even with the potential bartering for labor costs, I didn't know how much this sort of renovation could cost. While I had a substantial savings I could throw at the renovation, I really hoped Davis wouldn't come back with an astronomical estimate. I tried not to worry over the details just yet and concentrate on getting as much as possible done before the end of the day and the start of the weekend.

Luckily for me it was the weekend of the once a month flea market held just outside town. When we were little our grandfather would drag Sean and me to the market and we would search for buried treasure. Each month we would tote home small objects he would help us polish and refinish, peeling the rust and grime away to make whatever it was shine. He taught us how to restore and refinish, hauling home old furniture for the store for himself to work on as well. He was long gone and our little treasures, for the most part, scattered to wherever the winds of childhood took them, but Sean and I still scoured the flea market once a month seeking objects that could once again be made beautiful to fill out the showroom.

Since neither of us kept a personal vehicle, we took one of the small delivery vans we used for the store. The sign on the side of the van advertising the store was magnetic and Sean always made certain to remove it before we left because he didn't want anyone to see the sign before he began his bargaining. The bargaining was Sean's favorite part of the excursion. Over the years he even learned how to keep his own special skill tucked away so that he could truly haggle with the sellers and not feel like he was taking advantage of them. He considered it a failure when they agreed to the first price he offered. My job was to pick the items we wanted out, his was to get them at workable prices.

This Saturday, we bundled up for the cold and I was more than happy to use the sights and sounds around us to block out any potential budgetary concerns. "I'm sure it will be fine," Sean assured me as we exited the van. He had a long scarf wrapped around his throat and a cap pulled low over his ears. The wind today had a bite to it.

"I know," I replied. "And I'm sure he will be fair with his estimates," I told him as we headed into the fray. "I just have no clue what to expect and that frightens me." We approached the first stall and began looking over the furniture, ignoring the small shiny bits our younger selves would have flocked towards. I pushed my worries away and studied some of the more interesting pieces, running my hands over the wood, checking both construction and potential maker's marks.

The cushions on the wooden lounge chair were ratty and a bit moldy but the wood was good. In addition an old trunk caught my eye. I told Sean which pieces I was interested in and whispered the limit of what I thought we should pay for them and then moved on to the next booth while Sean began to haggle with the owner.

There were few people at the flea market as the weather had warned most of them that staying inside would be a much better prospect. We took our time moving from booth to booth and while I concentrated on design, Sean was in his element. I knew one of the things he missed most about the courtroom was the chance to argue against a worthy opponent. Unfortunately, he hadn't learned how to keep his skills in check prior to the Commission's ruling and these days this was as close to he got. After mastering his abilities he filed an appeal to rescind the restriction, but had been denied.

"You miss it don't you?" I asked as Sean and I finally made our way back to the van to begin loading our purchases. My ears felt like ice and I rubbed them trying to warm them up before they fell off the sides of my head in protest.

"Miss what?" he asked. Sean was studying the odd shaped objects and trying to determine the best way to fit them inside the vehicle.

"Arguing in the court room," I replied as I helped tug a trunk into the depths of the van.

"Sometimes," He admitted. "Does it show?"

"Only when you are haggling."

"Well it doesn't help that things have been a bit quiet lately. Very routine, you know. The most excitement lately has been you buying a building and even with that, figuring out how to keep the apartment budget separate from the shop's budget was the highlight of my involvement. That didn't actually take that long."

"Did you want to be more involved?" I asked.

"With the apartment?" he asked. I nodded. "Not the construction work or any of the dirty bits, but I wouldn't mind being a part of things."

"Well we do need to figure out some of the non-dirty bits," I told him. "Like finding tenants and making sure they have what they need and other management type stuff," I said running out my mental list. At the moment I hadn't much thought beyond shielding the apartments and making them livable. I wasn't quite sure what else was involved. "If you want the job of figuring out what to do once the construction settles, I will be happy to pass it on to you. For the shielding bits the regulations say the building has to be under my sole ownership, but beyond that legal bit, I am willing to make you a full partner in this crazy thing if you are interested."

Sean immediately brightened. "Really?" he asked.

"Really."

"And I could come up with a whole big management and marketing plan?"

"If you'd like."

"I would."

"Really?" I asked. I helped him heft a chest of drawers into the van. "That sounds absolutely horrendous to me. Are you sure you would want to do something like that?"

"Of course. I like planning."

"Weirdo," I replied with a grin. "You can't be that bored."

"Only a little bored. And I really do like planning."

"Then we are settled," I told him as we finished loading the last of our things. "You plan the whole management thing."

"And you handle the dirty bits," We shook on it and locked up the back of the van. I noticed Sean's steps were a little lighter as he moved. I wondered how bored he had really become. He handled the business side of things as well as his various contract jobs with ease. I knew he was capable of more, I just hadn't realized he wanted more.

"*Yet another thing to worry about.*" I told myself.

Chapter 8

Despite the foray into the flea market and the multitude of projects demanding my attention, I was relieved when Tuesday rolled around and the time for my meeting with Davis drew near. Sammy was less than thrilled with my vague mid-morning timeframe, but added my meeting onto his calendar on the line above his lunch break and agreed to send Davis back when he arrived. Determined not to let my nerves show, I pulled out an old carved wooden room divider from the back storeroom.

I picked up the three paneled wooden divider on a whim one weekend because I liked the general look of it. It had a thick coating of white-ish paint and looked as though it spent an hour or two being dragged behind a truck on a dusty highway. I took the hinges out of the panels, separating them, an effort that required much paint remover just to excavate the hinges from their latex entombment. It was a bit like finding the center of the tootsie roll pop, without all the licking.

Then, I began working on the first of the panels. As I stripped off layer after layer of paint, I realized the carvings were much more intricate then I first believed. The multitude of paint layers had glopped together, obscuring the details and making the design look clunky. As I worked I began to like the design more and more. Delicately I worked on the edges, trying to remove all of the paint without scarring the wood beneath, wondering what the original design entailed.

I became lost in my task as more and more of the pattern emerged. Finally, I straightened, giving my back a chance to stretch after being bent so long. I jumped with a start as I realized Davis was standing there watching me work.

"I didn't want to interrupt," He said smiling at me. It was barely nine when I started on the panel. A glance at the clock told me it was now quarter to eleven.

"Time flies," I replied, setting my heat gun and paint scraper down.

"May I?" he asked gesturing towards the piece. I nodded and he stepped forward, trying not to step on the drop cloth beneath the panel set to catch the fallen bits of paint. He traced the edges of some of the carvings where I managed to unearth them from their paint cocoon. "Nice, delicate. It will be a beautiful piece when you are done."

"Not bad for a five dollar find huh?" I replied, smiling at his interest.

"Five dollars, impressive. A lot of work, but impressive."

"Thanks," I told him. I looked around for a seat to offer him. There wasn't anything. "Um, we have a room in the back we use for meetings sometimes." I didn't point out that the only time we used the meeting room was when we needed to decide who was doing what on a project that involved multiple people and coordinated timing. "I *think* there are chairs back there."

"Or," he countered as though realizing the possible state of our back room. "There is a coffee shop across the street. I think they also serve sandwiches if you wanted to make it an early lunch. That way we can sit down and have a table."

"As I think we sold our table, that might be a better plan," I replied, remembering we had been using a giant twelve seat dining table as our meeting space. A visiting designer fell in love with it and had to have it for one of her projects. I was fairly certain it had been shipped out the week before. I dusted myself off and looked into the mirror we nailed to one of the walls to make certain my face was not streaked with paint. Sammy insisted on its placement as those of us in back routinely appeared looking like we were in the process of applying war paint, which he thought frightened the customers. I washed off my hands and pulled my wallet and keys from the drawer where I kept them during the day. I shoved the items in my pockets and was ready to go.

"No phone?" he asked.

"Oh," I replied. I looked around. "I'm not sure where I left it. I know I brought it in today in case you had to call to change anything."

"Is that it," he asked pointing to one of the shelves. I looked up and saw the phone.

"Yes," I picked it up and added it to my back pocket. "I put it where it was out of the way."

"That's all?" he asked. "No bolt cutters or flashlights?"

"Do you think I'll need them?" I asked smiling back at him.

"I'm fairly certain the café will have a knife with which to cut your sandwich if you wanted and they also have this newfangled thing called electricity, so I think you should be safe leaving your flashlight behind."

I shook my head. "That basement was dark and you know it," I replied feeling oddly comfortable with him. I led him away from my work area and towards the front. "We're heading out to lunch," I told Sammy who had apparently expected as much and nodded, an unconcerned look on his face.

"The basement was shadowy, not dark," Davis corrected as we left the shop.

"Shadowy is just a lighter degree of dark," I told him. I noticed he was carrying a folder. "Are those my estimates?"

87

"They are." He waved them at me. "And you get them once we are inside." We crossed the street and after placing our coffee orders, we slipped into one of the many available booths. While I was certain the place would be jam packed as the lunch crowd arrived, as it always was when I decided to leave the workshop for a bite, we appeared to have beaten the lunch rush.

Our coffee orders were called and Davis retrieved them, leaving the closed folder on the table. I resisted the urge to open it until he returned. He smiled at the closed folder as he handed me my coffee.

"Not even curious?" he teased.

"I figured I could wait five more seconds." I replied smiling. Davis seemed much more relaxed and somehow friendlier than he usually was on a job site. I wondered if it was because I was usually the one making him stay late or if this was just how he was when not actually working on site.

"Such restraint," he replied, opening the folder. He turned it so I was looking at the pages right side up, even though he had to look at them upside down. Slowly, he began to explain the various estimates. We had gotten lucky with the permits and inspections. Both the electrical and plumbing were up to code and ready to go with minimal alterations.

"What's this?" I asked spotting two separate lines for insulation, each with their own price. Davis leaned over the sheet trying to read upside down. I started to turn the page around to face him, but he stopped me.

"I think this might work better," he replied. Davis stood up and slipped into the booth next to me so we could both read the page right side up. His leg was warm where it pressed against mine and his aftershave or cologne or something gave of a pleasant, spicy

88

smell. I tried to ignore both, trying to think only professional thoughts, as he read the item on the list.

"Ah yes," he replied. "One is for regular rolled insulation and one is for sprayfoam insulation. It would be your call as to which we used. We would only use one obviously rather than both, so only one would go on the final tally."

"Okay," I replied trying to concentrate on the estimates instead of his nearness. We debated timelines, cost and effectiveness between the two before moving on. Davis ticked off my preference and drew a line through the other. We continued through his list. There were several places where he knew I could shave a little off of the prices if I was willing to do some of the work myself. In those places he separated the materials from the labor and let me make the decision.

"And I can give you a basic cabinetry plan for each of the kitchens, but if your people are doing them in house then you will have to do your own estimation for the build out," he told me. "I have installation estimates for those though." He flipped the page and his arm brushed mine.

"I'll have to see what we can use of the old ones before I can get a final tally," I told him, pleased that I sounded steady and professional instead of breathless and giggly. I tried shaking off the feeling. While I always found Davis attractive, hitting on my contractor didn't seem like the brightest of ideas. "Can we reuse any of the bathtubs and sinks?"

"I'll have to take a closer look at them in a stronger light," he told me. "They may be salvageable."

"Oh," I replied, unable to help myself. "Could the reason you couldn't see them be because it was dark in the basement?"

Davis laughed and tugged my ponytail lightly. "Shadowy," he corrected.

"Uh huh." While I knew I was going to be writing a slew of rather large checks in the near future, I was pleased that the final tally didn't seem astronomical. It was something my savings could manage which I found to be a relief. We finished going through the estimates and I expected Davis to slide back to his side of the booth. Instead, he stayed in place. The reason turned out to be less titillating than I thought as he dropped his voice to ask about the regulations regarding shields.

"Pretty much what I told you is right," I replied. Over the weekend I double checked the new regulations and quickly covered the details for him.

"If you are still interested in bartering, at least for your percentages, we could definitely work something out."

I nodded. "That sounds fine to me," I replied.

"Good," he said sounding relieved. "The kids had a bit of a scare recently, although luckily nothing major and I think everyone will rest easier once there are shields in place. At least everyone is hoping the nightmares will stop anyway."

"I can see that," I replied nodding, feeling a slight stab of disappointment that Davis was a family man despite not wearing a wedding ring. "My first scare gave me nightmares as well as a scar on my leg," I told him sympathizing. "I'm surprised you don't have shields already since you spend so much time waiting for me to put the shields up, especially since you have kids. I thought you would have worked up a deal with the Commission to shield your place."

Davis chuckled. "They are my brother's kids actually, not mine. Personally, I like the Commission to stay out of my business as much as possible, although since my nephews had a run in with the shadows, I have been thinking about talking to them to arrange something. I'm just glad things worked out this way instead."

"I understand about the Commission. One of the reasons I tend to forget to turn on my phone is so they have to call the office and leave a message with Gina instead of calling me directly."

"Even Malak?" he asked.

I laughed, my disappointment fading, and shook my head. "Malak doesn't call me," I told him. "The Commission calls him and tells him when to pick me up. Or at least that's how I assume it works, I've never really asked."

"So the Commission assigned him?"

"Yup." I replied nodding.

"I always wondered why you put up with him, but I guess you have no choice," Davis mused and then flushed as he realized what he said. "I mean, unless you like him."

"Honestly, I stopped really thinking about him a long time ago. I suppose if something attacked and I screamed loud enough to be heard over his audio books, he'd come help me out, which is technically his job." I shrugged. "Thus far it hasn't been an issue as they tend to back off once the shields are locked in place."

Occasionally on a job I saw one of the shadow creatures lurking on the edges of construction sites, but I was always either with enough people to keep them away or in too well lit an area for them to feel comfortable attacking. The shadow creatures preyed upon lone travelers in darkened spaces. While they naturally shunned the light, experience taught them to be cautious of groups.

"Personally, I wouldn't count on that," Davis said with a frown. "He doesn't seem the sort to risk himself to come to another's aid."

"You don't like him much do you?" I asked, already knowing the answer.

"I don't like his attitude and the way he talks to others," Davis said shrugging. "He belittles my crew, whenever he condescends to talk to them that is and then there are those audio tapes. Every time I get near the car for any reason he turns them off and waits for me to leave again as though he doesn't want me to hear the precious knowledge he is learning from them."

I laughed at Davis' response. "I think it's because he's embarrassed, not because he is hiding knowledge." I told him.

"Really," he said dryly setting off another spate of chuckles on my part.

"Really, all of his audio books fall into two categories, self-help and trashy romance. So unless you want to self-actualize or listen to tales involving the phases 'heaving bosoms' and/or 'throbbing members', I wouldn't worry about it."

"Well, I do like heaving bosoms," Davis said after a moment of thought, a twinkle in his eye.

I chose not to take the verbal bait. "So you want me to shield your brother's place," I said when he seemed disinclined to continue.

"Yes, we have gotten off track haven't we?" He shook himself and pulled out a sheet from the back of his stack of papers. I saw it covered with more familiar looking math. "The house is nineteen hundred square feet and you estimated twenty dollars per square foot which makes the total shielding cost $38,000." He looked at me and I nodded. "Fifteen percent would be five thousand and seven hundred which needs to be paid to the Commission leaving $32,300 for your tally, correct?"

"Sounds right," I said running the numbers in my head. "I would file the form electronically and the Commission will e-mail you a bill for the $5,700."

"I figured it was something like that," he said. "How long do they take to process the request?"

"Well, the last time I sent in the request, the person I was doing the work for had a bill in their inbox in less than an hour. I can file the form as soon as we are done here and you can have the bill today more than likely. I think they give you thirty days to pay it."

"So it has to be paid before you do the work?"

"Not necessarily," I said. "Any time after I send in the request it can be done. Technically speaking, it isn't a request to do the work, but a request to send a bill for the Commission's fifteen percent." I shrugged. "If you wanted, we could send the bill after this meeting and I could go straight over to the house and put up the shields or we could wait and send the form after I've put up the shields depending on your time frame. I brought my laptop in with me this morning just in case you wanted to either file immediately or just look the file over to see if you had any questions. The form is all ready, I just need to add the details. Of course there might be people home and watching so shielding right now might not be a good idea, depending on your brother's neighbors."

"Actually I was going to ask about that. Would you mind working on the shields really early in the morning instead of late at night? I figure a weekday before people start getting up and getting ready for work might be a better plan than at night. Lights flashing at night tend to get the neighbors curious, especially in the suburbs."

"I don't think they are any less curious in the city," I told him. "But I see your point. Early morning would work. I'll just have to switch Winston's schedule and ask Sean if he'll take Winston out in the morning while I take the evening on whatever day we choose."

"Winston?" he asked.

"Dog," I clarified.

"Really, what kind?"

"Half English Staffie and half American Pit," I replied.

"So half English, half American. I'm guessing you named him after Churchill then?"

"Of course," I replied pleased that he caught the reference. He shook his head. "All right then, I know Christy is anxious to get the shielding in as soon as possible. If you can settle Winston, would you mind tomorrow?"

"Tomorrow is fine, I'll need an address though." I thought for a moment. "Christy?"

"My brother Mike's wife and mother of the two boys currently having nightmares. Also our receptionist."

"Ah, I see."

"And the woman who thinks you're a spaz," he added with a grin.

"You said she didn't," I protested.

Davis laughed. "Actually she just thinks you were hunting me down for more personal reasons."

"More personal reasons?" I asked, frowning. "Wait, she thought the reason I sounded so scattered was that I was calling your work to ask you out on a date?"

"She is of a romantic bent and has been trying to marry me off for years. Well not just me, all of my brothers actually. She and Mike were high school sweethearts so she's been part of the family for a long time and has a hard time understanding why a couple of us haven't managed to find our way to the alter."

"A couple of you, how many brothers do you have?" I asked.

"Seven actually," he replied. "There are eight of us boys, no girls."

"Wow, I always wondered what it would be like to grow up in a large family. Well, I mean we had lots of aunts and uncles, but in my generation, it was just my cousin Sean and I."

"Really?" Davis asked, surprised. "My dad had nine brothers and my cousins were practically legion growing up. All boys. We were sort of our own little gang."

"That explains why there are so many Davis males listed in the Davis Construction company I suppose."

"It was my grandfather's company and over the years we all sort of got sucked in at one point or another. All of us had at least part time jobs with the company in high school. Most of us ended up sticking."

"Sean and I both got pulled into the family furniture shop the same way," I replied nodding.

"Family business, huh? Can I ask you something?"

"Sure."

"In the mirror over the counter I can see a very well dressed man who looks a little like he might be related to you behind us looking like he is trying to get your attention. Would that be Sean?"

I looked over Davis' shoulder. Sure enough my cousin was making encouraging signs and smoochy faces, clearly not realizing Davis could see his reflection in the mirror. I could feel Davis chuckling through the places where our limbs touched and flushed as I frowned at Sean and turned back to the table.

"Sorry about that," I apologized. "My cousin is also of a somewhat romantic bent."

Davis chuckled again. "Well tell him I'm flattered, but he really isn't my type." Davis winked at me. "Did you want to actually stay for lunch or do you need to get back?"

As I could see Sean settling into a booth, I opted for skipping lunch. Davis seemed amused as the two of us slipped out, threw away our now empty coffee cups and headed back to the workshop. As nearly everyone in the back was gone for lunch, the space was strangely quiet. I opened one of the drawers in my workbench and took my laptop out if the one I kept clean. It was the place where I usually stashed purses, keys and the occasional snack and guaranteed to be the one place safe from paint and other workroom fall out. Finding a cleared spot on my workbench, I placed the laptop, turned it on and pulled up the required form. As the room divider currently being worked on took up most of the available space, Davis slipped in behind me, looking at the form over my shoulder.

I typed in the square footage and cost. Davis added the names and addresses along with the e-mail address to receive the bill. In no time, the form was floating through the ether towards the Commission.

"So James Rutherford will look at it and sent us a bill, due in thirty days?" Davis asked as I powered down the laptop. He took a step back as though realizing how close we were standing. He shoved his hands in his back pockets.

"Actually his secretary will double check the math, send you a bill, print it out for the files and add it to the spreadsheet. I think James reviews those quarterly. I think if you pay late, she highlights your name in red and types up a notice with a late fee for James to sign. Otherwise your line just has a check mark in the paid in full category."

"So good to know James earns his five percent of the fifteen," Davis said wryly.

"Five percent?" I repeated with a frown.

"Didn't you know? Of the Commission's fifteen percent, which is standard on nearly every service they provide, including your shielding, the person in charge of organizing things gets five percent of every payment that comes in on top of his salary. As your handler, Malak only gets two percent on top of his salary, leaving the Commission a whopping eight percent. Well, at least for you anyway. Most of the other services don't require a handler, or at least a paid one isn't assigned."

"I didn't know that," I said. "When I started working for the Commission, they just explained the fifteen percent was a required fee."

"How long have you been working for the Commission," Davis asked.

"Since the age of twelve, so twenty years," I said. I rolled my eyes at myself. "And yes, I realize I should have asked for a break out at some point."

"Not really much reason for you to," Davis said with a shrug. "Knowing who got what didn't really change the fifteen percent."

"I suppose not," I replied. I took a lot of jobs over the years and even though the percentages James and Malak received from each wasn't terribly substantial, all those payments had to add up. While I thought of the five percent for James as basic bureaucracy at work and could justify it as an incentive not to take bribes and such, the two percent Malak received sort of bothered me. He clearly didn't want to be on site with me and in a pinch I had much more faith in Davis, or whatever contractor was managing the site, helping me out than Malak.

"I wonder how much that adds up to," I mused. How much was Malak paid to listen to audio books and chauffer me to and from job sites and airports? "More than cab fare, I'd guess," I decided, thinking about my records at home and wondering if I should take the time to figure it out or if such an act would only bother me more.

Davis cocked an eyebrow at me. "Malak's two percent." I told him.

"Ah," he said nodding. "Well I can't help you with the how much, but over twenty years, probably a lot would be my guess. Did they actually send you out with him when you were twelve?"

"My Aunt Lou, Sean's mom went as chaperone, but he was there."

"You aunt? Not your mom?"

"No my parents were killed in a car accident when I was ten. I lived with my grandparents after that. In the beginning there was only one trip per month, although some had several projects on that one trip. She thought of it as our girls' getaway." I smiled at the memory. "After the construction projects we would be in the motel room painting our toe nails and putting on facemasks to clean out our pores."

"Is that what removes drywall dust?" He asked with a grin. "I'll have to remember that."

"Well, Aunt Lou was fond of the mint julep mud mask," I told him. "It not only smelled great, but looked as though she smeared frosting all over her face."

"I do like frosting."

"I wouldn't suggest eating it."

"Too bad," Davis replied. "So for tomorrow…?"

"Yes tomorrow," I said snapping back to business. "Why don't we plan on that and I'll talk to Sean as soon as he gets back from lunch. If he has any issues with swapping Winston related playtimes, I'll let you know."

"Great," He replied. "I will need to know where you live so I can pick you up," he continued after we settled on a time. I gave him directions, which as my apartment was only a little over two blocks away was not that complicated. In truth, I could have just walked him out to the sidewalk and pointed as I could see my apartment building from the front of the shop.

"That works," he said nodding. "I was thinking maybe after the shields we could grab some breakfast then head over to the apartment building. That way, if you are so inclined, you could refuel and get the shielding up there before we begin the insulation and drywall."

"That works for me," I said mentally rearranging my schedule. We both turned towards the door as a Mason and Greg came back from lunch. Mason nodded and went over to his workstation. In moments, he had his ear phones on and a belt sander in hand. I waved Greg over before he could do the same.

"Greg, this is Davis, he is the contractor for the apartment building."

"Oh yeah," Greg said with a smile as he shook Davis' hand. "You're the one needing the cabinets."

"I actually have a preliminary layout plan in my truck," Davis replied. "We'll need better measurements and a look over at what is stashed to see if it is re-useable. I'm actually heading over now if you've got the time."

"I do actually," Greg replied. "We'll also need to get the old cabinets, the ones that are salvageable, over here."

"You can use the van," I told him. I handed him the keys and the two men walked off discussing countertops and work triangles. I left them to it and turned back to my work in progress. As I continued to strip paint from the encrusted surface of the room divider, I mentally began calculating figures in my head wondering exactly how much the two percent came to after so long. I knew Malak was there 'just in case' but as he never really did anything but complain about being there, it kind of irked me.

"I suppose I can think of it like paying insurance." I told myself. I sighed and continued to work.

A few hours later, more of the pattern emerged from the paint and I was ready for a break. I thought Sean might have made it back from lunch, so I left the workshop and headed over to his office. I found him sitting at his desk, typing away at his computer. As I entered, he looked up and grinned.

"You and your hunky contractor certainly looked cozy over coffee," Sean teased. He wiggled his eyebrows suggestively.

"He didn't want to be overheard when he asked about shields," I explained.

"Oh, I'm sure that's why he was sitting oh-so-close," Sean said with a laugh.

"He also didn't want to read his estimates upside down."

"Uh huh."

I frowned at Sean. "You do know he could see you making faces at him in the mirror on the back wall, in the same mirror you were using to look at him?"

The smile dropped from his face. "He could?" I nodded. "Oops, what did he say?"

"That he was flattered, but you weren't his type."

Sean grinned. "That's because *you* are his type. You did ask him what his type was, right? You didn't let a good opening line like that slide by unacknowledged, did you?"

"No," I replied. Sean sighed and shook his head. "Do I need to list the many reasons why hitting on the contractor I'm currently working with is a bad idea."

"I'm pretty sure many good and very naughty movies start with the lady of the house and the contractor scenario," Sean informed me. "Not to mention several divorce cases. I do not know what I am going to do with you. The man is clearly into you. *Please* tell me you will at least ask him out when this is over and he is not your contractor."

"I'll think about it, if you stop making the kissy faces every time he is around."

"I'll do my best," Sean replied. "Although I'm not quite sure how good my best will be in this case."

"Try," I replied. Sean grinned unrepentantly. "Also I wanted to know if you wouldn't mind switching Winston duties tomorrow so that you would take him out in the morning and I'll take him out after work."

"I can do that," Sean agreed with a nod. "Are you going out someplace tonight?"

"Nope, Davis bartered for a shield for his brother's place. We're going out super early tomorrow morning."

"Not quite as titillating, but it is a start I suppose. While you are here though, I need to run something past you."

"Shoot," I said.

"Well as I was beginning my plan for marketing and managing the building, I thought that the best place to advertise shielded apartments would be in *The Whisper*," Sean began.

I nodded. *The Whisper* was an on-line newspaper requiring a subscription with a password to read. It featured all of the news and gossip for the magical community. "They do have classifieds," I said. "Sounds like a good idea."

"I thought so too. I went through their ads looking for similar postings and found no other apartment listings, or their ad rates, so I called to ask. I talked to someone on the sales desk and told her what I was looking for. She put me on hold for a moment and then transferred me to the news desk."

"The news desk? For an ad placement?"

"No," Sean said shaking his head. "While I was on hold she told Wendy Watts what I was looking for and Wendy wants to know if she can interview you, and I suppose me, for an article. I told her I'd talk to you and get back to her."

"An article," I repeated. "About an apartment building?" I felt a little flutter of unease in my belly.

"A shielded apartment building," He corrected. "From what she said, I gathered they are somewhat rare." He shrugged. "Or it could just be a slow news day."

"Riiiiight."

"So what should I tell her?"

"Well, we aren't doing anything wrong. It's not illegal so there is nothing to hide. If she wants to interview me about it, I suppose I would be fine with it. It won't be a very interesting article though, I can almost guarantee that."

Sean nodded. "It's free advertising right? And as one of the few people around who can legally create shielded apartments, you are doing a good thing as well as a legal thing. I'll call and set something up."

"Thanks," I told him. "I think I'm going back to the workshop." Somehow focusing on my room divider looked like a much safer prospect.

Chapter 9

Morning came early. Winston was thrilled when I awoke long before sunrise, but looked somewhat morose when my early morning did not translate into immediate park time. "Sean is taking you out this morning and I'll be taking you on our run after work," I told him. He tilted his head to the side as though listening, but not really believing me. As usual I felt guilty for interrupting his routine.

A knock sounded on the door and I went to answer it. I smiled as Davis held out a cup of coffee in a to-go cup. I took it automatically.

"It's too early to go without caffeine," he told me stepping inside.

"Thanks," I said taking a sip. It was fixed just the way I liked. "I just need to get my shoes."

He nodded as I turned to leave. "I take it this is Winston?" he asked before I left the room.

"It is," I confirmed. "I'll be right back. Winston be nice."

I went into the bedroom and emerged a second later, my work boots in one hand and the coffee in the other. They weren't as heavy duty or as beat up as the ones Davis was wearing, but they had protected my feet over countless job sites. I may not have been doing any of the heavy construction work on those sites, but I learned very quickly that when walking around on worksites, the proper foot gear was essential. My first job site resulted in a nail through both sneaker and foot and required a not so fun tetanus shot right after the screaming pain of the large nail being removed. It was not something I wished to repeat.

Winston was clearly fascinated by Davis' work boots and was sniffing them like they were dipped in buckets of his favorite scent prior to arrival. I set the coffee down on the table and pulled out a kitchen chair, seating myself so I could lace on my boots.

"I think it's probably the different scents from the various job sites that he finds so fascinating," I explained my dog's fascination with his feet as I laced on my first boot.

"And here I thought he loved me for me and not just my foot wear." Davis said with a smile.

"I'm sure given the chance, he would adore you," I told him as I moved to the second set of laces. "I'm also sure if you weren't in those boots, he'd carry them off to his secret hideaway under my bed. He doesn't think we know anything about that. Sean and I take turns cleaning it out when he isn't in the apartment. Mostly because there is no way he'd let us take his treasures if he were here."

I finished tying my laces and stood. "He doesn't realize the things are gone?" Davis asked, bending down to rub Winston's head.

"Sort of," I confessed. "After we clean out some of his collection, weeding the mostly chewed tennis ball collection from ten to about three, that sort of thing, he wanders around looking over the apartment as though he is certain something changed, but he can't quite determine what."

"Ah," Davis said straightening. I picked up my coffee and my keys and we headed towards the door. Winston grabbed his leash from its place by the door, holding it in his mouth, and waited for me to clip it to his collar.

"No Winston," I said taking the leash from him and putting it back in its place. I picked up my coat and slipped it on. "You aren't coming this time. Sean will take you out when he gets up."

Winston shook his head and snorted. He then turned around so his back was facing us and sat down, giving us his version of the cold shoulder. I motioned Davis towards the door and the two of us quickly slipped out before Winston could look over his shoulder at us and decide to make more of a fuss waking Sean, and possibly the neighbors, up. Davis held his laugh until we were halfway down the hall.

"I guess that certainly showed you," he said.

"I guess it did," I said shaking my head. "Winston likes his routine." We took the elevator down to the street level. While the residents had a gated parking area behind the building, Davis did not have a copy of the gate code and parked on the street. At this time of the morning there was no traffic and few cars parked on the street. The morning birds had yet to begin their chirping and the world felt cold and abandoned.

I shivered wishing my jacket was heavier, although I knew the temperature wasn't the sole reason for my shivers. Even though I did go out after dark, I always made certain to go out with groups and I stayed in well-lit areas. Even with Davis next to me, the street felt too lonely with just the two of us on it. It made me feel like a target.

We were about ten feet from Davis' pick-up truck when I heard the sound of claws scrabbling on the concrete. We both spun around at the sound and I threw a shield around the two of us so we were protected. From my perspective it looked like we were standing in a soap bubble. If anyone happened to be looking down from one of the apartment windows, they might catch a glimmer of blue from the streetlights, but nothing else. Anyone who managed to see more would no doubt have magic of their own and it wouldn't matter what they saw.

"I can hold the shield while we move to the truck," I told Davis letting him know we could move and didn't need to stay in one place. I shivered as I saw gleaming red eyes peering hungrily out of the shadows at us. After that first attack when Sean and I were children, I practiced a lot with moving while maintaining a shield, after all, neither Sean nor I had anything but the shield and run away method of dealing with such things. It turned out, Davis did.

"Will the shield let my attack pass through?" He asked his voice was calm and steady.

"Yes," I replied, thinking of Jimmy's little electric sparks. After a hit, the shadow creatures would yelp and maintain a cautious distance, preferring their prey not to fight back. The distance often helped with the running away part. Davis nodded and my eyes widened as I saw three of the shadow creatures slinking around the edges of the light cast by the streetlamp. With the exception of the first attack when I was a child, I had never seen more than one at a time. Davis cupped his hand and drew power from himself in much the same way I did to create a shield. Instead of a blue-ish soap bubble however, Davis looked like he was clutching a pulsing red sphere about the size of a baseball.

His baseball looked rather angry and kept spitting out little red-gold sparks. Davis pulled his arm back as though the red ball were an actual baseball. He threw it directly at the nearest of the shadow creatures like a fast pitch, putting his whole body into it. The ball not only hit, it stuck. In awe I watched as the ball stretched out to become a blanket, covering the strangely shaped creature. The red covering pulsed twice and then seemed to turn black. For a second it looked as though the creature was frozen in place under its now black blanket. Then one of its legs began to crumble away beneath it, tilting it precariously to one side. The lean became more pronounced as gravity took over and it began to fall to the sidewalk.

I peered through my shield, realizing the creature had in fact turned to ash, or something like it, and was disintegrating as I watched. As

I studied the first creature, Davis finished off the other two. I turned to look as the other two shadow creatures disintegrated, the ash blowing away on the icy breeze.

"Handy," I said, my voice sounding somewhat breathless.

Davis smiled at me. "It's a lot easier to pull off from behind a shield, especially when there's more than one."

"Yeah," I replied feeling somewhat dazed. I stared stupidly at the last of the ash floating away.

I wasn't sure what was showing on my face, but Davis closed the short distance between us and slipped his arm around my shoulders. "You can let the shields down now Alice," He told me, his tone gentle. "If there were any more of those things out there, they would have fled."

"Yeah," I repeated, nodding. "Right sorry, just old memories." I shook my head and let my shields drop. The coffee cup was less than steady in my hand and Davis guided me to the passenger's side of his truck, keeping his arm around me. I wondered how bad I looked and tried to push away the memories. I was no longer a child and, thanks to Davis, the shadow creatures hadn't even laid so much as a claw on my shield, even if I could still hear the echoes of their scratching in my mind. I slid into the truck, Davis' arm sliding off my shoulders. He closed the door and walked around to his side. I took a small sip of the coffee and tried to relax.

"*Everything is fine*," I mentally told myself as he settled himself behind the wheel.

"Did you hurt your leg?" he asked. I blinked in surprise and looked down. My hand was rubbing the old bite scar through my jeans the same way Sean rubbed the scars on his arms. I stopped and balled my hand into a fist in my lap.

"Sorry, no that's just…"

"Where you were bitten the last time you were attacked?" he guessed. I looked over and he shrugged. "You mentioned a scar."

"So I did," I replied, remembering the café. I opened my fist and reached for the seatbelt, fastening it into place as Davis started the engine. I sighed as heat rolled out of the vents.

When the car didn't move, I looked over at him. "We can put this off for another day if we need to Alice. I mean if you are too shaken…"

"I'm fine," I told him smiling weakly. "Knowing that I'm putting up shields for other people to safely sleep behind helps with my personal freak out."

Davis smiled and put the truck in gear, accepting my answer. I took slow and steady breaths to calm myself. "That was quite a nifty trick of yours back there." I told him as I settled. "Much better than hitting them with a handy piece of scrap wood."

"Scrap wood?" he asked, sounding slightly amused.

"It was my plan B in case Malak didn't arrive," I told him not mentioning that I thought he or one of the other contractors could do the hitting. "Put up my shields and hit them with a piece of scrap wood, preferably one with old rusty nails sticking out of it."

Davis chuckled. "I'm not so sure that would work," he said conversationally.

"Because shadow creatures don't get tetanus?"

"Not that I'm aware of," he replied.

"Well, it was still a good thought," I told him. We drove in silence for a while. I had the feeling Davis was searching for a neutral topic to keep me calm.

"So," I said helping him out. "Sean came up with something interesting. He is handling the post construction bits dealing with the apartment building."

"Like…" Davis prompted, seeming relieved at my topic choice.

"Like renting the apartments," I replied. Davis nodded. "Anyway he thought putting a posting in *The Whisper* might be a good way to get tenants who actually could use a shielded apartment."

"Sounds like a good plan," Davis replied knowing about *The Whisper*.

"I thought so too, apparently Wendy Watts thought otherwise."

"Did she now?" Davis replied.

"She wants to interview Sean and me for an article about it."

Davis nodded. "Shielded apartments are rare."

"So I've heard. The reason I'm bringing it up is that I want to know if I can mention that you are working on it or if you don't want Davis Construction mentioned."

"Because we don't want to be tied to something as nefarious as a mid-range apartment building?" he asked with a grin.

"I just meant that since it seems to be turning into a bigger deal than I planned," I began.

"Planned?" he repeated with a chuckle.

"Planned, accidentally got into, whatever, I just figured I'd ask if you still wanted to be involved with me since she may end up asking you questions as you are in charge of the construction."

"Oh, I'm involved with you now am I?" he asked grinning.

"With the building," I clarified, blushing.

"Well, that's not nearly as fun, but probably best until the building is done."

"That's what I told Sean," I said before I thought about it. "And it was a simple question."

"You told Sean you wouldn't go out with me until after the building was complete? Fair enough." He teased.

"That's not…," I began my face radiating heat.

"You can mention Davis Construction to the reporter," he continued over my protests, chuckling a little. "And give her my number if she wants to call me for details."

"Was that so hard?" I asked.

"What? Getting you to stop thinking of the shadow creatures?"

"Getting me…," I started then realized what he did. "That was sneaky."

"It was," he admitted. "But now you aren't shaken up *and* I know you like me." He wiggled his eyebrows at me.

"I didn't say that," I told him.

"I'm pretty sure you did," he countered.

"I didn't."

"Did, and we are here," he added. "So no take backs."

"No take backs?" I said. "What is this kindergarten?"

"Nope if it were kindergarten I would have pulled your pigtails and shared my cookies with you at lunch time."

He grinned at me and I shook my head. I looked away from Davis and out the window as he pulled into a driveway and parked. We were in an average looking suburb and I could see the house was one of the few on the street with lights on. The front yard had a decorative border composed of paving stones separating it from the sidewalk. I hoped they continued around to the back as they would make excellent anchors for the exterior shield. While I technically only needed between three and five exterior anchors, using all of the paving stones would mean that the shield would remain stable even if some of the stones were removed.

"We should take care of the yard before the house as it will be the most noticeable," I told him, switching into work mode as we exited the vehicle. Davis nodded and we walked towards the front door. Before we could knock, the door swung open and a large man, slightly older than Davis, but looking remarkably like him, filled the doorway. I was guessing this was his brother, Mike.

Davis introduced him as we stepped inside, my assumption proving correct. I was then introduced to Christy. She smiled, but looked nervous. "Would you like some coffee?" she asked.

"I appreciate it," I told her. "But we should probably get the outside done before the neighbors start waking up."

"Of course," She said. All three of them looked at me as though waiting for instructions and I realized that even though Davis was familiar with my shielding, he always maintained a distance, letting me work in peace.

"Right," I said realizing they really were waiting for instructions. "The back yard?"

"Of course," Christy said shaking herself. She led me to the sliding glass doors and opened them, letting in a wash of cold air. "Do we need to stay out of the way?" She asked as the four of us stepped into the back yard. She pulled the cardigan she was wearing over her t-shirt closer. It looked more like a nervous gesture than a warming one.

"Not really," I said. I decided some explanation might help with her nerves. "The exterior shield will link to the edges of the property so the yard is safe, or shielded." I looked around and saw that while a privacy fence had been added to the yard, the pavers were still lining the edge in places even though it ceased to be a smooth continuous line.

"The pavers will be my anchors. Then, I'll go inside and put a secondary one inside. It will stick to the walls, floor and ceiling as though I just added an invisible layer of paint to everything. The shield will start like a ball in my hands and then expand like a bubble. It will expand over you so you won't bother it when it touches you, and you won't be harmed by it either. Sean, my cousin, said it feels kind of strange for a second as it passes through you. He described it as momentary tingles like when you get when your foot falls asleep, but it doesn't last."

It wasn't a great description, but I personally didn't feel anything when the shields touched me, mostly because they were still a part of me at that point, or at least that was my guess. Sean was the only person I ever had describe to me what my shields felt like so I wasn't entirely certain he was the norm. Occasionally when I saw others react they sort of shook themselves and looked vaguely surprised. Of course he also told me he didn't remember feeling anything when I threw the shields around us for defense when the shadow creatures appeared, so even though I shielded Davis earlier, this would be new to him as well. If Sean was the norm of course, one being a rather small sample of the population at large.

Neither Sammy nor Darcy ever commented on those shields to me.

Usually people weren't around when I placed my shields. Even the contractors, like Davis, who escorted me through the work zones tended to stay out of the range of the shields as I put them into place. The three of them nodded their understanding and I tried to ignore my audience as I knew I had to get started before the neighbors were up and about.

"Okay," I said. "Here goes." I pushed everything from my mind and concentrated on the shield. I heard a soft gasp as the ball of blue appeared in my hands. I thought it might have been Christy as it sounded female. I pushed power into the sphere, expanding it slowly, not just for stability, but so the others wouldn't be startled. When it was beach ball sized, I let it roll out of my hands and on to the ground. When it was large enough to accommodate me, but not yet touching the others, I stepped inside of it, showing the three watching there was nothing to fear. I kept the rate of expansion steady and heard soft sounds of surprise as it expended wide enough to include the watching trio.

I kept pushing more power into it, increasing the size, letting it flow over the house like a giant dome, the lower curve of the bubble sinking deep into the ground below the foundation. I didn't know if any of the shadow creatures could fly or burrow beneath the ground, but I didn't like to take any chances. My sphere reached the edges of the yard and I focused on the paving stones. I could feel them with my power the same way I could feel my teeth with my tongue. One by one I tied the power to the stones. When I was certain it was locked in place, I severed my connection. Around us the shield flashed bright white, causing startled exclamations from Christy and Mike, before it disappeared.

"Well," I said, satisfied. "That would be the exterior. It covers the front yard as well, down to the sidewalk. How about the interior?"

Christy looked dazed but nodded and led us all back inside. As we turned I caught sight of three little boys peering into the yard from one of the windows. Their eyes were wide. I smiled and followed the adults into the house, wondering if the boys would sneak into the hallway to watch the interior shields go up.

If they did, I didn't see them. As before, I let the power spill to my hands, expanded it and let it flow over the walls. I let the bottom flow over the basement floor below us and pushed the top so that it draped the roof's rafters in the attic. The sides coated the interior of the exterior walls. As before, it flashed brightly white as I locked it into place.

I looked around and saw small patches of shimmery blue in spots on the walls. "That will fade," I assured Christy not wanting her to think I ruined her walls.

"Do we have to… do anything to it to keep it… running?" She asked lifting a hand towards one of the shimmery spots but stopping before actually touching it.

"No," I replied shaking my head. "It's pretty much done. In a few hours, you won't even be able to tell it's there."

She nodded. "And what about cleaning?" She asked. "Do I need special cleaner or something to keep it from washing off?"

I smiled. This wasn't the first time I had been asked that. While I was normally called in during either construction or renovation, not everyone opened their walls when they wanted a shield. I had assured many a nervous homeowner that just because they couldn't see the shield any more; it didn't mean that they had worn off.

"No, what you do normally will be fine. The only things that would affect it is if you start knocking down walls, the exterior ones, or digging up the basement floor. For the exterior shield you would only have an issue if you start digging up the decorative pavers around the edge of the yard. Actually, since I used all of the pavers as anchors instead of just a few you should be all right there as well even if a couple of them went missing." I didn't want the couple to worry that the entire shield would come crashing down if one of the pavers happened to be knocked askew by a lawnmower or something.

Christy looked as though she wanted to ask more questions, but couldn't quite decide what to ask. "If you come up with any more questions, you can always call and ask later," I told her. "It's a lot to take in the first time you see a shield go up." She looked relieved.

"Thanks," she replied. "Would you two like to stay for breakfast?" She asked.

"Actually, I am using Alice as an excuse to get waffles before we head to the apartment building to get started there," Davis said quickly. Christy accepted the excuse and both she and Mike thanked me, Mike looking rather amused for some reason. As we left I thought I saw Mike slip something to Davis when Christy wasn't looking.

Back in the truck, I looked at Davis as he backed out of the driveway. "Waffles?" I asked.

"I like waffles," Davis replied.

"And you need an excuse to eat them?"

"Ah well, truth is Christy isn't much of a cook," He began. "And she has recently gone on this healthy sort of thing, turkey bacon, egg white omelets, sneaking tofu into places where it really doesn't belong and completely without warning." He shuttered. "Don't get me wrong, I have eaten tofu and know it can be done right, just not by Christy. Last time I had breakfast there, she cut it into little bitty cubes and added it to the cereal. It bonded to the milk and made some sort of weird slime creature. I could almost swear it started to rise up from the bowl. You shouldn't have to defend yourself from your breakfast cereal."

"Not usually no," I replied with a laugh. "And what did your brother slip you? A ransom note from the Cheerios?"

"Saw that did you?" Davis said with a laugh. "Actually since he is showing up this morning to help with insulation and drywall, he wanted me to pick up something for him to eat."

"So he's helping with the building?" I asked as we headed back towards the section of town I was more familiar with.

"Yup," Davis replied. "Actually you are getting most of us at some point or other as we move from job site to job site. That way we can quickly cover the tradeoff for the shield with time."

"Really?" I said frowning. "You aren't putting off other work to help me out are you? I know we negotiated labor for my percentage of the shield cost, but…"

"You aren't pulling us off other jobs," Davis assured me. "Mike just finished a job and won't be needed on a different site for a few days. Same with the others, they are either just finishing jobs or not ready to be put on others. As they start new jobs, others will finish what they are working on and come in to take their places. We are used to running multiple jobs and this causes no problem. Besides, none of the rest of us have kids, so we all felt like helping Mikey out." Davis shrugged as he pulled into the parking lot of a diner. The sun was just starting to come up, turning the cloud filled sky a pearly gray.

"As long as I am not taking advantage of you," I said as we exited the vehicle and headed to the door of the diner.

Davis laughed. "I thought you decided to wait until after the job was finished to take advantage of me," he teased as we went inside.

I sighed. "That's not what I said."

"It's what I heard," Davis replied. He looked at the hostess. "Table for two please." The hostess nodded, picked up two plastic coated menus and led us to a booth. We settled ourselves. It was early enough that we beat whatever morning rush the diner boasted. On the other side of the diner counter I could see some of the morning wait staff filling sugar, salt, and pepper shakers while others topped off syrup carafes and wrapped silver wear in napkin blankets.

"I think you heard what you wanted to hear," I said opening my menu.

"So I didn't hear that you wanted to take advantage of me? I must have gotten it backwards. Clearly, that means that you want me to take advantage of you."

"How do you figure that?" I asked looking at him over the menu.

Davis smiled. "I am having waffles, do you know what you want?"

I frowned and quickly looked over the menu. The buttermilk pancakes seemed like a good idea, the long burning energy of carbs useful since I still had the apartment shields to put up. "I think so," I replied. The waitress wandered over, took our orders, both of us ordering coffee with our respective platters, and went to put the order in. Davis also arranged for an egg sandwich of some sort packaged to go and delivered with the check.

"Clearly you want me to take advantage of you," Davis said after the waitress left. "Otherwise you wouldn't have added in the yard, since it wasn't included in the square footage."

118

I sighed. "That has nothing to do with you," I told him. "It was for those three little boys."

This time Davis frowned, his eyes narrowing. "How did you know there were three?" he asked.

"I saw them looking out of the window when we were in the back yard."

Davis chuckled and shook his head, his good mood returning. "Christy wanted them asleep so they wouldn't be scared. I'm not quite certain what she thought went into making shields. She might have thought it involved sacrificing a goat or something."

He grew quiet as the waitress brought a plastic carafe of coffee and two mugs. "She wasn't born in the community so to speak," he said when she left again. He added a packet of sugar and a dollop of milk to his cup. I did the same.

"She's normal?"

He nodded. "Or as normal as people really get I suppose. That's why she asked about cleaning the walls," Davis continued.

"I figured she asked that because she was a mom." I replied with a smile. "She's not the first one," I told him. "Even with folks born to the community, they ask what they have to do to maintain the shields. I'm usually asked something similar any time I arrive after the drywall. People always think it wears off since they can't see it. They are much more comfortable with it if it is protected by the insulation and a layer of drywall so they can't... damage it somehow."

"Really?" He nodded slowly. "I can see that I suppose."

"She must be having a really hard time with all of this," I said, trying to picture how someone not born into the magical community would deal with the everyday reality of our lives, especially attacks by shadow creatures.

"Well like I said, she and Mike were high school sweethearts so she's been around the lot of us for quite a while. We try to keep the crazier stuff out of the way, but the shadows are a bit much, especially when they went after the boys," he told me.

I looked around and realized that while people had started coming into the diner now, no one was seated near us, or at least near enough to be overheard. "Can she even see them?" I asked. Most people born without some ability of their own couldn't even see the creatures.

"No, but she is sensitive enough to hear them," He explained.

"Wow," I said to myself. I took a sip of coffee. Seeing the shadow creatures was bad, hearing their claws and howls and growls, but not being able to actually see them sounded even worse somehow. I shuttered. "I'm guessing the boys aren't the only ones with nightmares then?"

"Nope," Davis confirmed. "Hopefully that will end now."

"Making me doubly glad I included the yard," I replied. "When I was little I woke up to find one of them pressed against the window watching me sleep," I told him. "It freaked me out for weeks after, although I never forgot to close the curtains again and whenever possible, I always include the yard. Especially when children are involved."

"You didn't on the Fausti job," Davis said as the waitress brought our breakfasts.

"I didn't," I told Davis as I watched him with his waffle. He smeared butter over the surface making certain every square was equally coated. Then as it melted he reached for the syrup and made certain to pour the same amount into every square. I was less methodical, giving a swipe of butter between each pancake in the stack and a light coating of syrup over the top.

"But I did cover the pathways," I reminded him. "It added $160,000 to their final bill and they decided that was better than paying for the square footage of the entire property on top of the buildings."

"So you don't always include the yard?" he teased as he cut a bit of his waffle, trying not to spill the syrup from its squared cells.

"All of the bedrooms in the Fausti house are on the second floor," I replied. "Even in the guest cottage. Besides I think the creatures can sense the shields. The more you have in an area, the less likely they are to come sniffing around in the first place. It's sort of like a flashing 'Do not Enter' sign. There were a lot of shields on that site."

"Now that's handy," Davis replied.

"Personally, it always makes me want to sneak onto the property of my old elementary school and add some shielding," I replied. "But that is not allowed."

"I take it you didn't go to one of the private schools?"

"Nope, regular public school all the way. My parents thought that since we made up such a small percentage of the population, we should learn to blend from the beginning. Luckily neither Sean nor I had abilities that could go too badly awry if the school bully knocked us down."

"Yeah," Davis said nodding. "We had issues with control when they first kicked in. Most of us have somewhat…defensive abilities."

"Defensive?" I replied with a laugh washing down a bite of my pancakes with the coffee. "I am defense, you, I think, fall more into the offense category."

Davis chuckled. "I only go on the offensive when I feel the need to defend," he said with a laugh.

"I can't imagine anyone attempting to bully you," I told him. "Although I'm sure you were much smaller when younger."

"I was," He replied with a laugh. "And luckily for me I had the entire Davis army watching my back. It's one of the benefits to a large family, especially as we were in public school too. With so many of us, most bullies considered it unwise to mess with us as they knew they would be taking us all on. It meant fewer chances for our offensive defenses to be triggered once they started to develop."

"And as they put Jimmy Lucas to shame, it was probably a good thing." I told him.

"Jimmy Lucas?" Davis repeated.

"He lived a few doors down from us and was our little group's defense," I explained telling him about the four of us uniting our skills for safety.

Davis chuckled. "This would be Jimmy Lucas the quarterback of the Northdale High football team?"

"Yeah, go Cougars." I replied. "Why you know him?"

"Please tell me you weren't friends."

"I wasn't," I said honestly. "I was the art geek and Sean was the brainiac gay boy. Jimmy put up with us because we helped him and his sister stay safe after dark. In addition his family was often born with multiple talents as opposed to just the one talent per person so he tended to think his station was a little above ours. When we graduated, his little sister who was about two years younger, joined another after hours cluster and I never saw him again."

"He was my brother, Scott's nemesis in high school. Scott was quarterback for Westbridge High back in the day."

"Our biggest rival," I replied with a nod.

"We were," Davis agreed. "Jimmy'd use that little electric stinger of his during games to help his team. It was much more subtle than anything we could do and he could hide it pretty well, at least he never got caught using it on the field. It used to drive Scott insane every time we played Northdale. He especially liked to use it on those with stronger abilities who couldn't risk using them in public."

"I can't say I'm that surprised, although I never actually saw him do it. It fits his personality."

"So you went to the games?"

"Quite a few of them," I told him.

"You know you probably saw me play then," Davis said with a smile. "I'm surprised we never met."

"I said I went, I didn't say I watched," I replied. "The school had pride points which you got for going to school functions and occasionally they came in handy, so I went to a lot of the games. Most of the time, my friends and I would play poker instead of watching the game. Football was never really my thing."

"Not a lot of school spirit huh?" Davis said with a grin.

"I had plenty of school spirit," I replied. "But most of the people I knew on the football team were Jimmy's friends and sort of cut from the same cloth as he was even if not all of them had his sort of abilities. Encouraging them never seemed like a terribly good idea. It was like rewarding a dog for biting the mail man."

"I can understand that. So are you any good at poker?"

"I'm okay," I told him. "I haven't played in years though so I am a bit rusty. As a friendly warning, never play with my cousin."

"Is he good?"

"He is scary good."

"I will have to remember that." The two of us finished our breakfast and the waitress brought both the extra sandwich Davis ordered for his brother and the check.

"Don't even think about it," Davis said as I began to reach for my wallet. He handed the waitress a credit card and she wandered off.

"You didn't have to buy breakfast," I told him.

"And you didn't have to shield the yard."

Chapter 10

When we arrived at the apartment building, the sun was higher in the sky and although it was still too early for commuters to clog the streets, I knew they were up and preparing to start their day. After a quick conversation with Davis about what was staying in the yard and driveway, I got to work on the exterior shield. While Davis budgeted for a new privacy fence around the building's parking lot, the fence posts were in good enough shape to stay. Their concrete footings served me well as anchors.

In the front, Davis pointed out a line of bricks, half buried in the overgrown yard that went around the front yard's perimeter. It looked like the remains of a long gone wall. As the only yard work planned was a trimming of the trees and painting of the building, they would be staying, giving me anchors there as well.

With only Davis as audience, his attention more on keeping an eye out for people passing by than me, it took less time to set the exterior shields. Davis still looked startled as the shields passed through him, but he shook off the feeling easily now that he knew what to expect. With a bright flash the shields were set and we moved inside. The building was still cold as the furnace had yet to be installed. Shadows filled the space and I could see my breath puff around me. Davis hefted a large flashlight to illuminate my path. We passed through the vestibule and I stopped for a moment, thinking about the building.

Due to the restrictions, I was never called upon to shield an apartment building. Once, one of the properties I worked on had a basement apartment to accommodate one of the owner's aging parents, but that was as close as I got. Davis waited patiently as I gave the situation some thought.

"Okay," I said. "I think I'll do one over-all shield for the building and then separate shields for each apartment building. It is a bit of overkill, but at least I can honestly say that each apartment has its own shield."

"Sounds reasonable," Davis said nodding. "Just let me know where to shine the flashlight."

I nodded. "I can set the overall one from here," I told him. I looked over my shoulder at Davis and realized that while one hand held the flashlight, the other held a camera. "Are you taking pictures of me setting the shields?" I asked. No one had ever done that before and I wondered if the shields would actually show up on film.

"No," he replied with a smile. "It's just in case someone sees the flash outside and asks questions. If they ask, then I am just going through the building with the owner, prior to work starting today and taking pictures for reference points."

"Smart," I replied nodding.

"I try."

Deciding not to delay, I began the overarching interior shield. It went up quickly and painlessly. Slowly, we moved through each of the darkened apartments, Davis lighting the way with his flashlight so I didn't trip and break my neck. The four-bedroom apartment on the upper floor was the last to receive its shield. By the time it was completed, I was glad I chose a carb-loaded breakfast and was wishing I ordered a second helping. I knew once Davis dropped me off at the shop, I would nip out and grab one of the breakfast sandwiches the deli next door offered before getting to work.

Outside, the sun was truly up and morning officially begun. Davis switched off the flashlight as the sunlight flooded in through the uncovered windows making it unnecessary. With no insulation, not only was the place very cold, but I could hear the noise of the traffic below. I shivered and rubbed my cold hands together.

"We'll be taking care of that today," Davis assured me. "Scott and Luke are handling the insulation and the furnaces should be delivered this afternoon."

"Furnaces," I said as we headed back to the stairwell and descended to ground level. "As in plural? I knew this place needed more than one."

"You could probably get by with one, but this will be more efficient and should anything happen to one of them, your tenants won't be completely without heat during repairs."

I shivered. "This is a good thing."

As we stepped out of the front door I blinked in surprise. While I was putting up shields inside, the Davis clan appeared to have staged an invasion. Everywhere I looked were men bearing enough similarity that I could tell they swam in the same gene pool as Davis. Mike retrieved the breakfast sandwich Davis picked up and was eating it while leaning against the truck and chatting with someone who could only be family. He was sipping coffee and looking amused at Mike's enjoyment of the illicit breakfast sandwich. The others were milling around in small groups as though waiting for something. As they spotted us leaving the building and began to gather, I realized it was us they were waiting for.

"Figured you were done when we saw the last flash from the top floor," Mike said as he polished off the last of his breakfast and wiped his hands on a napkin. He tossed the used napkin in the now empty box and put both in the passenger's seat of Davis' truck. "Thanks for that by the way. Christy put the tofu in the egg whites this morning. I think she thought it would melt like cheese.

It burned, but it didn't melt. Not as pleasant a start to the day as waffles."

He shook his head as Davis and the Davis male holding the coffee chuckled. He introduced himself as Scott.

"Westbridge High quarterback," I said. "Nemesis of Jimmy Lucas."

Davis chuckled. "I'll explain later," Davis told his brother.

"Is there anything else you need me for?" I asked, turning to Davis. Scott gave a snort of laughter that he tried to hide in his coffee cup and Mike smiled broadly at the question.

"I think we're good," Davis told me, shooting his brothers a dark look. They seemed unrepentant. "Do you need a ride back?"

"No, the shop is close. Oh and Greg said to tell you he should have a list of what is officially salvageable and what needs to be scrapped, as well as a time line by this afternoon."

With my part in the morning's proceedings complete, I turned to leave as Davis called the milling legion of Davis men together. I left them to get started and as I walked I tried to decide what sort of breakfast sandwich I would get from the deli. Slow burning carbs or not, the energy from the pancakes was gone and I needed to refuel before beginning my actual work day.

Sammy had already opened the showroom for the day when I arrived and to my surprise, he and Sean were chatting when I walked in. Sean followed me back into the workroom, leaving Sammy to continue his normal morning routine in peace.

"You know I think his OCD is getting worse," Sean said once we were safely in the back.

"You didn't try to touch anything up front did you?"

"No," Sean replied. "I remembered from the last time. But today I got here as he was opening up and told him I wanted to catch you before you were buried in a project, so I waited out of the way. Every time he passed the light switch, he had to touch the plate and then look at me as though my merely being there when he was going through his routine was enough to disrupt him. Usually it's only a problem if I try to touch something."

"I haven't noticed any other changes, but I have been sort of preoccupied. I'll keep an eye out," I told Sean. "Usually he only gets worse when there is a lot of stress. If I notice anything I'll have a chat with him."

Chats with Sammy about his stressed out behavior were always an interesting challenge. While he told me about his condition before being hired, he didn't like to discuss it. However when he was stressed, he needed to tell someone what was going on to make him stressed in order to actually relieve the stress. Saying it out loud was part of his process, as though acknowledging it made it more manageable. The problem was telling him you noticed he was stressed without pointing out that his compulsions were somewhat worsened and what caused you to notice something was up in the first place. Sean was always happy to leave that particular task to me.

"So what did you need to see me about?" I asked, unwrapping my bacon and egg sandwich and leaning against my workbench.

"I thought you were going to breakfast with Davis," Sean asked with a frown.

"I did," I told him. "I worked on the shields for his brother's house and then we ate. Then I took care of the apartment building, so I needed to eat again."

"Ah," Sean replied nodding. "Everything go all right?"

"Yup," I told him, deciding not to mention the attack just outside our building. Davis eliminated the creatures and with luck, more would not come slinking around. I didn't see the point in causing Sean to panic.

"Good," He told me. "I spoke with Wendy Watts and scheduled a time for her interview. She'll come here, but as I didn't know the state of your conference room, I figured a few days from now wouldn't be a bad idea."

"As the state is somewhat desperate," I replied. "I appreciate it. At the moment there are only three rickety folding chairs back there. I'll see what we can pull from storage to make it at least usable for the interview. I also talked to Davis about it and he said he is willing to talk with her as well if she feels the need."

Sean nodded. He handed me the note with the date and time of the scheduled interview and left me to finish my sandwich in peace. Once I felt a little less hollow, I washed my hands and went to find Sammy. He was fluffing pillows on the sleigh bed in a bedroom vignette he arranged to display some of our more recent showroom additions.

"Nice," I said as he stepped back. While the bed was traditional, Sammy arranged the grouping so the room looked like a mix of old and new so the bed would seem classic rather than old fashioned. The mix he chose worked well.

"It did come out rather nicely," Sammy said. He crossed his hands in front of himself as he studied his handiwork, looking for flaws. He wore a monogrammed signet ring on the ring finger of his right hand and I watched as he tapped the ring with the index finger of his left hand. Tap, tap, slow count of three, tap, tap and then another slow count. I waited knowing that he would need to tap the ring twelve times, each time tapping twice and each with a three count between the paired taps. I mentally counted in my head as I looked over the scene. Sean was right, Sammy was stressed.

Sammy sighed and uncrossed his hands. I turned away from the bedroom scene to look at him.

"Did Sean manage to speak with you?" He asked.

"Yes," I said nodding. "I actually wanted to talk to you about that. I know we have been awfully busy lately and things have been somewhat stressful. I have a small project I would like you to help me with, but I want to make certain your plate isn't overly full."

Sammy looked down at his signet ring for a second and sighed, realizing his stress was showing. "It's Princess Buttercup," Sammy said shaking his head. "She went and swallowed a sock." He shook his head as I pictured the rather stout bulldog Sammy kept as a pet.

"Oh poor thing," I said. "I thought she was over her sock phase."

"I don't know how she got it," Sammy continued shaking his head as the words tumbled out. "I've been so careful since her last episode. I don't even know where she got the sock from. I took the poor dear to the vet yesterday and they had to extract it. Now she's laid up with giant plastic cone over her head. *And* it wasn't even my sock. It was pink and fuzzy. I don't have any socks that are pink and fuzzy," Sammy said sounding affronted by the thought that someone would think he did. "So now she is stealing someone else's socks. One of my neighbors is probably running around half mad trying to find a missing fuzzy pink sock."

Knowing that having one sock without a match would drive Sammy completely bonkers, I nodded in understanding. Actually thinking about someone searching for a missing sock as well as wondering how his darling bulldog, Princess Buttercup, managed to acquire said sock was probably the source of the stress.

"Do you need time off to take care of her?" I asked, knowing he would probably spend the time off trying to figure out the identity of the original sock owner.

"No," Sammy replied shaking his head. "It's just gotten me a little out of sorts. The danger has passed and I'm sure someone will come looking for their socks soon. I am perfectly capable of taking on another project if my assistance is needed."

"If it's not too much then," I replied. I explained about the interview with Wendy Watts. Sammy being of the magical community, needed no explanation of *The Whisper* and was thrilled that he would be allowed to do something with our small meeting room in the back. I knew he felt the room was a waste of space as it served no proper function and he looked thrilled to be able to give the room purpose.

"It will be presentable by the time of your interview," Sammy assured me. "Hopefully it will manage to stay that way at least for a little while." Even though he knew we were in the business of selling furniture, it always irked him when someone visited our backrooms and fell in love with a piece in progress circumventing the usual purchasing systems, i.e. showroom and website. Understanding the business though, he kept his personal, procedural irritations mostly to himself. Sammy moved to the counter and made notations in his calendar. I left him to his planning and returned to my room divider. While up front with Sammy, the others arrived in back.

"Sammy's bulldog ate a sock and had to have it removed by a vet, so he is a bit out of sorts today," I warned everyone as they began getting ready for the day's work. All of them nodded, familiar with Sammy's stress. "He's also going to be making our back room look like an actual meeting space," I added so they would know he might be passing through the workroom. Message delivered, we all went to our separate spaces and got to work.

The day passed more or less predictably. Everyone worked on their individual projects, occasionally asking for assistance from one of the others. Sammy took frequent trips to the mostly vacant meeting room, tape measure in hand. Even though he wrote down the room's measurements, I knew he would measure the room three times before he was satisfied his measurements were correct. Knowing his procedure, we all left him in peace, not wanting to derail him when he was already somewhat stressed. Over all while I worked, I tried not to think about anything but the piece I was working on. I tried not to fret about Davis and what he might uncover as he worked. I tried not to think about the shadow creatures that attacked us. Most of all, I tried not to think about the upcoming interview.

Sadly it was the upcoming interview that worried me the most.

I knew what I was doing was legal, I just didn't know anyone else who was doing it. Admittedly, I didn't know that many people capable of shielding. I met several during testing, when the strength of my shields, and therefore the cost the Commission could set for them, was determined. I thought about the day I was tested as I finished one panel of the room divider and moved to stripping paint off of the second panel.

Jeffrey, the man who held James Rutherford's place before him, led a group of us to a field owned by a member of the Commission. I remembered seeing signs for a wilderness preserve of some sort and figured the privately held land was further insulated by government-held land. We were trekked out into the middle of the space in a conga line of four wheel drive vehicles. There were about twenty people in the caravan, although only two of us were to be tested that day.

I was by far the youngest in the group. The other person to be tested that day was a man in his twenties whose blonde facial hair was still patchy and who looked like he hadn't quite grown into his limbs yet. In truth, he reminded me a bit of Shaggy from the Scooby Doo cartoons, with significantly less personality.

Set up in the field were six small sheds. They were the kind you could buy pre made at a garden or hardware store and looked like miniature houses. A couple of them even had small porches on the front as though they were meant more to be children's play houses rather than used for storing gardening supplies.

Each of us was told to shield three of the sheds. Once finished, we were sent back to one of the vehicles to wait while the others took turns testing the shields. Aunt Lou sat with me and tried to make small talk with Kevin, the Shaggy look-alike. His answers were mostly mumbles and usually consisted of only one word at a time, so she soon gave up and we sat in silence. The car where we waited was parked next to a rather large oak tree. It blocked most of the view of the testing, which I was fairly certain was intentional. All we could see were blasts of crackling light. It smelled like a lightning strike and I wondered what would happen if the grass around us caught fire.

Eventually all six of the shields were broken and everyone filed back into the vehicles so we could conga back to the main house. Everyone was quiet on the drive back to the house.

"There were eight people waiting," I remembered as I continued to delicately strip paint from the carved wood. "Maybe nine."

They had all been older than my grandfather and all were capable of shielding. Once Jeffery announced our levels, they greeted each of us offering congratulations to both me and Shaggy, and stayed long enough to share a cup of fruit punch and doughnuts. From some of the comments made, I was fairly certain that the fruit punch was due to the fact that I was twelve, my early development causing me to be younger than most during my test. Kevin was invited out for a more adult celebration when Aunt Lou and I headed back to town.

I wasn't sure where Kevin was from and I had no clue where the other eight or nine people lived, or if they were still alive by this point. That was the only time I met them. Our paths never crossed again and none of them looked like they were planning to work on apartment buildings. In fact none of them, including Kevin, looked like they were planning to go on any job sites given both their age and their clothing. I thought the clothing might just be because they dressed for the celebration, but I was certain their age meant they were either retired or significantly slowing down their activities in construction sites.

A few of them looked disappointed that it was only Keven and me being tested. Most of them looked surprised that I was being tested. I wasn't sure if it was my age or gender that threw them off as I was the only female in the crowd, barring Aunt Lou. If there were any other people capable of shielding, I hadn't been invited to their testing.

"Or they are in another region and the regions don't mix," I thought, although the thought felt odd. I knew James, and Jeffrey before him, were in charge of coordinating things, Commission-wise, for my region and I knew that others held the same position in different regions. I even met some of them as James sometimes sent me to different regions to work, their coordinators sometimes meeting with me before I set to work. *"And if I can go to different regions, why wouldn't we meet?"*

It was a question I never thought to ask, like the percentages James and Malak received. I usually thought about my shielding projects in terms of the disruptions they made to my normal life not as me being part of a group. When I was in middle and high school it was whether or not the list of projects would take over my entire spring or summer break or if I would still have time to relax like the others my age.

In my college years, I worried over completing papers and studying for exams between jobs and dealing with the havoc disappearing one weekend a month did do my social life. While many of my friends were from the magical community and understood being required to work with the Commission, many weren't. Nearly every guy I dated who was not from the magical community, assigned somewhat nefarious reasons to my routine disappearances.

Usually another man.

"And Sean wonders why I date poorly," I muttered to myself as I realized it was getting close to the end of the day and began cleaning off my tools. Admittedly, the dating aspect did get easier once I was out of college. I started working at a large design firm and it was well known that my grandfather was in ill health. Everyone merely thought if I was out of town, I was visiting him. Once I went to work for the family business, the stock excuse of dealing with a client covered nearly everything.

I shrugged to myself as I finished putting things to rights and got ready to leave. It was probably my fault for not dating more people in the magical community. If I had, then I wouldn't need a cover story. I could just tell him, whoever he was, that I was working for the Commission. Such thoughts brought me back to thinking about Davis.

Admiration for his physique and warm smile faded, leaving me with thoughts about the building and potential unexpected disasters, which led to thoughts about the reporter. I sighed, somewhat disgusted with myself and wishing I could keep my thoughts to just ogling Davis. They may have been inappropriate, but they didn't turn my belly into a pool of acid worry. I noticed everyone else left the workshop and I locked up before leaving the darkened building.

When I arrived home, Winston capered around the apartment as though I had been kidnapped and finally returned to him after extensive ransom negotiations. He spun around in circles wiggling and barking excitedly as I changed into running clothes and slipped on my sneakers.

"It was just one morning," I told him as I began to stretch, pleased that someone was that excited to see me even if it was somewhat unwarranted. Taking no chances, he picked up his leash from its resting place and placed himself directly in front of the doorway, eyes following my movements. "You are getting as bad as Sammy," I told him.

I finished stretching and took the leash from Winston's mouth, clipping it to his collar. Winston tugged me through my warm up section of our pathway and we hit the park at top speed. I could see the other dog owners in the park and occasionally tossed a few of them a wave with my free hand. Dogs barked out greetings, but Winston ignored them. He was on a mission to make up for his morning run and nothing was going to stop him.

Both of us were panting as we headed back towards the apartment. Daylight was fading and I was beginning to feel a little nervous as the overhead streetlights buzzed to life and the shadows lengthened. We were moving at a normal walking speed to cool down as we approached the building and when we passed the spot where Davis turned the three shadow creatures to ash, I found myself staring.

There was no sign of them on the street, no sign of anything really, and Winston and I moved past the unremarkable patch of asphalt. We climbed the stairs to the apartment and I opened the door, letting us both inside. I unhooked Winston's leash and he immediately went to see what was in his dog bowl. As Sean filled it when he arrived home, it was full and Winston lost no time in devouring its contents as though he hadn't been fed in weeks.

"Well don't we look spiffy," I said as Sean emerged from the back. Sean turned and posed as though walking a runway. "What's the occasion?"

"Dinner," Sean told me, his face fighting a grin.

"Really anyone I know?" I kept my voice sounding innocent.

"Jake," Sean replied. "Don't make a big deal of it."

"I wasn't going to," I assured him. "Tell him I said hello."

"I will," Sean said nodding. He checked his cuffs, straightened his tie, which was already ruler straight, and touched his perfectly styled hair. He sighed heavily, his grin slipping as his nerves began to show.

"God, I wasn't this nervous on our first date. Not that this is even a date really. We're just going to dinner to catch up." Sean once again checked his cuffs, tie and hair. "What if he wants to have dinner with me to tell me he's met someone else? That they are head-over-heals in love with each other and adopting a dozen babies from China."

"I don't think your ex is inviting you to dinner to tell you he is adopting a dozen babies from China," I assured him.

"You don't know, he could be," Sean said. I could see the panic rising in his eyes.

"I think they only let you get one at a time, or maybe two if they are a matched set like twins. I don't think you can take a dozen at once."

Sean frowned his hands stilling. "You know what I mean."

"I do," I conceded. "How did he look when he ran into you the other day? Did he look happy to see you?"

"Well yes."

"Did you ask him out or did he ask you?"

"He asked me."

"Did he mention a new boyfriend? Or that he had something he wanted to talk to you about?"

"Well no, but why would he?"

"Did he do or say anything that made you think he was dating someone else?"

"No, he just said he wanted to reconnect now that he was back in town. He could be waiting to spring the new guy and Chinese babies on me."

"Do you think he would do that in public and at dinner?"

"No, he'd probably tell me in private."

"And where are you going for your dinner?"

"Mama Leonie's."

"Where you had your first date?"

"Yeah," Sean gave me a half smile.

"I don't think he's telling you he is adopting babies with another man. I think he wants to get you naked."

"Really?" Sean asked, a hopeful gleam in his eye.

"Really," I replied. "And for the record, since I have been up since well before the sun, I am going to bed early and will probably sleep like the dead, hearing nothing of any sort until morning." Sean smiled. "Feel better?"

"Much."

"Good, now I am going to sleep," I told him stifling a yawn. "Have a good time."

"Night," He called as I headed down the hallway to my bedroom. "And may pleasant thoughts of naked contractors dancing in your head follow you into your dreams." I heard Sean chuckling as he left the apartment, all nerves forgotten, or at least buried. A few minutes later, I was clad in my pajamas and slipping between my sheets, eyes already heavy.

"Please don't let Jake be in love with someone else and adopting a bunch of Chinese babies," I prayed as I closed my eyes.

Chapter 11

Whether due to Sean's suggestion or the day's events, thoughts of Davis did follow me into sleep. Unfortunately, the dreams fell more into the nightmare category than the fantasy one. The dreams were jumbled and the topics shifted and blurred together. In one dream Davis and I were attacked by the shadow creatures and both of our skills failed. I couldn't get my shields up and Davis managed to miss when he threw the red balls of energy at them. Disturbingly, I heard an umpire like voice calling one, two and three strikes before declaring us out and letting the creatures tear into us. A row of babies in carriers watched from the sidelines. I couldn't tell if they were Chinese or not but they were all holding boxes of popcorn.

In other dreams, Davis called to tell me the building's foundation crumbled and I raced down the street only to find the apartment building listing sharply to one side like a ship after hitting an iceberg. In still others, Bradford demanded to know why I would shield an apartment building and not shield his friend's apartment. He then hurled books at my head until I was buried in half a library's worth of texts. Sometimes James would show up to lecture me, before, after or during the book throwing.

The dreams cycled through over and over again, sometimes, just for fun, blurring together so that Bradford threw books at the apartment building and Davis and I turned to ash and fell to the ground, James lecturing us while the creatures licked up our ashes as though we were their favorite ice cream. Weirdly, several times Davis danced naked in the background when I had to deal with Bradford or listen to a lecture by James. I woke up early, twisted in the sheets and feeling like I had been running most of the night. Slowly, I untangled myself.

"At least I can blame Sean for the naked dancing parts," I told myself as I got out of bed. "And the babies. I just know they were Chinese." Winston and I went on our normal run and when we returned, I put on the coffee before leaving Winston to his breakfast while I showered. Sean still wasn't awake when I returned to the kitchen and I realized that even with an extra lap around the park, I was still up earlier than usual.

"So even with the nightmares the early night helped," I told myself. As I settled with my first cup of coffee I pulled out the new rules and regulations booklet. Slowly, I read over each one of the rules regarding shielded properties. Sometime in my dreams, I realized I was nervous about the fact that I was creating shielded apartments when I knew of no one else who had and I needed to reassure myself that what I was doing was in fact legal. I read the booklet cover to cover, even checking the date of the edition to make certain it was the latest copy of the regulations and not an older copy that had accidentally gotten into the pile. The booklet was less than a month old.

"And I was right," I told myself, shoving the booklet away. Nothing I was doing was against the regulations. Everything was perfectly legal. "So why is everyone making such a fuss? There can't be that great a need for shielded apartments."

While the shadow creatures were dangerous, if attacks were so common *The Whisper* would have reported something and pressure would have been put on the Commission to change the rules. It was after all their job to keep us all safe. That was why we put up with the regulations they set. When the rules were revised, more would have changed had it been a problem. The only thing that appeared to have changed in this latest edition was that if the person providing the shielding for one of the private schools had a child, they could trade their shielding for tuition credits for their child or children. As I had no children, the few times I was called in to shield a school I waived my fee. The change didn't affect me much.

"I suppose if I had kids it would mean more," I decided, still sipping my coffee. Winston finished his chow and arranged himself in the sun. "And they were just revised," I continued, looking at the booklet. "Clearly there wasn't that big of an uproar over them." Despite my apparent conviction, the whole thing still left me feeling uneasy.

Annoyed with myself, I got ready for my day, deciding to go in a little early since I would be taking off time later in the week for the interview and didn't know when Davis would call to let me know there were small jobs on site that I could work on. As I was getting ready to leave, Sean shambled out of his bedroom, poured two cups of coffee, tossed me a grin and headed back to his room.

"No Chinese babies I guess," I told Winston as I gave him a quick belly rub before heading out to the shop.

On my walk to work I decided to give into my thoughts about Wendy Watts. Instead of trying to push her and all thoughts about the interview from my mind and being annoyed with myself when worries circled around like sharks, I decided to deliberately think about it. As I reached the shop and began my day, I tried to decide what sorts of questions she could ask me and how I would respond. I ran the interview over in my head from a dozen different angles, my imaginary questions ranging from the serious to the ridiculous.

"Why did you buy the property," I imagined she would ask when thinking of more serious questions. I decided telling her I happened to be attending a foreclosure auction when the property came up and I decided it would be a good investment, would sound better than using the words 'accidental purchase because no one bid against me after I was stupid enough to raise my number'.

"And how exactly do you plan on taking advantage of Davis once the project is complete," the Wendy in my head asked me in my sillier thoughts. As I was thinking of a response, a throat clearing cough caused me to look up. When I saw Davis standing there, I felt heat scald my face and was certain I was scarlet from my neck to my hairline.

"That's quite a reaction," Davis said, eyes sparkling with amusement. "Want to share your thoughts with the class?"

"I was thinking of something else," I replied stupidly as I turned off my heat gun and set it to the side, making sure it wasn't near anything that could burn.

"Would that something else be something *naughty*?" he asked wiggling his eyebrows at me.

"I was just thinking about the possible questions Wendy might ask during the interview and what I might say," I told him, certain the flush on my face deepened.

"I don't think she asks those sorts of questions," He replied. "So, you set up an interview?"

"Sean did actually," I said. I gave him the details. "You aren't ready for me now are you?" I asked wondering why he had stopped by the shop. I thought I had time before I would be needed at the apartment building.

"No, I told you I'd wait until the building was done," He replied with a grin.

"I meant with the smaller jobs at the apartment building," I said.

"Oh that, no it will be a few more days before we are ready to turn you loose with a bucket of primer and a paint roller in the first of the apartments. I was just checking on the cabinets with Greg and figured I'd stop by and see if you wanted to grab lunch."

I blinked in surprise. "Lunch?" I looked over at the wall clock and realized it was a little after noon. "Oh, lunch."

Davis grinned at me and shook his head. "I wanted to go over paint colors if you had the time."

"Sure," I replied. I quickly washed up and made certain I looked reasonably presentable before we left the shop.

"Your room divider is coming along nicely," He told me as we left the shop and headed to the deli next door.

"Thanks," I told him. The deli was packed, and while I was certain we'd make it to the counter to order, I doubted we would find a table.

"Are you leaving the wood natural?" He asked as we took our place in the noisy line. His size made him seem like a large boulder in the middle of a swift moving stream, the current of people swirling around him, but not making much of an impact. As a much smaller obstacle, I was less insulated and received jabs and slight inadvertent shoves as people flowed around us. Noticing my difficulty, Davis pulled me in closer, his hand resting on my back. The buffeting stopped and he left his hand in place as the line slowly moved forward.

"Um no," I told him feeling somewhat distracted by his warm hand on my back. "There are still small traces of the paint imbedded in the details that I can't remove without damaging the design, but more importantly, it was never built to be unpainted. You can see where some of the wood was cobbled in and doesn't quite match."

"So what are you going to do with it?"

We made it up to the front and placed our sandwich orders. We each paid for our lunches and Davis slipped his hand off my back.

I tried not to feel disappointed. We shuffled along, getting our sandwiches quickly. As I thought, there were no available seats.

"Back to the shop?" I suggested. Earlier I saw Sammy moving a table and chairs into the conference room in anticipation of my interview and thought it would be as good a place as any to eat. Davis agreed and we headed back. The shop was empty and quiet when we returned. The small conference room felt further secluded from the rest of the shop. Not only did Sammy manage to find a table and chairs but he added a buffet to the side, placing a vase filled with flowers in the center. Mirrors were placed on the wall, reflecting each other and the room, so it felt more spacious. Everything looked ready for my interview the following day. I made a mental note to thank Sammy for his efforts.

"Sammy really out did himself," I said as I sat down across the table from Davis.

"Sammy?"

"Store manager," I clarified. "I needed a place to have my interview with Wendy Watts. A few days ago this just had three old folding chairs. Now, it looks respectable."

"Very nice." Davis said. We each unwrapped our sandwiches and began to eat. "So you never said what you were planning for the room divider." Davis prompted.

"Oh, I guess I didn't. Actually given the detail, I was thinking of having it sprayed in kind of a cinnabar color, you know that sort of red-orange color of cinnabar bracelets. The pattern sort of reminds me of one of those bracelets."

"That would be bold," Davis replied looking as though he was trying to picture what I was talking about.

"It would be a statement piece I suppose," I admitted.

"Are you worried about the interview?" He asked.

"A little."

"Are you going to tell them it was an accidental purchase?" He asked, smiling.

"No, I was planning to keep that to myself. I was going to go with, it seemed like a good investment."

"Probably a good idea. Don't worry, your secret is safe with me."

"I appreciate it. So, how are your nephews? Nightmares leaving them and Christy?"

"Slowly but surely," Davis replied. "Now that the yard is shielded, the boys have started begging to be allowed to have a camp out in the back yard. Christy is not quite that relaxed about it, but has agreed to a barbeque."

"Isn't it a bit late in the season for campouts and barbeques? Apparently my neighbor tried it while I was on the Fausti site and it didn't turn out so well."

"I should have said, a barbeque come spring," Davis added. "She's also managed to convince them that it is too cold to spend a night out of doors right now, so they are planning for the summer. I think their non-magical friends spun tales of summer camps and nights under the stars and they got jealous."

"Ah," I replied. "Not exactly the norm for us." By the time my friends were going off to summer camps, my leg already sported a shadow creature bite mark and even though the camps sounded like fun, nothing was going to get me to camp alone in the unprotected dark.

"I suppose not. But the cookouts should be fun."

"Because who doesn't love grilled tofu," I replied.

Davis' smile dropped. "I didn't even think of that."

"Maybe you can claim grilling as a manly thing and then you only have to worry about the side dishes."

"I like the way you think," Davis said nodding in approval. "Of course, she could be over her tofu thing by then. Her food crazes don't seem to last that long."

"Was there something that started her love of tofu?"

"I think it was one too many articles about cholesterol and hormones in meat. She seems to read a lot of articles about nutrition and GMOs and other stuff, but only seems to fixate on one ingredient at a time. She went through a brown rice phase and then she went through a no- carb phase, and if I remember that was followed by the no gluten phase and now we are in the tofu phase. Luckily for Mike, she drops one phase before she starts the next. I'm not so sure he would survive if he had to go through the gluten and carb free life at the same time she was inflicting tofu. I think he's secretly hoping that that caveman, paleo diet will attract her interest soon."

We chatted amiably as we ate our sandwiches and I found myself liking Davis more. While he was always friendly and good looking, on the work sites, he was boss which didn't leave a lot of room for casual conversation. It was nice to find I liked him as a person as well as a fantasy.

After lunch, we made decisions on paint colors, he headed back to the apartment building and I headed back to my room divider. I traced a hand over the wood, studying the design. The carvings definitely reminded me of the cinnabar bracelet sitting in my jewelry box. It had been my grandmother's and I always found it intriguing as a child. I remembered sitting on her lap as she told me stories about how it was made. My favorite involved a red hot stone taken from inside the heart of a volcano and placed under ground. There ants would swarm the rock, taking little pieces and leaving behind the delicately carved bracelet. I even tried my own version when I was little and got into a whole lot of trouble when I heated one of the charcoal briquettes for my father's grill up to a white hot heat and dropped it into the center of an ant hill in our back yard.

Neither my parents nor the ants had been happy that day. From then on my grandmother added the words 'skilled artisans who trained for years' to each of her more fantastical tales.

I smiled at the piece and decided cinnabar was the right color. Something so bold might turn off some buyers, but we would have to place it in such a way that it accented a room's design rather than clashed which was certain to attract others. I was certain that between Sammy and me, we could come up with something. I finished the second panel and began work on the third and final panel, a mental plan in place.

The rest of the day passed in relative quiet as I tried not to think about the upcoming interview. When I left for the day, I went home and spent a great deal of time looking through my closet. While I would be working in my habitual jeans and t-shirt combo, I wanted to look nice during the interview. I also didn't want to be stumbling around the work room in a skirt and heels. I pushed aside both my date wear and paint spattered clothes. Sadly, this left me with a limited selection to choose from. I picked through the remaining selections finally coming up with a pair of gray wool slacks and a blue cashmere sweater. I figured with a bit of shoe polish, and only the toes showing, my work boots would pass.

I hung the interview outfit on the back of my bedroom door, folded a pair of jeans and a t-shirt and stuffed the not so dressy clothes into my messenger bag. Once Wendy was through with me, I could nip into the bathroom, change and get back to work.

"Now, I just need to tackle those boots," I told myself narrowing my eyes as I looked around the room. "If I were shoe polish where would I be stashed?"

Chapter 12

The next morning, I woke to a gray sky, rain sheeting down. "Oh, this is going to be fun," I told myself, knowing Winston's reaction to the wet. Sure enough, he was ready and eager to go, right until we hit the side walk and he could see the rain hitting the pavement. Winston tilted his head up, looking at me as though he thought I had gone completely insane.

"I don't control the weather." I told him. Delicately, he extended a paw out from under the area sheltered by the overhang. He touched it to the wet sidewalk and picked his paw immediately back up, holding it as though the paw were now injured, a low whine in his throat.

"Yeah, rough, tough fighting dog bred for life in the pits, that's you." I told him. I opened up the large umbrella I brought with me and stepped out onto the side walk. The rain hit the fabric of the umbrella hard and I thought there might be a little ice mixed in. It was certainly cold enough for it.

Winston snorted, shook his head and followed. He kept close to the building, walking as much as he could on the strip of dry concrete covered by the building's eaves. When we reached the end of the building, Winston hung his head as though being led to the gallows. Instead of going to the park, he moved into the trees separating the tenant parking from the street, quickly did his morning business, turned and headed straight back to the apartment building at a brisk trot.

"So no run today?" I asked as we stepped back into the stairwell. Winston snorted and tugged me back upstairs. "How is it that you hate the rain so much, but as soon as someone turns a sprinkler on in a yard, you think it is the most magically, delightful thing ever?" I asked as I filled his bowl. He ignored my question in favor of the food. "Oh well, I need the extra time to look presentable I suppose."

I left Winston, took my morning shower and dressed in my interview appropriate clothes. Since I had the time, I even added a bit of makeup to my face, something I rarely remembered to do. Once ready, I settled myself with my coffee, mentally running through the possible answers to Wendy's questions in my head.

"Morning," Sean said joining me and interrupting my mental recap. I was insanely grateful for something else to think about for the moment. "Ready for your interview?"

"I suppose," I replied not wanting to think about it. "I take it your date went well the other night?"

Sean grinned. "It did and we are going out again soon."

"So… are you two back together?" I asked.

"We are just keeping things casual and seeing where they end up."

"Uh huh," I replied, swallowing my comments about where they ended up the night before so as not to dent my cousin's happiness. "So what's on your agenda today?"

"Well, the morning is all about website management," He told me. "It needs to be done and I figured it would keep me close. We sold a few pieces so those images will need to be taken down and we have several new pieces to add." Sean took a sip of his coffee. "I'll also be shooting a list over to the workshop of designer requests."

I nodded. A large portion of our clientele was made up of designers. Several of them sent messages when they were looking for specific pieces. Often they would send pieces to us to be refinished for a specific job. Sometimes when they knew what they needed but didn't have it, we had a piece that suited, but had yet to be refinished or reupholstered and we could work with them on specifics using the color and fabric of their choosing. We also built things from scratch for them and a few sent us standing requests. For those designers with standing requests, we sent images of items prior to posting them on our website giving them the chance to purchase the item before it became publicly available.

"Anything I should keep in mind?" I asked.

"We have a standing request from Lucy Mays for interesting lamps."

"Interesting lamps?"

"I think she just wants non-typical lamps, but I am calling to clarify and will add any notes I get to the list."

"Well, it is a little more specific than John Charles and his standing request for 'seating'," I reminded him.

"True, but John Charles does end up buying about ninety percent of the seating related items we show him."

"This is true. Speaking of which, Cole is working on a piece he may find interesting. I think it might loosely qualify as seating to the broadminded, but as Charles always snaps up the more unusual items, it might be worth sending him an image. He should be finishing it up in the next day or so."

"I'll check with him for a photograph." Sean told me. "Mostly I'm keeping to the office until Wendy leaves in case she wants to talk to me after she interviews you. Oh, and on those lines, I have the bulk of the apartment building website set up. We'll need pictures of the finished and staged apartments to add to it, but now not only does the Ravenwood Arms have a website, but future tenants can pay rent on line as well as log maintenance requests."

"Nice," I replied nodding.

"Also I did the legal paperwork so that The Ravenwood Arms is part of the Appleton Property Management Group."

"Since when is one building a group?" I asked.

"One building now," He replied. "More can always be added later."

"Can we just finish one building before building a real estate empire?"

"Of course," Sean said. "However the legal set up separates your personal finances from the business ones. You remember we talked about this when dealing with the furniture store. It was the whole 'if something bad happens the business is liable but you are personally protected' thing we went over."

"I vaguely recall your lengthy tirade on the subject and then, as now, I thank you for taking the steps to legally protect me and the business." I told him.

"Which means you remember signing the paperwork and know that it is important, but nothing else," Sean translated.

"Pretty much, yeah." I replied nodding.

Sean shook his head. "You know the legal stuff is important?"

"I do, which is why I sign the paper work you put together. I was just thrown off by suddenly being a group."

"I wouldn't worry about it. I just wanted you to know the name before the interview."

"And if Wendy Watts asks about the group thing?" My stomach tensed at the thought of explaining the legal aspects.

"Just tell her to talk to me about the name," Sean assured me. I felt a little bit better.

A little while later I headed towards the shop. As I walked, huddled under my umbrella, I was certain the rain was at least half ice. When I reached the shop, I went in through the back so I wouldn't drip water all over the show room. While I knew Sammy would set out floor mats and have a slew of towels ready to prevent slick, wet floors and possibly calamitous spills, I didn't see the need to add to the mess. Since I hoped to stay clean until after the interview, I left my work-in-progress sit. I put my bag of work clothes under the bench, taking out the rules and regulations booklet before I did. I set it on the workbench next to my laptop. I didn't think I would need it, but brought it anyway, just in case.

I powered up the laptop and went to the site Sean gave me. There I typed in the password to take a look at the as of yet non-public site. It looked good, very professional and user friendly. It even included a downloadable application for potential tenants to fill out. I could see where pictures would be placed and how it would enhance the page.

"Not bad," I decided.

"Is that for the apartment building," A voice said behind me causing me to jump and let out a small yip of surprise. I spun around and saw a woman grinning sheepishly at me.

"Sorry, the manager sent me back." She held out a hand. "I'm Wendy Watts."

"Alice Appleton," I replied, introducing myself as I shook her hand. Wendy Watts was put together head to toe. Her hair was an artfully arranged mass of glossy black waves, her make-up flawless and her outfit put together so perfectly that not only did the shoes and purse coordinate, but her umbrella matched as well. Even her manicured and painted nails matched. She looked like she stepped directly off of a magazine page. It was somewhat unsettling.

"And yes, this is for the Ravenwood Arms," I told her. "It won't be public until we finish construction and take some pictures."

"May I?" she asked, stepping around to the workbench.

"Sure," I told her moving aside so she didn't have to hip check the mostly stripped wooden panel. She looked at the laptop, clicked around a bit, then smiled and stepped away.

"Is that the shielding regulations booklet?" She asked spotting it as she backed up carefully to avoid damaging her outfit.

"It is," I told her. "I didn't know if it would be useful or not, but figured better safe than sorry. I thought we could use the back conference room for our talk," I continued picking up the booklet to take with us. I powered down the laptop. At the other workstations the others were taking tools out and getting ready to begin their tasks for the day. I knew several of them were dragging their feet so as to keep quiet. "It's about to get loud in here."

"Of course," She replied smiling and looking around. I led her back to the meeting room and as soon as we moved around the corner and were out of the direct line of sight, I could hear a belt sander fire up as Cole began working on a dining room table. A second later and the sound of Greg's table saw was added to the mix.

"I see what you mean," Wendy said with a little laugh as we entered the meeting room and I closed the door. The sound was significantly muffled, but not gone.

"So," I said as we settled ourselves at the table. "You have some questions?" I put the booklet on the table instead of clutching it like a security blanket.

"Direct and to the point," She said pulling not only a notebook and pen from her giant luggage-like purse, but a small digital recorder as well. "I like it." She opened her notebook and made a quick notation before turning the recorder on. "Interview with Alice Appleton of the Ravenwood Arms Apartments," she said into the recorder. She then listed the date and turned to me. "So you recently purchased an apartment building named The Ravenwood Arms," Wendy began. "How did that happen?"

"A friend of mine wanted to go to a foreclosure auction," I said. "She's fond of home improvement shows, heard about the auctions, and thought it would be fun."

"And you went to help her buy a property?"

"No," I replied with a laugh. "I went to try and talk her out of buying a property. She is the least handy person I know and I didn't want her getting in over her head either physically or financially. Luckily, she was out bid on everything she tried to buy."

"But you weren't?"

"No, I ended up buying the Ravenwood. I thought it might be a good investment."

"And you are planning on putting a shield on the apartment building?"

"Actually, I already put the shields on the apartment building," I told her. "The parking lot and yard have a shield and the building has an overall shield. In addition, each apartment has an individual shield as well."

"That sounds quite thorough," Wendy said, her pen scratching away.

"Well, you know the old saying, if it's worth doing, it's worth doing right."

"Of course," She said with a smile. I tried not to look at the notes she was taking. I could only control what I said, not what she thought of me. "You know that shielded apartments are rather rare?"

"That is more than likely because of the restrictions." I replied.

"And what are the restrictions?"

I quickly outlined the details of who was allowed to shield apartment buildings, which buildings they could work on and what the specifics were. She asked me to find the relevant legal codes in the booklet and I did, handing her the booklet. She read the regulations out loud, including the section numbers of the rules and the page number that the specific regulation was printed on. I guessed it was for the recorder so she would have specifics later without taking my book or writing it all down long hand.

Satisfied with the legalities, she then asked me about my shielding experience and even about how those capable of shielding were tested and ranked. She asked how I took my jobs and what the process of shielding involved. I walked her through taking a call from James Rutherford, Tom Malak picking me up and shuttling me to whatever site I had been contracted to shield, shielding the site and reporting back into James when the project was complete.

I left out the part about Malak's audio books.

Throughout the interview, her face remained politely interested. I had no clue if she knew all of the information I was giving her or if it was all new information. At no time did her mask slip. I decided she was not a woman with whom I ever wished to play poker. I thought she might even give Sean a hard time.

"And work on the Ravenwood Arms is proceeding?" She asked shifting back to asking about the building.

"Yes, I'm working with Davis Construction to get the building ready for occupancy," I told her.

"And have you worked with them before? Is that why you chose them?"

"I have shielded several sites where they were responsible for the construction or renovation of the property and chose them because they do good work and are locally based."

"Excellent," Wendy said. She clicked off the recorder and closed her notebook. "I think I have enough. Thank you for meeting with me." She put her notepad and recorder into her bag and we both stood. "I was hoping to talk to your cousin Sean before I left. He's the one handling the legal set up, right?"

"He is and his office is right next door. Actually, if you use the back exit of our building, the awning for our loading dock and his almost meet so you could actually stay dry."

"It is quite the nasty day isn't it?" She commented looking relieved that a sprint through ice edged rain in heels wasn't imminent. "You know they are predicting snow over night?"

"Really?" I said wondering how that would affect Davis and his crew. I hoped they had the furnaces installed and working so they didn't have to work in the cold. "I thought we still had a few more weeks before first snowfall."

As we chatted about the weather, I led Wendy to the back door and opened it. We stepped onto the sheltered stoop and I pointed the door she needed and gave her directions to Gina's desk, knowing Sean's assistant would take it from there.

"It was a pleasure meeting you," She told me.

"Likewise," I replied. I watched her walk to the edge of our loading dock and step over the three inch gap onto the loading dock of Sean's building. She waved as she let herself into the building.

"Well, that wasn't so bad," I told myself. I looked at the rain falling from the sky and tried to decide if it had gotten colder or if it just felt that way because my coat was inside. "Standing out in it without a coat isn't helping," I told myself.

I turned and went back inside, closing the door firmly behind me. As I did, I pushed thoughts of the interview away and decided there was nothing I could do about it now. I also decided I would stop by the apartment building after work and hope that Davis didn't interpret it as snooping. With that in mind, I retrieved my work clothes, changed in the bathroom and got back to work.

The rest of my day passed smoothly and I resisted the urge to call Sean and ask how his interview went. I also resisted calling Davis to ask if Wendy contacted him about the building. I figured when I stopped by, he might tell me. I also tried to tell myself I was stopping by as a property owner checking on progress rather than snooping around to find out what Wendy asked. In the end, I only half believed myself. By the time my workday ended and I was ready to leave the shop, the rain stopped. The clouds still loomed heavily as though promising they weren't finished.

"We just might get that snow," I said as I pulled my coat closer. My interview clothes were in my messenger bag and I clutched my umbrella in one hand. It was closed since the rain stopped, but I knew if I left it behind the sky would open up immediately, soaking me in freezing water. I walked quickly and was soon at the Ravenwood Arms. At the building, I noticed the gate to the parking lot was open and, when I looked, the lot was full of trucks that seemed accustomed to being on construction sites. All of them had some form of tool box built in or some sort of rig used to move large panes of glass, drywall or other large flat items. To my surprise, the fence surrounding the parking lot had already been replaced.

"At least they aren't working outside now," I said to myself as I walked back around to the front door. "I guess they wanted to finish the outside work before the season turned completely."

I opened the front door and stepped inside. The small vestibule now had a light fixture with no more dangling electrical wires in evidence. In addition, the beat up silver mail boxes were replaced, keys were placed in each of the locks, tags with apartment numbers dangling from them. The security door had been re-installed, although I saw it had yet to have a lock added to it. I wondered why they put up the door before finding a lock for it, but as I pushed it open, it soon became evident. As the door swung open, a wash of heat hit me.

"I guess the furnaces are working," I said to myself, pushing the door closed behind me. I opened my coat and slipped it off. Spotting what looked like an army's worth of outerwear, I added mine to the mix. Next to the much larger garments, worn, no doubt, by the Davis men, my coat looked like it belonged to a child.

"That family does breed them big," I muttered to myself. I shoved the long sleeves of my t-shirt up to the elbows. While I was certain the heat wasn't turned up full blast, compared to the icy wind that tried to peel my skin from my bones on the walk over, it felt deliciously warm inside. Hearing the sounds of tools and men, I headed in. Poking my head into one of the apartments I saw several of the Davis men at work. Mike was on a ladder and installing a light fixture into what would be the apartment's living room. Two others I couldn't name were finishing the installation of the kitchen floor, while another was taping the seams where sheets of drywall met.

"Alice, hi," Mike said as he saw me in the door way. He put the final screw into the fixture and descended the ladder. "Last time I saw him, he was on the top floor."

"Oh," I replied surprised by his reaction even though it was probably more than obvious who I came to see. "Okay, thanks. I'm glad you guys got the furnaces going. It's a miserable day outside."

"Is it still raining?" he asked.

"The rain stopped, but it doesn't look like it wants to stop for long. We might actually get some snow tonight. The sky sure looks like it."

As Mike looked like he wanted to take the ladder into the other room, I left and headed upstairs. I found Davis in the large four-bedroom apartment. My eyes went wide as I took in the change to the apartment. Instead of basic framing indicating where walls should be and exposed wiring with uninsulated walls, the exterior walls had been covered with drywall, and the interior walls were complete. They looked like actual walls instead of suggestions as to where walls might go if someone were inclined to place them. The floors were covered with brown paper and I guessed that it was protecting new flooring and that I was no longer walking directly on the subfloor.

"This actually looks like an apartment," I said as Davis walked over.

"Well that was what we were going for," He replied with a laugh. "I was actually going to call you about that. We finished the sanding on this apartment and it is ready for its primer coat and paint, if you still want to help out to cut costs. We are still working on the lower floors, but if you wanted to start up here, tomorrow would be a good time."

"That was quick," I said.

"There is still a lot of work to be done," he warned me. Davis walked me through the apartment, showing me their progress as the rest of the crew packed up and got ready to head out. While he was right, there was still a lot of work to do, I was impressed by how much they had gotten done. Around us the building quieted as the others left for the day. Davis took me through the other few floors and pointed out their progress. By the time we finished the tour of the basement, we were the only ones left on site.

"Well I finished the piece I was working on today," I told him. "The final coat of lacquer needs to dry but it can do that without me watching it, so I am all yours."

"Are you now?" he asked with a grin.

"For the painting," I added.

"So tomorrow morning we will have you on site, then," He said.

"Will that be a problem?"

"Nope." He replied. "And since I'm sure you will be wearing sensible shoes, I won't have to worry about you breaking your neck."

"Sensible shoes?" I asked, looking down at my boots.

"Wendy Watts stopped by for a tour," he explained.

"Oh," I said, somewhat surprised. "I thought she would call, but I didn't think she would stop by." I thought about the shoes she was wearing. They had very high, very skinny heels. "Not in those shoes at least."

"We had a few tense moments," he said with a frown.

"I'm sorry."

"Not your fault," Davis said with a shrug. He looked past me and frowned out of the window. I turned and looked, following his gaze. Outside, fat flakes of snow were drifting from a sky that had gone a dark murderous gray.

"You walked?" he asked.

"I did," I replied.

"I'll drive you home," Davis told me.

"I brought a coat, I'll be fine," I told him.

Davis shook his head. "It's not the cold, it's the dark. Or the things in the dark rather."

"Oh, well there is that," I replied.

"And it isn't out of the way," He said before I could protest.

"Thanks, I appreciate that," I told him, knowing whatever protest I brought wouldn't really matter. Besides, the thought of not walking home in the dark was a pleasant one. I knew I could hold my shields up as I ran like hell for a few blocks, but I didn't really want to. I jumped as the cell phone in my back pocket buzzed to life.

"The phone is actually on?" He said with a smile.

"It's Sean." I told him. "I left it on in case he had issues with his interview."

"Go ahead and answer it, I want to check the locks anyway." Davis went to make certain the building was secure for the night as I answered Sean's call.

"Where are you?" He asked even as I said hello.

"The apartment building."

"You aren't walking home alone in this are you?"

"No," I assured him. "Davis is going to be driving me home."

"Good," Sean replied. "And as thanks, ask him if he wants to join us for pizza. Jake is here and we figured it would be better than going out in this mess."

"I'll ask. After all he also gave Wendy a tour today which definitely deserves a thanks as I don't think he enjoyed having her on the property. How did your meeting with her go?"

"Not bad," Sean said. "She asked about the website and the rates, checked out our application and asked about our timeline. It was all quick and painless."

I felt a tight coil of tension I hadn't realized I was carrying around in my belly loosen a little. "Good."

"I'm not surprised she visited Davis though, apparently she is being quite thorough. She called James Rutherford's office."

Davis returned from his inspection. "She called James?" I asked, the tension winding tight again. Davis lifted an eyebrow at my tone.

"Yup, she asked several questions and wants to see you in action. James called and wants you for another job. He left a message for you to call him ASAP no matter what time you got the message. He left his cell number rather than the office one."

"Okay, I'll call when I get home," I told him. "Which will be shortly."

"Ask about dinner," Sean said before he hung up.

"And goodbye to you too," I said into the dead phone.

"So who called James," Davis asked as we headed towards the coats. The multitude of outerwear was reduced to two jackets, my messenger bag and umbrella.

"Wendy," I told him. "She asked if she could watch me on a job and now James has a job for me."

"So you might not be painting tomorrow?"

"I don't think he would arrange a job that quickly," I said. "But it will probably put a dent in my painting time. Good thing you budgeted for painters in the first place." I said knowing that he put the payment for painters in his estimate and it was up to me to decide how much work I could do to lower the amount."

"And it will be a much more pleasant surprise for you at the end," he said.

"So we get a television style reveal?" I asked with a smile.

"I'll work on my game show diva presentation style."

"I appreciate it," I replied. "Sean mentioned he and Jake were ordering pizza instead of going out tonight and we were both invited to join if you were interested."

"Oh, are you asking me out for dinner?" Davis asked, with a grin.

"In for dinner actually and it is with my cousin and his …" I fumbled for a term. "Casually seeing where it is going but was once the boyfriend he was head over heels in love with…friend," I finished.

Davis laughed. "Oh, a double date then. And I thought you were going to wait until after the job was done to take advantage of me or did we decide I was going to take advantage of you?"

"It's just pizza," I reminded him.

166

"Well neither of us is dressed for a night on the town," he pointed out. "Although you do appear to be wearing make-up."

"I wanted to look nice for my interview." Davis scanned my current clothing. "I have other clothes in the bag. I wore them when Wendy was around."

"With your bolt cutters and flashlight?"

"I don't always carry them."

"So do your clothes match the cinnabar?" Davis asked.

"Cinnabar?"

He moved forward and picked up my left hand. I looked down and could see a smear of paint on it. "You know I had to look it up when I went home to make sure I knew what you were talking about. The color looks good on you."

"It looks better on the room divider, I promise." My heart was thumping loudly in my chest and I was pleased that my voice came out sounding fairly normal. Davis smiled slowly and I felt my heart skip a beat as he slipped a hand up to my neck and stepped a little closer.

"It looks pretty good here," he said, gently stroking the side of my neck. I vaguely recalled pushing a strand of hair back from my neck sometime after painting the room divider.

"It must have transferred from my hand," I said feeling breathless.

"Do you mind if I don't wait until the job is over?" he asked softly.

"No," I replied. His hand slid to the back of my neck while the other went around me, his hand resting on the small of my back. I went up on my toes as he bent down to kiss me, meeting him halfway.

"Do you have any idea how long I've wanted to do that," he asked when we finally broke apart.

"No," I said with a smile as he eased back.

"A long time. It just never seemed appropriate at a job site." He shook his head and looked around. "Until now that is. Maybe it's the lack of Malak. I'm not a big fan of audiences." Davis shrugged. "We should probably get you home before your cousin worries too much." He picked up my coat and handed it to me. "I could do with some pizza," he told me as I slipped it on.

"I should warn you," I said as I picked up my bag and umbrella. "It comes with a side of smirking cousin."

"Are people who are starting something casual with an ex-love still allowed to smirk?" He asked. We stepped outside. The snow was falling rather heavily now and I was glad we didn't have that far to go.

"Probably not, but I doubt it would stop him." I said as Davis made certain the front door was locked. We walked back to the parking lot where his truck was the sole remaining occupant. We got inside and he drove out of the gates. I took the gate key from him, slipped out and locked it behind us. Once I was back in the passenger seat, he drove to my apartment building. I typed the key code into the box by the gate and it mechanically slid open, Davis parking in the protected lot. After parking, we went upstairs.

"Let the smirking begin," Davis said as I fitted my key into the lock and we went inside.

Chapter 13

We entered the apartment and I was fairly certain the smirking began long before we arrived. Sean was in his element as gracious host and as we entered the apartment, we were each presented with a first snow cocktail, which proved to be a super cold martini. I was fairly certain both Jake and Sean were on their second already.

Winston slowly circled Davis and after his initial inspection, the dog placed himself between Davis and the door. His placement was also calculated to be far enough away from Davis to keep him in view without moving too much, but close enough to be able to inhale whatever scents were wafting from his work boots.

Davis eyed Winston. "Perhaps I should invest in odor eater type inserts," he said.

"I wouldn't worry over much," Sean told him. "He never took any notice of my shoes until one day I stepped in something squishy by the dumpster when wearing leather shoes. For weeks afterward I had to put the shoes on a shelf whenever I took them off, despite cleaning them really well. Then one day, poof." He snapped his fingers. "Any lingering scent was gone and he no longer cared. The evil eye he's giving you is because you disrupted his schedule last time he saw you."

"Speaking of which, did you get him to go out when you got home? He only did a quick dash this morning due to the rain." I asked.

"Briefly. We did a short run post rain, but pre snow, although our little delicate flower here was disturbed when his paws got wet. We had to wipe them down with a towel upon our return because he gave me the pitiful face." Sean looked at me and frowned. "Something wrong with your drink?"

"No, but I think I probably ought to call James before I imbibe, especially since lunch was only a quick sandwich."

"Ah, good call. The number is on the table. By all means give James a call, then you can fill us all in. I can call for pizza while you do. The usual?"

"Works for me," I replied.

As I moved over to the table, Sean turned to Davis. They discussed pizza toppings and before Sean moved to place the order he announced, "Jake is a part of the community, so don't feel you need to hide."

"Good to know," Davis replied with a smile.

"I was thrilled to hear about the apartments," Jake told him. "I can't believe there aren't more of them. Personally I always make sure to live in a high rise to make up for the lack of shields at my place."

"I have the feeling there will be far more applicants than apartments when they are available," Davis replied. The two of them settled themselves on the couch while Sean stepped away to call in the pizza. I left them to their conversation and dialed the number James left with Sean. It rang twice before being answered.

"Alice, so good of you to call," James said as he picked up his end of the line.

"Sean said it was important I return your call as soon as possible." I replied.

"Yes, but with you being so *busy* these days, I hadn't anticipated you returning the call so promptly."

The comment was delivered dryly and I'm certain meant as some sort of criticism. It was a tactic James used often. He would imply some dissatisfaction with my behavior and if I rose to the bait, he would use it as an opportunity to try and get me to change whatever behavior annoyed him, without actually saying he was annoyed. Usually, he tried the tactic after I refused a job he wanted me to do even if he knew it was just due to scheduling conflicts.

Recently, it had been used for the fact that I didn't answer my phone immediately when he called, forcing him to send a message through the office where it would have to go through both Gina and Sean before it reached me. I discovered if I just stayed silent until he continued, he would get to the point of the conversation without relaying the passive aggressive lectures. The silence stretched.

"I received a call from Wendy Watts of *The Whisper* today," James finally continued when it was clear I wasn't going to comment on my busy schedule.

"Did you?"

"Yes, after hearing about this apartment building you bought, she wants to see you put up a shield first hand. I don't suppose you have any additional jobs you've managed to line up on your own?" There was a tone of disapproval in his voice and I frowned. I don't know why he disapproved of my taking a job on my own. He never had before. Shielding Mike and Christy's house still required me sending the fifteen percent to the Commission, five of which still went into his account apparently. While I didn't take outside jobs often, he was never upset by the ones I took as long as I followed the rules. Or at least that was always the case previously.

"No," I replied, keeping my tone even and my annoyance down. I always found it hard to make a one word response not sound surly, but I gave it my best as I didn't have anything else to add.

"Then it is a good thing I have provided you with one," James said, his voice crisp. "Mr. Malak will pick you up outside your apartment at precisely two pm tomorrow. Ms. Watts will meet the two of you in my office when you arrive. I trust you will have a pleasant evening." With that James hung up, skipping the normal pleasantries. I pulled the phone away from my ear and stared at the darkening screen for a moment.

"That was odd," I said, half to myself.

"What was," Sean asked. I saw the three men sitting in the living room and went to join them, taking a seat on the couch near Davis. I took a large sip from my martini.

"He didn't give me a chance to refuse," I replied. "Usually he calls, tells me there is a job and when I would need to be ready for it, and then lets me check my calendar to see if my schedule will allow it. This time he just told me that Malak will be picking me up at two tomorrow afternoon and that Wendy will meet us in James' office. He sounded kind of annoyed."

"Maybe it's because he didn't get paid for the apartment building?" Sean suggested.

"It would be a chunk of change," Davis said, nodding. "The one bedroom apartments are about 1000 square feet each, the two bedrooms are about fifteen hundred and the four bedroom is 2500 square feet. That's what, 11,000 square feet total?"

"You forgot the basement," I told him. "That would up it to about 13,500 square feet." I muttered to myself as I did the math. "Twenty bucks per square foot, fifteen percent for the commission, five for James. It's substantial," I said nodding and taking a sip of my martini. "Especially if you count the parking lot and yard in the square footage, which the Commission would do."

"Maybe he thinks it is going to be a more common occurrence as you buy more buildings," Jake surmised. "After all, you did list yourselves as the Appleton Property Group. It practically implies you will be adding more properties. Properties he won't get a percentage of."

"See," I told Sean. "I told you group sounded like more than one property."

"He wouldn't know that it's a group as it hasn't been made public yet," Sean said waving off my concern. "He could just be ticked off that he is missing his five percent of Ravenwood."

"I think he's also upset I took a job outside of his office," I said thinking over the short conversation.

"You mean Mike's place?" Davis said frowning. "We paid their fifteen percent already and were e-mailed a receipt as soon as the money cleared their account."

"I'm sure you did," I replied. "He's never been upset when I took jobs outside his office before. In fact he was always happy with them as the Commission didn't need to deduct either Malak's fee or the traveling expenses from their percentage."

"I wonder why this time is different," Jake wondered.

"Maybe they are afraid Davis Construction will apply for a permit," Sean suggested.

"A permit to do what?" Davis asked, frowning.

"Work with Alice," Sean clarified. All three of us looked at him blankly.

"I really am the only lawyer in the room aren't I?" he said shaking his head and sighing dramatically. "In the rules and regulations booklet there is a section dealing with independent contractors," He explained. "Apparently construction companies that have a Commission issued license and have completed a specific number

173

of jobs with that certification can apply for a permit to work with someone who is Commission certified to shield."

"Davis Construction is licensed by the Commission," Davis replied. "And have been for three generations, so we have a whole slew of projects completed. Odds are we have enough projects to qualify."

"I vaguely recall seeing that," I said. I set my drink down and went to retrieve the rules from my bag. I returned and as I settled back down on the couch, I began flipping pages. Davis moved in close to read over my shoulder.

"Ah, here it is." I said as I found it. "I didn't pay it much attention before because the construction companies were all arranged through the office. Let's see," I scanned the page, reading aloud. "Construction companies licensed by the Commission and who have completed Commission based projects totaling no less than twenty percent of their total jobs for any given year, can apply for a permit to work directly with the individual establishing the shields. Instead of remitting fifteen percent to the Commission for each of the projects completed under permit, the individual completing the shields must remit no less than twenty five percent to the permitted company."

"So maybe James thinks that this apartment building might be your way of testing the Davis Construction Company before they apply for a permit?" Jake asked.

"Could be," I said handing the booklet to Davis so he could look over the details. He took the booklet, but didn't move away from me.

"We'd certainly qualify, but you'd make less money with the twenty-five percent going to us instead of just giving the fifteen percent to the Commission. Admittedly, I wouldn't be listening to an audio book while you worked and could be counted on to do more than wield a nail encrusted piece of scrap wood."

"I thought you said that wouldn't help," I replied with a smile.

"Which is why I'd do more." He said with a wink.

"And if you went with Davis Construction," Sean said. "James would lose a lot more than just the percentage for your apartment building, even if you don't buy more buildings. As it stands you do at least two projects a month for them. That adds up."

"One to two, yeah," I replied.

Sean shook his head. "I checked the calendar. It *was* one or possibly two a month, now it's at least two to three a month and has been for the last three years."

"Are you sure," I said frowning.

"I was pretty sure with my schedule, but I compared it with Sammy's calendar to check."

"And we all know Sammy's calendar," I muttered. "That does explain why my rainy day fund has gotten larger."

"I don't know Sammy's calendar," Davis replied.

"Ah Sammy is a bit…obsessed with his schedule. He doesn't deal well with surprises," I explained. "It's one of the reasons I make James call the office instead of my cell. It helps when adding to the calendar."

"Makes sense," Davis said nodding. "Christy keeps our calendar and she gets irritated if we don't put everything down on the office board. I think it comes with being an office manager."

"Well how can you deploy your minions if you don't know where they are?" Jake added with a smile. "At least that's how I'm pretty sure my assistant views me, as one of her minions."

The pizza arrived and we continued to talk, conversation straying from talk of the Commission to local restaurants and various travels. Jake regaled us with tales of his overseas adventures and Davis pitched in stories from construction sites. Eventually the pizza was consumed and Jake and Sean disappeared into the back, leaving me alone with Davis. Since both Sean and Jake had multiple martinis, I knew Jake wasn't driving anywhere and would more than likely stay the night. During the meal, Davis slipped Winston several slices of peperoni and he was no longer favored with suspicious canine glances.

"It must be strange having a roommate," Davis said as I cleaned up the remains of dinner. Outside the window it looked as though the snow finally stopped falling.

"It usually works out all right," I told him. "Neither of us really date that much and we know how to stay out of each other's way, so it is rarely a problem."

"You know," Davis said as he slipped on his coat. "I don't think we should call this a first date."

"You don't?" I replied with a smile. "I thought you decided this was a double date."

"I thought about it and I think our first date should occur after each of us has had a chance to shower off our day and get all cleaned up. And it should end at my place, since I have no roommates."

"Oh really," I said with a little laugh as I walked him to the door.

"Yup. Plus, this way if Wendy, James or Malak ask about me you can honestly say we have never been on a date. I have the feeling our socializing would not be received well."

"Because we work on projects together?" I asked.

"Because it would make him definitely decide Davis Construction was looking for a more permanent alliance," Davis said.

"As in permits? Are you thinking of applying for one?"

Davis nodded. He picked up the booklet with the rules and regulations in it. "Would you mind if I borrow this?" he asked.

"Not at all. I think I've covered everything I need."

"I want to go over the details of the permits. Of course it will have to be voted on as it wouldn't be up to just me. I won't do anything but look without talking to you first, but I want to see what the permit application entails, especially if James is going to be annoyed about the possibility of us even considering applying."

"Fair enough," I told him. We reached the door and Davis bent down, giving me a rather chaste kiss goodnight.

"Do you still want to paint in the morning?" He asked, opening the door.

"I might as well," I told him. "I can probably work until lunch time before coming home to pack and get ready to go."

"Then I will see you first thing."

"First thing then. Drive safe it's bound to be slick out there and people are always a little crazy with the first snow of the season."

"I'll be careful," he assured me. "Goodnight."

"Night," I replied. As Davis stepped away, I could see a little red glow around his right hand. While the building and parking lot lights generally kept the shadow creatures out of the gated lot, I had the feeling if any attempted a run at Davis he would be more than ready for them. Davis disappeared into the elevator and I closed the door. As I readied myself for bed, I found myself grinning.

The next morning Winston and I went out for our morning run. The world was coated in a blanket of white and the early morning sun made the ice crystals sparkle like diamonds. As the moisture was settled on the ground and no longer falling from the sky, Winston was in a better frame of mind. He wasn't however in a running mood. The sidewalks had yet to be cleared and Winston did not care for the way his paws sunk into the fluffy mass and were wet with clinging bits of snow when he picked them up.

"All right princess, I won't make you stay out if you don't want to," I told him, my words puffing white around us. He walked over to the small stand of trees, did his morning business and was more than pleased to return to the apartment. Given his lack of interest in the park, I had extra time.

Unfortunately I also realized that shoveling the snow from the sidewalk in front of The Ravenwood Arms was my responsibility. As our building manager shoveled the sidewalks in front of our apartment building, we didn't keep a shovel in the apartment. Luckily we kept one at the shop to clear the sidewalk in front of both Sean's office and the furniture shop.

"And if I borrow it to shovel out the Ravenwood's sidewalk I'll have to do the shop's as well so they aren't at a loss. I suppose it's a good thing I'm ready early." Plan in place, I fed Winston, took a shower and got dressed. I put a layer of thermals under my jeans and tucked the jeans into my snow boots. Thus prepared, I filled a thermos full of coffee and headed off to the shop.

At the furniture store, I pulled the snow shovel from the closet, leaving everything else as it was so as not to interrupt Sammy's normal routine. It was too early for him to arrive, so the building remained dark. I put the ear buds of my i-pod into my ears and selected a playlist that was filled with high energy songs. Then I got to work. I started in front of Sean's building and worked my way down the sidewalk. When I finished clearing out both his building and the shop, I hefted the shovel over my shoulder, picked up my thermos and marched over to the Ravenwood.

While several of the neighboring buildings had people shoveling their stretch of sidewalk when I arrived, none of the construction crew were in evidence. There was only a two inch accumulation, but I took care of both the sidewalk and the drive into the parking lot. I was standing in the drive, contemplating the white covered lot when Davis arrived. In addition to his normal work gear I noticed he had a shovel and a plastic container filled with pellets to sprinkle on the sidewalk to keep it from getting icy.

"I haven't gotten around to picking those up yet," I told him as he began to sprinkle them over the path.

"But you did get everything shoveled." He told me, He finished and handed me the container so I could sprinkle the mix on the stairs to keep them from being a hazard. While I was occupied, he drove his truck from the drive into the lot, crunching the parking lot's snow under his tires. As the trees protected a large chunk of it, the show wasn't as heavy in the lot.

As he walked back to join me in the front, the other vehicles started to arrive. We went inside and dropped our coats in the designated outerwear pile. I sipped my coffee to warm up as the others arrived and gathered. After issuing the morning's instructions to the rest of the crew, Davis helped me haul my painting supplies up to the top floor.

Once established and given my orders, he left me while he worked on another part of the building. I pushed my sleeves up, turned my high energy music on and sang to myself as I applied the primer coat to the walls. I was in my own little world as I worked and was for the most part left alone. Occasionally Davis stopped by to check on me, smirking when he caught me singing along with my music. I wondered how last night would affect working on site together, but was pleased to see that it really didn't change anything. Davis was still professional. I wondered if that was due to the fact that most of the crew was his family. I had the feeling his brothers would probably tease him as badly, if not worse, than Sean would tease me if the situation were reversed.

When noon rolled around, I turned in my roller and as everyone else broke for lunch, I headed back to my apartment to pack. The night before, I thought about packing so that I could stay on site longer. I decided against it though as I didn't want Winston to associate Davis with breaks in his routine. I figured the lunch time packing would at least distance the event of me leaving from Davis' visit to the apartment.

While Winston was thrilled to see me during the day, rising from his patch of sun to give me an enthusiastic welcome, he was less pleased by the appearance of my suitcase. As I placed the case on the bed, Winston came into the bedroom, and sighed heavily as he sunk down onto the floor. His eyes rolled up to watch me as I moved from closet to suitcase.

"I won't be gone long," I told him. As the words left my mouth I realized James hadn't said how long the trip was going to take. Along with allowing me the right to refuse, he always let me know the duration of my time away. "Crap." I added.

Normally I would pack not only work clothes, but something halfway nice to wear should I decide to actually eat in a restaurant instead of getting take-out at an all-night drive through. Most of the time, the hours kept during these trips didn't allow it, but I liked to be ready if it did. This time, I didn't bother and merely packed extra underwear, t-shirts and jeans. Since James neglected to tell me where I would be taken to put up these shields as well as how long I'd be gone, I made certain to have a mix for different climates.

"Layering is always an option," I told myself. I had to sit on my suitcase to get it zipped. I sighed and spent the remaining time in a spirited tug of war with Winston and his favorite rope chew toy. His jaws locked on the knot on his end of the rope and he threw his muscle into trying to wrench it away from me, his stub tail wagging so fast it was a blur. It took not only all my arm strength, but my heavier weight just to hold on as his powerful muscles shook and jerked.

When it was time for me to head downstairs, I let Winston win, releasing my end of the rope. Satisfied with his conquest, he took his prize to his dog bed and flopped down to revel in his victory, giving the toy a few vigorous shakes to let it know who was boss. I picked up the handle to my rolling suitcase and left the apartment.

Chapter 14

I exited my building just as Malak turned the corner in his black SUV. The day warmed slightly as it progressed and I stood back from the curb so that Malak wouldn't splash me with the expanding pool of icy slush gathered on the street side of the curb. He pulled up and I dodged the splash his SUV created. I heard the click as the back unlocked and I placed my suitcase inside before taking my place in the passenger's seat.

Malak didn't say a word as I got in, barely even waiting for my seatbelt to be fastened before putting the car in drive. If anything, he looked grumpier than usual. I thought about reminding him that James was the one who decided on this particular excursion, but decided not to waste my breath. If Malak wanted to be grumpy, he could be grumpy. As we headed to the airport and our meeting with James, I wondered if Malak would behave any differently with the reporter around. Would he forsake his audio books and seat in the car? Would he trail me around the site, watching both what I did and taking notes on the reporter's actions for James? Despite my annoyance at the impromptu summons, I found myself curious.

We arrived at the airport and Malak parked. Still silent, I followed him through the security doors, the wheels of our rolling suitcases first making a low sound against the concrete sidewalks, then changing pitch slightly as we hit the tile of the interior corridor. This time there was no shouting and no Bradford in evidence. In James' office, Marcie smiled at us, got up and walked into the inner office to let James know we had arrived. As soon as she returned, she sent us back. We parked our luggage by her desk and walked into James' office.

Wendy Watts arrived before we did and was decked out in an emerald green suit. The shirt under her jacket gleamed silver. Once again she carried a large purse. This one was silver to match the shirt and earrings. Her suitcase, a wheeled number like mine, was a hard shelled case, also in silver. I wondered if all of the outfits packed inside would match the luggage as well or if she would only coordinate with the luggage on travel days. Her nails were painted a metallic green that reminded me of beetles and they shimmered slightly when she moved her fingers. As much as I liked the color, I decided it would creep me out to wear it. I didn't need to look at my fingers and think 'bugs' as I worked. I glanced down at my short unpainted nails and realized any polish I put on them would no doubt be quickly destroyed anyway so it was a moot point.

"*I could always paint my toes*," I thought, trying to remember if I still had any nail polish in the apartment that hadn't dried up. My thoughts regarding self-beautification were interrupted as James began to speak. While Wendy occupied one of the guest chairs, Malak and I remained standing.

"Ms. Watts will be accompanying the two of you on this trip," He told us. Malak's eyebrow shot up in surprise and I found myself surprised he didn't know. I always assumed he knew more than I did. I suppose what they say of assumptions was correct. Apparently today, both of us were asses.

"There are two jobs during this trip out, one tonight and one first thing in the morning," James handed Malak a file and I watched him open it and scan the directions. I knew it would contain not only the location of the two sites, but the hotel and rental car information as well. I also knew first thing in the morning meant only a few hours down time between sites at best.

"The first is a shielding of both a house and yard, the second is of the house only," James continued, handing me a sheet with the break out of the properties. The first property was a new construction and as usual I was being called in post electric and pre insulation. The second property was a renovation. The kitchen was gutted and both it and the living room were getting a makeover to create an open floorplan. Both projects were being managed by the same contractor, Greg Timmons. As I worked with him nearly as much as I worked with Davis, I had no problems with him.

"Ms. Watts is here to observe. You will behave as you normally do on any other job site and should she have any questions, you will answer them."

Both Malak and I nodded and a moment later, James was shaking Wendy's hand and sending us out of his office. This time it was three of us in a row as we left the office and headed towards the airport. We were quiet as we waited for the plane to be ready. Finally, we boarded the plane. As usual, Malak headed to the private compartment, leaving me to entertain Wendy. She stared at the closed door as we took our seats.

"I hope you don't mind me watching you work," She said, turning to me a look of concern on her face.

"No problem," I told her smiling. She glanced back towards the closed door. "He does that even when it's just me," I told her. "I wouldn't take it personally if I were you."

"Oh," Wendy replied. The plane began taxi-ing down the runway. "So what happens now?"

"Well Malak has the logistics file, but usually when we have two projects we will do one after dark and one before the sun comes up. What will more than likely happen is we will land, pick up the rental car and more than likely check into our motel. Then when it is dark, we will go to the site, meet the contractor and I will shield the first site. Then it's back to the motel to sleep, off to the second site before dawn, more than likely checking out of the motel before we go, and after shielding we will fly back."

Wendy nodded. "Seems reasonable," she replied. "Do you do anything to prep before arrival?"

"Not really."

"Oh, well then I am just going to relax and enjoy the ride." Wendy pulled out an i-pod and a sleep mask. In moments, she was zoned out in her own little world. As I was used to flying more or less alone, I didn't mind. I pulled a battered copy of *'To Kill a Mockingbird'* from my bag.

In an attempt to keep my brain from atrophying, I decided to start re-reading classics and in fact downloaded a list entitled '100 books every person should read'. It not only gave me a strange sort of satisfaction to be able to cross each one off the list, but I found the books I only read as part of a school requirement years ago to be infinitely more enjoyable now that I didn't have to break the story down for my English teacher. I considered it a double win.

The flight passed quietly with the exception of some minor turbulence about an hour in. During the few minutes where the plane did its impression of a Mexican jumping bean, Wendy didn't move and I had to put my book down so I didn't get sick. After that, the pilot took us to a slightly higher altitude and the ride smoothed out.

When the plane began its descent, Wendy pulled off her mask and put it and her i-pod back in her bag. I put my book away and Wendy pulled out her compact to make certain her make-up hadn't smudged. By the time we landed and rolled to our arrival gate, she was camera ready, should anyone around actually have a camera, and Malak was opening the door in the back.

In the airport, I ducked into the restroom while Wendy followed Malak to the rental car booth. I spent too many hours on site not to know using the facilities before leaving the airport was a must.

While the building sites usual had a row of port-a-johns available, I was not a fan.

Especially at night.

On an empty construction site.

As I washed my hands, I took in my appearance. While I was wearing no make-up today, I was pleased to see my hair wasn't sticking up in strange spikes. Of course on this flight, I hadn't slept so I was more or less expecting normal. I stuck my tongue out at my reflection, dried my hands and went to join the other two. Somehow I thought in my absence, Wendy would question Malak. If she had, she had done so while I was in the restroom because both of them were now standing silently waiting for me. Malak held the keys to the rental car and was tapping his foot impatiently. Wendy was checking something or other on her phone.

Malak led the way out to the lot of rental cars and we all piled into a red Ford Fusion. Under his breath I could hear Malak complaining about the color of the vehicle. While I could barely catch the muttered words, I heard his rant about how police paid more attention to red vehicles than others many times before. I guessed the rant was voiced low for Wendy's consideration as I usually got the full volume version. We loaded our bags into the back and Wendy took the back seat. I wondered if she was being gracious, didn't want to sit next to Malak or wanted to keep both of us in sight in case we did something noteworthy.

"Maybe it's a combination of the three," I thought as Malak went through his mental vehicle check list. I fastened my seat belt as he checked the gas gage to make certain it matched the paperwork the agency handed him. He then checked to make certain the audio equipment was in working order. Malak started the car and plugged his I-pod into the car's audio system to make certain it worked. For a moment, the speakers blared an audio clip of a newscast. It wasn't a recent one, just one he recorded to use as his

sound check when others, usually me, were in the vehicle. Satisfied, Malak turned off the music and switched to his GPS app. As expected, it gave directions for our overnight accommodations since he already programed the locations into the unit.

It was already dark as we pulled out of the airport parking lot, the sun having set about an hour before. Before anyone could ask, the GPS announced that we had a two hour drive ahead of us. Wendy seemed to be watching the two of us as Malak turned onto the interstate. I guessed that since she knew we had been taking these trips since I turned twelve, she was expecting to see some form of comradery. If so, she was disappointed as Malak maintained his sulky silence. After a while, realizing she wasn't missing anything, Wendy put her head phones in her ears and listened to her own music.

"Destination on right in point two miles," the GPS finally announced. Malak took the appropriate right and we entered the parking lot for the small road side motel where we would be sleeping. I was more relieved than usual to reach our destination. Somehow with Wendy along for the ride, Malak's silence seemed more oppressive.

"Not exactly the Ritz," Wendy muttered, half to herself, as we exited the car and walked. "Is this normal?" she asked.

"Pretty much," I replied, shrugging.

"Oh," she replied looking the building over. I wondered what she expected. It was a pretty standard older, middle of nowhere motel. In the lobby we got our keys and room assignments. Our rooms were in a row and we quickly deposited our luggage before heading out to the job site. Wendy looked excited as we left the motel and I noticed that while she still wore her skinny heels, she carried a pair of tennis shoes in her hand. I decided I'd have to tell Davis she at least learned something from her tour of the Ravenwood Arms.

Malak already had the site's address programed into the GPS and it swiftly and efficiently guided us to our destination. In a very short time, we glided up to the edge of the site. A car was already parked in front of the newly created building. As we pulled up, Greg stepped out of the waiting vehicle parked in front of the house. Once parked, Malak reached for his I-pod, turning off the GPS and pulling up his audio book. I caught sight of the cover as I unbuckled my seat belt. Tonight's selection was called 'Betrayed' and featured a busty blonde in a ball gown.

"*I guess that answers that*," I told myself as I opened my door. Apparently Malak *was* going to behave as usual. As I got out of the car, Wendy following, I wondered what the reporter would think of that.

"Well Alice, we meet again," Greg said with a smile as I walked over. "As usual you look spectacular in the moonlight."

"Thanks, Greg," I replied returning his smile. Greg had graying hair and deep grooves fanning out from his eyes and bracketing his mouth. I had the feeling they were carved by years working in the sun and from lots of smiles. Greg reminded me of my Uncle Derrick, an electrician whose deep and abiding love of fried foods contributed to the massive heart attack that took him out a few years prior.

He looked over my shoulder. "Rutherford said you were bringing someone along." He said before I could ask him how he was doing. I turned to look at Wendy. She stopped to change her shoes, slipping her heels into her monster purse. "He said she wanted to see a shield go up first hand."

"Yup," I replied. "Wendy Watts from *The Whisper*." I introduced her as she walked over.

"Greg Timmons," he replied shaking her hand. He turned to me. "Ready?"

188

"I am," I replied. "Is there anything I need to know?"

"Not really," he replied with a shrug. "It's a new subdivision, so no neighbors yet as the surrounding homes are still under construction. We spaced six inch pavers along the property's perimeter for you to use as anchors for the exterior shields since the family requested it." Greg pointed out one of the pavers as we passed. I looked down and nodded at the half buried paver. Wendy stooped for a closer look.

"Back yard's got more cover if you want to get the outside done before we go inside," he continued.

I nodded. "That would work." I told him.

He gestured to the side of the house. "Gate's unlocked. I'll get the back door unlocked and meet you there. Lights are already on."

"Thanks," I replied. I headed to the side of the house, Wendy following along behind.

"What happens if there is an attack," she asked nervously, eyes darting to the shadows.

"You stand next to me and I throw shields around us while we both scream our heads off," I told her. "Unless you have a skill that would be useful in an attack." I paused to look at her.

"Not really," she said. I turned and opened the gate leading to the back yard. At the moment yard was more of an optimistic connotation as the area was still bare dirt. I could see the squared off spots indicating the half buried stones. Before our arrival, Greg set up construction lights. It helped me not only see what I was doing, but provided bright enough light that if anything was lurking in the darkness, it would be kept away. Wendy moved in close, actually stepping on my heels as I moved to the center of the back yard. Her eyes were watching the edges of the yard. In the shadows, outside the lighted zone, I thought I saw some form of movement. As I knew the shields would cause whatever was out there to leave, seeking easier prey once they were locked in place, I decided it was time to get to work.

"You'll need to move back a bit," I told Wendy. She looked at me as though I just advocated her skinny dipping in a pool of piranha while covered in barbeque sauce. "Not far," I assured her. "I just need a little space to work."

Her mouth formed an oh shape and she took a few steps back. I smiled. "Thanks." She seemed relieved I wasn't asking her to go too far. Satisfied Wendy wasn't breathing down my neck, I returned to the business at hand. I ignored Wendy as I spilled power into my hands and formed the beginnings of a shield. When my large, and still expanding, soap bubble reached beach ball size, I dropped it to the ground, still pushing power into it. I expanded it, hearing Wendy's start of surprise as it grew large enough to cover both of us. I continued expanding.

I heard the sizzle of electricity and jumped as one of the large construction lights turned off making a slight snapping sound. The light on its stand fell to the ground with a crash as something gave the electrical cord a sharp tug. The sound of breaking glass seemed loud in the now only half-lit yard. I turned my head in the direction of the failed light. As my eyes adjusted to the darkness on that side of the yard I could see something was indeed tugging on the cord. One of the shadow creatures had the cord in its mouth and was shaking it the way Winston shook his tug-of-war rope toy. The creatures red eyes looked at us and I heard Wendy let out a startled cry.

I knew both of us were safe inside the shields and I thought about yelling for Malak, but thought we were still okay at the moment. I continued expanding the shield, even as the shadow creature stalked forward. As my shields met the creature, I was encouraged when it took a step back. I pumped energy into the shields, forcing it to expand and driving the creature slowly from the yard. When I reached the perimeter, I locked the shield in place. The shadow creature yelped as the shield flashed bright white and I was relieved when it fled into the darkness, defeated.

"Oh my god," Wendy said sounding shaky. I felt about as shaky as she looked, but kept it inside. I hadn't known before that my shields could actually shove one of the shadow creatures back before. Theoretically, I suppose I should have known something like that would happen. Personally I hoped never to need to try it again, but I was thrilled it worked this time at least.

"What happened to the light," Greg said. He was standing in the open sliding glass door leading to the back yard, a puzzled frown on his face.

"You didn't see?" Wendy asked. Her voice trembled.

"No, I was on the phone," Greg replied frowning at the half darkened yard. "What happened?"

"Shadow creature attacked the power cord," I explained grateful that I didn't sound as shaken up as I felt. He blinked in surprise at me.

"The yard is shielded?" he asked. I nodded. He walked over to the darkened lamp, stood it upright again and picked up the cord. He reeled in the length and swore as he found the cord shredded. "Since we are working on most of the block, the generator is in the next yard over," he told us. I looked over into the darkened yard next door. Dimly I could hear the rumblings of the generator. With the cord mostly in darkness, it was vulnerable.

"I didn't think they would attack the cord," Greg said apologetically.

"Lesson learned, I suppose," I replied, quelling my own fears. "Shall we move indoors?"

"Yeah," Greg said dropping the cord. The three of us moved into the house, Greg moving protectively between Wendy and the darkness as we both saw she was shaking slightly. I was proud of myself for not looking terrified. I didn't mind Davis seeing me freaked out by three circling shadow creatures on the street in front of my apartment. Having the other contractors I worked with thinking I was a scare-dy cat on site was something else entirely. Luckily, Greg didn't think I was in any form of distress. I was happy to let Wendy play the damsel in tonight's drama.

Normally, he would leave me be while I set up the house shields. Due to our scare and Wendy's presence, he stuck close, shivering as the shields passed through him and sunk into the building's structure. When we were done, he escorted us back to the car, eyes scanning the darkened street. I opened the car door.

"Rachel's lower lip quivered in reaction to the Duke's callus remarks," Malak's audio book spilled out before Malak could turn the sound off. My lips turned up in a small smile as the other two frowned at the snippet. Greg shook his head as he returned to his vehicle and Wendy and I slipped into the Ford. Without a word, Malak put the car in gear and took us back to the motel. As we drove, Wendy looked between the two of us as though wondering what was going to happen. Malak drove in silence until we pulled into the motel parking lot.

"We leave at two am, have the bags packed and ready to go since we aren't coming back after the second job." He announced as he parked and turned off the car's engine. I nodded and he got out of the car, walking to his room without looking back.

"Is that normal?" Wendy asked as the two of us got out and headed to our rooms.

"Pretty much."

"Oh," Our rooms were next to each other and when we reached the doors Wendy looked at me as though she wanted to say something but wasn't entirely sure what. She shook her head as though dispelling the thought. "See you in a few hours," She said finally, opening her door.

"Night," I said, opening mine.

Alone in my room, I allowed myself a moment of reaction, shaking from the near miss of the shadow creature's attack. Once settled, I set the alarm on my phone and got ready for bed. There was after all only a few hours before I had to place a second shield.

"At least there are almost never any shadow creatures around when I place shields in the morning," I told myself. Then I remembered the three had attacked outside my building in the early morning and sighed heavily. I ordered myself not to think about it and closed my eyes.

Sleep was elusive and I drifted in and out of consciousness, not really sinking into deep slumber. When my alarm went off I was already half awake. I groggily rubbed my eyes and turned off the alarm. Knowing rolling back to sleep for a few more hours was not an option, I stumbled to the bathroom, stripped and turned on the shower, using only the cold water. I yelped as the icy droplets hit my warm skin, but the cold shower did the trick and by the time I toweled off and dressed, I was more or less awake.

In very little time I was back at the car, loading my suitcase in the trunk. Malak's bag was already loaded and I gave him my room key. Wendy trudged over, looking less put together than usual. Her snazzy suit was slightly rumpled and she was already wearing the sneakers instead of the heels, as though she couldn't be bothered to change on site. She handed Malak her room key and as he left to turn them into the clerk, Wendy shoved her bag in the back next to mine.

"This is cruel and unusual punishment," Wendy informed me as we slipped into the car. The woman had dark circles under her eyes and her royal blue silk blouse was misbuttoned.

"This is just a quick indoor shield, then we'll head back to the airport," I told her. "You might want to fix your shirt." She looked down and sighed at the misbuttoned garment. She finished fixing it as Malak returned and we began our drive to the second site.

The second job of the trip was located closer to the airport. Again Greg Timmons met us on site and we left Malak in the car.

"Does he always stay in the car?" Wendy asked as we followed Greg into the house. Greg snorted in derision, but otherwise stayed silent, letting me field the question.

"For the most part," I answered.

"But isn't he supposed to be here to keep you safe?"

"That's what I was told," I replied. As Wendy still seemed skittish, Greg stayed inside with us, instead of leaving me alone to work. Again he shivered when the shield passed through him.

"I will never get used to that," he said shaking his head as I expanded the shield so that it covered the entire house. Wendy looked at the shields quizzically as I worked and I realized she had been a little too spooked by our encounter at the first job site to ask any questions. Even though she looked exhausted now, she was calmer.

She was quiet until I locked the shields in place and they flashed brightly. Then she pulled out her digital recorder and the questions began. Luckily, they were the questions I was expecting. Like Christy, she wanted to know if the shield would wear off the already finished walls that existed throughout the house or if special cleaners needed to be used or preservation work done to maintain them. I answered each one of her questions. When she was done, she turned to Greg and asked about his experience with shielded properties, me, others like me and Commission based projects in general. Greg gave her calm, clear and concise answers to her questions and soon she was satisfied. Wendy turned off her recorder, and tucked it back into her silver bag.

This time, Malak had his audio book turned off before I opened the car door. Wendy and I slipped inside as Greg returned to his own vehicle. I knew he would be heading back to his construction office and catching some sleep before his crews began arriving. We headed back to the airport, the drive shorter as we were closer than the day before. Once again silence reigned as we drove. After skipping dinner and completing two jobs, my stomach felt cavernously empty. As I could feel sleep waiting to claim me though, I didn't insist on stopping to eat.

We arrived at the airport, Malak took care of the rental car and in a short while we were once again aboard one of the Commission's private planes. Malak secreted himself in the back and without a word, Wendy put her sleep mask over her eyes and her head phones in her ears. I settled myself in my seat and instead of pulling out my book; I leaned back and closed my eyes, more than ready for a little sleep myself.

Chapter 15

We arrived at the small airport that served as home base and Malak reported to James that all had gone well with no problems at either site. Wendy shot me a glance at his statement, but kept her mouth shut. James was all smiles and good will.

"Excellent to hear," He beamed. "Did you have any further questions?" he asked Wendy as he completed the paperwork and sent it to the printer.

"I think I learned all I needed," she replied, her smile bright and empty. I wondered what exactly would make it into her article and was somewhat nervous about the fallout.

"Good, good," James said. Marcie walked in the printed sheets and James scanned the information before signing both copies and passing them to me. I looked it over. It was the standard payment page I saw after every job. I signed the pages, handed one to James and folded the other into a square to slide into my back pocket. As I did, my stomach rumbled loudly. I felt my face color.

"Well, I won't keep you then," James said. He waved us towards the door as though shooing ducks into a pond. No one commented on my rumbling stomach. The three of us went into the parking lot and Wendy got into her red Fiat while I joined Malak in his Escalade. She waved as she left the parking lot. As usual Malak remained stoically silent for our drive back to my apartment.

The flight was a long one and I managed to get enough sleep that my stomach was more of a concern than sleep was. It was only a few minutes past eleven am when I arrived home and my body was still wanting dinner rather than breakfast. To quiet it, I ordered Chinese from the local take-out place I favored and played with

Winston until it arrived. After lunch, I thought about taking a nap, but didn't feel like settling down. Instead I took myself to The Ravenwood Arms, figuring that if I couldn't sleep, I might as well paint.

"Well now, I didn't expect you back for at least another day," Davis said with a smile as he handed me a paint roller.

"Got back a little while ago and wanted to get back into a normal schedule," I told him as I began on my section of wall.

Davis nodded, familiar with the middle of the night job site excursions. "How did it go?" Davis asked as he picked up a brush and began doing the cut work around the windows and doors.

"It was …interesting," I decided. "James had me do two jobs, one on a new build and one on a renovation, I suppose so Wendy could get a feel for both types. We had some issues on the first site." I told him about the shadow creature attacking the power cord and about my shields pushing it back.

"I didn't know they were smart enough to go for the cord," He said frowning.

"Me neither," I said with a little shudder. "Something to remember for the future though."

Davis nodded in agreement, then tilted his head in question. "Was Malak any help?"

"No," I said shaking my head. "But to be fair, I didn't call him. I used the shields to push the creature back and it fled when I locked them into place. Greg stuck close by as Wendy was pretty shaken." I smiled chuckled to myself. "When we opened the car door he wasn't quick enough to turn off his audio book so we got to hear a bit. Greg and Wendy both seemed surprised by his selection."

Davis smiled. "And what was this trip's choice?"

"*Betrayed*," I replied and relayed the snippet we overheard before Malak turned it off.

Davis laughed. "I wonder if that will end up in Wendy's story."

"No clue," I said shaking my head. "She kept asking 'is this normal' during the trip so I don't think it was what she expected." I frowned wondering how Wendy's tale of the Ravenwood Arms would affect not only my working relationship with Malak and James, but my ability to rent out the apartments. "I suppose if no one wants to rent the apartments, I could move into them." It wouldn't earn me any money that way, but it would at least keep me from having to pay rent elsewhere.

"I don't think you are going to have a problem renting the apartments, regardless of Wendy's story," Davis assured me. "Although I did wonder if you were planning on moving in."

"Did you?"

"Something your friend mentioned when she stopped by yesterday."

"Friend?" I asked wondering who had stopped by.

"Gracie something or other," Davis clarified. "She was looking for you and seemed in awe of how good the building looked."

"Ah that friend, Gracie was the one who took me to the auction in the first place."

"So she saw your accidental purchase?" He asked. I finished my wall and moved on to the next.

"She did," I confirmed. "Since she was outbid on everything she tried for, I figured I would be too. Alas, here we are." I smiled. Thus far my accidental purchase hadn't been that big a problem, but I wasn't going to tempt fate by saying that out loud.

"That explains why she was looking for you," Davis said. "She mentioned another auction coming up and wasn't sure if you were moving here or still needed a new place."

"Another auction?" I shook my head. "Do you know she has managed to break her thumb with my hammer, twice in the time I've known her? She does not need to tackle a house renovation on her own."

"Well she did manage to almost step in a paint pan and trip over a power cord in the ten minutes or so she was here."

"Did she?"

"Yup, Scott caught her and made sure she managed to leave the property in one piece."

"Remind me to thank him," I said as I continued to roll paint on the walls.

"I don't think he minded," Davis said. "In fact, I think he ended up with her phone number."

"Really?" I thought about it. "Well she is single, the two of us are actually the last unmarried ones in our group, everyone else paired off a while ago. You might want to let him know that she knows nothing about the magical community though, despite being my friend for a number of years."

"I thought as much since she asked if you were away again escorting another shipment to its destination. But Christy is going to be disappointed."

"Why?" I asked frowning.

"I think she was hoping you had lots of single friends you could throw at some of my unmarried brothers and cousins. She figured since you seemed both nice and smart, you'd have classy friends."

I laughed. "Glad I come off as both nice and smart. Unfortunately most of my classy friends are married. Many married with children at this point."

"Oh well, yet another of Christy's matchmaking schemes gone awry." We continued working companionably for a while. "So were you looking for a new place to live?" he asked.

"Not exactly," I said slowly. "Sean and I are pretty packed in the apartment," I told him. "So I mentioned to Gracie that we were either going to have to move or have a mass clear out soon. That is when she started mentioning the foreclosure auctions."

"That makes sense."

"It's also why we put your coat in one of the bedrooms the other night instead of the coat closet," I told him. "Adding coats to the closet is a fight best done without company present."

"I'll remember that," Davis told me. "Although in all fairness, my front hall closet is much the same even though I live alone. It seems to be where all of my extra junk ends up. That's why I bought a free standing coat tree a few years back."

"I thought about getting one of those," I replied.

"Every winter it topples over at least twice a week. You have to balance the coats just right to keep it steady."

"I think maybe I'll just clean out our closet instead."

"Probably a good idea." We both continued to work for a while. "So if you were to move, would it be with Sean or on your own?"

"I think it would depend on where Sean lived," I replied. "If he were to buy a house I would make sure it was shielded. If he were to get another apartment…" I let the thought trail off.

"He would be unprotected unless it was in a building like this," Davis concluded.

"Something like that," I replied. "I wonder if he'd want to move in here," I said, half to myself. It wasn't something I thought about. Over all the two of us were comfortable living with each other and had more or less been roommates since graduating from college. Neither of us needed a roommate to pay bills, but then neither of us felt the need to buy a house for just one person. In Sean's case not buying a house meant he had limited options if he wanted to live in a shielded space. In fact on that score, living with me was his best option. I wondered if I could bring up the topic without making him think I wanted him gone.

Davis let the conversation drop as I thought about broaching the topic with Sean. Soon after, he finished the cut work in the room and left me while he went to work on another task. I decided sooner was better than later and decided that if Sean was home when I got there, I would talk to him about it.

"Maybe he could be a building manager of sorts," I mused thinking that might be a better way to bring it up. All in all, I decided to play it by ear.

As the day drew to a close and the shadows began to lengthen, I bid good night to Davis and his crew and walked home. My late night and early morning was beginning to catch up with me and I tried not to rub my eyes like a sleepy child.

Sean beat me home and was just bringing Winston in from his playtime in the park when I arrived. "Well I didn't expect to see you up and about," He said as we walked into the apartment, Winston immediately going to his food bowl for his evening ration. I filled the bowl as Sean hung up the leash and slipped off his jacket. "So how did it go?"

I relayed the trip's highlights and Sean shook his head. "And Malak reported everything as normal?"

"Yup," I replied.

Sean shook his head again. "I can't wait for the story to come out. I wonder if she'll mention the audio books."

"I have the feeling he would not be amused," I replied. "I also don't think James would approve." I didn't know what James' relationship with Malak entailed, but I couldn't see James being too happy with a reporter stating that the handler the Commission sent to keep me safe during my jobs was more or less useless.

"Good," Sean replied. "Malak should either do the job or be replaced." The words had more heat to them than I expected.

"Well in either case, we will have to wait for the story to see the repercussions. There was something else I wanted to talk to you about though if you have a minute."

"Sure," Sean said flopping down onto the couch. "Shoot."

"Well," I said, sitting across from him. "I was talking to Davis earlier and he mentioned Gracie stopped by and after talking to her he wondered if I was planning to move into the apartment building. Apparently she said something about why I was going to the foreclosure auction in the first place."

"Because we are busting at the seams?" Sean replied.

"And because she can't be trusted with power tools," I added. "But mostly because of the busting at the seams. So, I was thinking you might like to move into one of the apartments. Not that I don't love living with you and I'm sure Winston will freak out at such a massive change, but I know that you don't really want to buy a house at the moment and that sort of limits where you can move and still be shielded. As well as where you can move and still be close enough to walk to work. Since by law I have to be the sole owner of the building, I figured that maybe the apartment could be one of your perks for managing all of the web and legal stuff and you could, I don't know keep people from burning the place down or something." I bit my lip and looked at Sean wondering how he would take the suggestion. Thankfully, he didn't seem offended.

"You would do that for me?" He asked, a half smile on his face.

"Of course," I told him. "Admittedly, if you didn't want to live there I would still shield wherever you lived even if it did bend the rules. You haven't been living with me just because of the shields, have you?"

"Of course not," Sean replied waving off my concern. "You are a great roommate. And since almost everyone in this building is at least a decade younger, living with you keeps me from looking like the weird older guy who lives alone. Of course if I did live in the building I would sort of be the building manager and therefore my age would make me look responsible. Are you sure you would be okay with that?"

"With you moving out or you moving into the apartment building?" I asked, relieved that he hadn't been offended by my question.

"Both I suppose," Sean said. "I know you bought it as an investment property so me living there as my perk for being your business partner would cut down on your profits."

"And it would insure my investment property was well looked after," I reminded him, remembering I never told him the building purchase was an accident. "Plus since you are going to be sifting through the applications for tenants anyway, I figure you will choose extra nice ones since they will be your neighbors."

"Oh, I get to pick my neighbors? That kind of power could go to a man's head."

I smiled. "Does that mean you are in?" I asked. "You can pick which apartment you want."

"I am so in," Sean said. He jumped up off the couch and gave me a hug. I laughed as he let me go and flopped back down onto the couch.

"Of course that means you will be the crazy single lady of this building, unless you were planning to take one of the other apartments."

"I hadn't thought of that." I told him.

"Now before I go into planning and packing mode, lord this means I have to actually find the back of my closet," Sean waved away the thought. "Before then, I want to hear all about Davis."

"There isn't much to tell," I replied with a laugh.

"Not much means there is still something," Sean said wagging his finger at me. "So I will pour us each a celebratory glass of wine, after all how long has it been since we've both had juicy gossip? And then you will spill your details and I will spill mine."

"I have the feeling yours will be much more salacious than mine, since Jake spent not just one but two nights here since being back in town," I told him as he popped up to open a bottle of wine. "Davis decided we shouldn't call the other night a first date since I had to deal with James and his issues with the current situation."

"Sounds fair," Sean said returning with the opened bottle and two glasses. He poured a generous portion into each glass and we settled in to compare notes on our current love lives, his qualifying more than mine as an actual love life whereas mine was still just potential.

When we finished, I rinsed out the wine glasses and left them to dry, recorking the half-finished bottle. Sean went back to his room and I could hear various bumps and thumps coming from his room. "I'm gonna miss this," I told Winston who looked like he was torn between watching me in the kitchen, hoping food would soon appear, and going to investigate what Sean was up to in the back. "But it's time, I suppose and he will be in a legally shielded place."

While the law may state I had the right to shield the homes of my under-aged relatives, it still frowned on apartments unless I met the criteria as I did with the Ravenwood. It also considered Sean a full-fledged adult capable of paying for what he wanted or needed. I would have shielded him anyway and trusted to the fact that few people, if any would be able to tell the apartment was shielded once I was done. In fact, I shielded the homes of all of those who worked in either the shop or Sean's office. Admittedly, they each lived in houses not apartment buildings so there would be little blowback should the shields be discovered. At best, I would be liable for the fifteen percent for each for the Commission. As their homes all met the criteria for shielding, it would just be a matter of money.

I decided that with Sean in sorting mode, I might as well give my own space a good clear out. I went into my room, opened my closet and frowned at the overstuffed space. Clearly I was overdue for a spring cleaning. I rolled up my sleeves and set to work.

The next morning I felt virtuous as I looked at the bags of items I planned to donate sitting in the corner of my bedroom. The things I found in the back of my closet astounded me. "I probably had enough Halloween costumes in there to outfit a squadron of partygoers," I told myself as I pried myself out of bed and got ready for Winston's morning run. "Who even needs that many wigs?"

The morning run blew the cobwebs out of my mind and I felt ready to face the day. After comparing schedules with Sean, and promising to keep my cell phone on during the day in case of emergencies, I headed off to the apartment building. Once there, Davis set me to work and left me alone.

The rest of the week passed in routine fashion, morning run, talk with Sean over coffee and working on various projects around the apartment building. The following week, I had to return to the workshop to work on a few pieces for one of our major clients and so missed the final two weeks of construction as Davis and his crew finished the work. At our apartment, Sean's belongings were slowly packed up and we made decisions about which furniture was officially mine and which items were officially his as he prepared to move. Winston started making circuits throughout the apartment, checking to make certain he hadn't missed anything when he was out on his walks. He stared at the accumulating boxes as though they were portents of doom and took to sleeping in front of the door in case we decided to sneak something past him in the night.

Cole and I were making a final check of the order to be shipped out and loading the last of it onto the waiting truck as Davis put in an appearance at the workshop. He watched as we finished up and as the truck pulled out I turned to him.

He held out the building's keys to me, jingling them like bells. "Construction's through and we are ready for staging. You have me, Scott and Mike to help with furniture moving as well as whoever you have ready."

"Nice," I replied taking the keys from him. In between working on the custom pieces for our client, I worked with Sammy to gather staging elements. Much was cribbed from our storage areas while other items were rented from a staging company to fill it out, after all we generally had only furniture, and the few decorative pieces we needed to stage our showroom on hand. It was the same company Sammy worked with to buy staging items for our showroom actually. In fact while some was rented, other pieces had been purchased so that we could use them in our show room displays once the apartments no longer needed the dressing, thus rotating our own stock and freshening the space.

"We are ready to go," I told him. "Everything is ready to ship over." I pointed to the store room. As I already talked to the staff and arranged for them to help, it was all hands on deck as we loaded the delivery van for the first shipment. It took several trips to get everything into the appropriate apartments and by the time everything was in place, the work day was over. Each apartment featured an ungainly heap of items.

"I'll be arranging them tomorrow," I told Davis as I let my crew go for the night.

"I can stop by and give you a hand," Davis said. Scott made a comment to Mike that I couldn't quite catch and both of Davis' brothers chuckled while he shot them a glare. The two men walked off unconcerned with their brother's ire.

"That would be nice," I told him. "We can get everything arranged and then Sean can take the pictures and decide which apartment he wants to claim."

"He hasn't decided yet?" Davis asked.

"No, he narrowed it down to one of the two-bedroom apartments, but wants to see it finished before he makes his final decision."

"I can understand that," Davis said nodding. "What are you doing tomorrow night after we get all of the arranging done and Sean takes his photos?"

"No plans, why?"

"I was thinking dinner," Davis said.

"As in a date?" I asked with a smile.

"As in a date. I figure arranging can't take all day and then we will each have time to go home, shower and change before I pick you up."

"I'd like that," I told him with a smile.

Chapter 16

I went home a short while later, my mind alternating between arranging the apartments and my dinner date with Davis. Excitement filled our apartment as Sean planned the last details of his move and I went through my closet. I studied my two favorite date dresses trying to decide which was more appropriate. I finally chose the blue one and made sure it was ironed, hanging it on the back of my door and pulling out the heels that went with it. As Davis had only seen me on construction sites or in the workshop, wearing appropriate clothing for the site and task I was performing, it would be quite a change from normal.

The next morning I woke up smiling. Even if everything went to hell, I still had that moment of satisfaction for a completed job. "And even if no one wants to rent the apartments, Sean has a place to live." I told myself. "And if they remain empty too long, I can take another one and Winston can roam the halls freely." Adding in the upcoming date just made the moment better.

Winston and I went on our morning run and when we returned, he made his circuit through the apartment while I filled his bowl with food and checked to see he had enough water. Satisfied that everything was in place, he returned for breakfast.

"This is going to be a hard week for him," I told Sean who looked sadly at Winston happily chomping away.

"I know," Sean said. "But I'll still get to play with him in the park right? You aren't revoking my Winston privileges are you?"

"Of course not," I told him. "I'm just not looking forward to the moping."

"His or mine?" Sean asked.

A little while later I headed over to the apartment building, arriving just as Davis pulled up. "Thanks for helping me to arrange things," I told him as I opened the front door.

"Not a problem," he told me. "It's kind of nice to see the thing through. Usually once construction is done I turn the empty building or house over to someone else. I don't get to see this part a lot."

I pushed open the front door and looked in the vestibule. Gone were the yellowed walls and bare wires. The walls were now painted a warm ocher which made the hanging light and the mail boxes stand out. The keys no longer dangled from the keyholes in the mailboxes. Instead they were on the large key ring Davis gave me, each tagged with their apartment number. The security door was closed and this time not only had a doorknob and lock on it, there was a security pin pad where the residents would have to type in a number to unlock the door. Davis walked me through the system and told me how to re-program the code when I chose. I typed in the current code and stepped into the hallway of the first floor.

The hallway now boasted pendant lights that matched the one in the vestibule and no longer required light from the open apartments to illuminate the space. While the sun still poured into the hall from the window at the end, I knew it would be well lit in the night.

"*Which is a good thing as each apartment has a door now*," I thought to myself as we moved into the first apartment and began arranging the furniture and other items trucked in the day before.

"So did you see *The Whisper* this morning?" Davis asked as we began shifting things around.

"No why," I said gesturing to where I wanted the couch. He picked up one end while I picked up the other and we moved it into place. I tried not to envy the ease with which his end was lifted.

"Wendy's article came out this morning," He replied.

"How did it look?" I asked, my stomach tensing up and nearly dropping my side of the couch. Since the interview I determinedly put all thought of it out of my mind.

"It was quite spectacular," Davis replied as he moved the coffee table. "You came out looking good, and I'm sure there will be a big buzz about this place."

"But," I asked as I hung a picture on the wall. "There is a but isn't there?"

"But," Davis continued as we moved around the apartment. "The article is likely to raise a few questions about the Commission. They didn't come off looking so hot. Neither did Malak or James for that matter."

"Really? I'm not surprised by Malak, but James?"

"It is quite the article," Davis said as we moved into the bedroom and rolled out the Turkish carpet I chose for the room. "You end up looking a bit…crusader-like."

"Crusader-like?" I asked as we shifted the bedframe into place.

"Yeah, finding ways around the system to help the little guy with apartments such as this."

"Why is that so crusader-like?" I asked butterflies dancing in my belly. "People buy investment properties all the time."

"You are only charging mid-range prices for these apartments."

"It's a mid-range district," I said frowning.

"But the apartments are shielded," Davis explained. "That makes them high-end even if they are located in the worst neighborhood in the city."

"Oh," I said frowning. I hadn't thought of it like that. We continued working, Davis taking directions as we made final adjustments and when finished, we moved on to the second apartment.

"Wendy did interviews with other people, asking how they felt about it. The apartment building that is. Most thought it was fantastic." Davis told me.

"Most?" I replied, my stomach turning into a pit of acid, killing the dancing butterflies.

"Bradford Addison, you know he's always advocating for a change in leadership," Davis said. I nodded, familiar with the man. "He wasn't pleased."

"As the last time he saw me he called me an imperialist dupe and an ignorant fool, I would imagine he would be pleased that I'm working on my own."

"Charming," Davis said frowning at Bradford's comments. "He apparently doesn't approve of you working on an investment property when there are so many of the elite who do not have shielded apartments. He thinks you should have offered to shield them before working on a property of your own."

"Does he not realize that would be illegal?" I asked.

"Apparently, he didn't and from what he said, doesn't really care, using it as another talking point for why the Commission needs change. Wendy and James both knew what he wanted was illegal and it was well pointed out making Bradford look a little foolish despite many people thinking the rules should change."

"Which I'm sure he loved," I said dryly.

"Probably not, but making him look foolish helps the Commission since he is the strongest advocate for a new world order."

"So even if they don't look so hot in the article, they at least look better than Bradford and his lot?" I asked.

"Basically."

"Well, that is something." I shook my head. "When we are done, I am so reading that article."

"I figured as much."

The two of us steadily worked through the building, making certain each apartment was staged appropriately. I tried not to worry about the article, knowing there wasn't much I could do about it. When we were finished, I called Sean to let him know we were ready for photographs. Instead of getting through to Sean's direct line, I got a busy signal.

"That's odd," I told Davis. "It should go to voice mail if he is on the other line or transfer to his assistant's desk." I tried dialing Gina's number and got a busy signal there as well. "Guess I'll have to walk over there," I said wondering if this was fall out from the article of if a band of rogue designers had taken over the building demanding the return of Art Deco and ottomans for all. Perhaps even now my cousin and his assistant had been taken hostage by Prismacolor pencil wielding hooligans. I shook the thought away.

"I can drop you off if you'd like," Davis said. "That way you will know what's up sooner."

"Thanks," I replied.

We locked up the building and I slipped into the passenger seat of Davis' truck. A short drive later, we pulled up in front of the office and shop.

"See you at seven," Davis told me with a smile as I unfastened my seat belt.

"See you then," I told him smiling back. I slid out of his truck and closed the door. As he pulled away I walked over to the door leading to Sean's office and let myself inside.

"Yes, the information will all be on the website and the website with be up before the end of the week," Gina said into the phone. All of the lights on her phone were blinking madly, indicating calls on the other lines. The usually calm and collected Gina looked slightly frazzled. When she spotted me, she waved me into Sean's inner office with barely a look as she switched lines to one of the other callers. I moved past her and into Sean's office.

"Yes, there is an application on the website and the website will be up before the end of the week," Sean was saying into his phone as I walked in. His head was tilted so that the phone was balanced between his shoulder and ear. His hands were busy at his keyboard as he tried to work the computer and the phone at the same time. He looked far more frazzled than Gina. He looked at me as I entered the room, eyes somewhat wild.

"This is insane," he said after ending his call and hanging up the phone. He ignored the ringing that began almost immediately as well as the blinking lights indicating every line was active.

"The article?" I suggested hesitantly, figuring I was to blame for the current dilemma.

"I haven't even had a chance to read it yet," Sean said. "But apparently everyone else in the world has. In addition to the calls, I've had almost five thousand e-mail requests asking about the apartments. At this point I'm just sending them a basic stock message to keep the server from crashing as more messages come in." He shook his head. "And the website isn't even public yet, I set up a separate e-mail account for the applications thinking we could keep things separate and we haven't even gotten that e-mail address out yet. I was going to post a notice."

Sean paused and took a deep breath. "It's insane."

"Okay," I said. "For the website to be ready we need the photos of the staged apartments right? Then it can be made public?"

"Right," Sean said nodding.

"And you have your digital camera ready to go?"

Sean opened a drawer, pulled his camera out and set it on the desk.

"Okay," I said, the constant ringing of his phone echoing through the office. "You go to the apartment building. Pick which apartment you want as yours, take pictures of the rest and we can get the website up and out." Sean looked from phone to computer, eyes wild. "I'll take over here while you are gone," I told him. "Then when the site is up we will set a pre-recorded message on the phones directing people to the website."

"Okay," Sean said running a hand through his hair. "Okay." He stood as I walked around to his side of the desk. He showed me the message he was copying and pasting into e-mails and covered the simple statement they were going over on the phone. "I would suggest letting them think you are one of the receptionists instead of the owner," Sean cautioned as he slipped on his coat and picked up the camera. "It keeps them a little more professional. The first few calls I answered with the standard 'this is Sean Appleton' and got a litany of horror stories pertaining to why they specifically needed a shielded apartment. I'm sure you would be worse off."

"Probably," I said nodding. "Thanks and once things are settled, we are both reading that article."

Sean left, looking a bit like he was fleeing the scene of a disaster, and I settled myself at his desk. I took a deep breath and picked up the phone. "Appleton Furniture, how may I direct your call?" I said into the receiver as my hands moved to the keyboard to begin replying to the swiftly multiplying e-mails. I listened to the caller and soon found Sean's stock phrases rolling out of my mouth.

"The application is on the website and the website will be up and running by the end of the week, please check there." I told the desperate sounding, apartment-questing man on the other end of the line. The call ended and I pressed one of the blinking buttons on the phone letting the next caller through the electronic gate. Time seemed to stand still as I repeated the same phrase over and over again, all the while sending out the standard e-mail response to interested parties. In the other room, I could hear Gina doing the same. There was no time for worry, regret or blame, just the endless stream of inquiries.

The afternoon pushed on and finally Sean returned, camera in hand. He took over the computer to upload the photos and finish the website while I continued answering calls. He muttered under his breath and I knew he wanted more time to fiddle with the photos and go through each one thoroughly making certain it was the perfect option. I knew from the creation and daily management of the Appleton Furniture website that Sean preferred to go through the photos separately, put the ones he wanted into the site, let it sit overnight and then look at it fresh the next day to see if he still liked the photos before even contemplating making the site active. I also knew there was a great deal of analyzing different shots for the perfect angle of presentation.

Today, there was none of that as Sean quickly clicked the photos into place completing the site and making it active. "Done," he finally called. He moved to the door. "Website is up, send them there," he told Gina.

"You will find all of the information along with the tenant application on the website," Gina switched her spiel, smoothly incorporating the new information with barely a nod to Sean. She gave them the website name and on the other phone I did so as well. Sean moved back to the computer, answering e-mails, the stock reply altered to reflect the change, while Gina and I continued answering phones.

We continued working frantically until the website availability had the desired effect and the calls began to slow. Sean managed to get ahead of the e-mails and sighed with relief as he no longer feared for the stability of the network. By the time the flood of calls dried to a trickle, it was close to normal closing time for the office. Sean went into reception and after having Gina set an outgoing message on the answering service, sent her home early. He then set the same message on his phone.

"So you haven't seen the article yet either?" Sean asked.

"No," I replied shaking my head. "I went straight to the building this morning and Davis mentioned it as we got to work. He said we looked good in the article, but not so much everyone else."

"Really?"

"Yeah, apparently James, Malak and the Commission look bad, but then Bradford made himself look stupid which might help with the fact we made the Commission look bad."

"Since he is the biggest threat to the Commission, making him look stupid helps them out," Sean replied nodding.

I looked at the phone and the computer for a moment. "I think we need to read the article."

"Yeah, but not here," He replied. "We are leaving the office in case anyone comes here in person looking for one of us instead of just going to the website. Personally, I'm surprised we didn't have people walking in to question us as well as calling and e-mailing."

"Yeah," I sighed. "Home is a better option." We both pulled on our coats and Sean began turning out the lights and closing the office for the day. As we stepped outside, I looked into the furniture store window. There were a couple of people browsing and Sammy was talking to someone at the counter. He was smiling and looked relaxed. Clearly the bomb that hit Sean's office had spared the showroom.

"Thank god for that," I muttered as Sean and I headed home.

Chapter 17

We arrived home a little earlier than usual and together, which was a rare occurrence and sent Winston into spasms of doggie delight. "He is not going to take this move well is he?" I said looking at Winston as he capered through the living room.

"About that," Sean said slowly. "Are you sure I should still move into one of the apartments?"

"Of course," I replied.

"But with all of the others…," He trailed off.

"And you not getting an apartment is going to leave room for all five thousand of them to cram in?" I replied, lifting an eyebrow at him.

"True," Sean said with a little sigh. "There are just so many."

"I know," I told him. I let out a small snort of laughter. "And I thought we were going to have trouble finding tenants."

"You?" Sean said. "This whole mess started when I called to try and *pay* for an advertisement." Sean chuckled and I joined him. Suddenly as though a dam had broken the two of us were both laughing like lunatics, tears streaming from our eyes, bent nearly double as the somewhat hysterical mirth came bubbling out.

Finally, the laughter tapered off and we both quieted. Winston barked once and then trotted over to the door, picking his leash up in his mouth and waiting for normality to resume.

"Okay," Sean said wiping his eyes and moving to the door. "I'll take Winston out and you start getting ready for your date. We can read the article together when I get back." It came out as half statement, half question, but I nodded in agreement with the plan.

"Deal," I told him. As he and Winston went off to the park, I headed to the shower.

By the time they returned, I was more or less ready to go. Giving my feet a break, I stayed barefoot, placing my heels next to the couch so I could slip them on at the last moment. I was adding a few basic items to my small clutch purse as Winston barreled through the living room. As Sean filled his bowl for the evening, Winston did his pass through the house making sure nothing had been removed in his absence.

"You know when we move your stuff to your new place, we might want to take him along to show him where you disappeared to," I said. "That way he might not freak out so badly when the stuff disappears."

"Might be a good plan." He looked over my outfit and made me turn so he could take it all in. "Very nice," he told me. "Better with the heels, but nice."

"Thank you." We both looked at the laptop on the kitchen table and sighed simultaneously. "Article?"

"Article," he agreed. Sean powered up the laptop and pulled up *The Whisper's* website, logging in with his password. "Oh," he said as it came up. "Front page. I thought I'd have to look for it in one of the sections."

"Front page?" I repeated feeling nervous. "I thought maybe lifestyle or local."

"It explains why we've been getting so many calls." Sean said. "Nice title too, *'Keeping the Shadows at Bay'*. That's going to catch a few eyes."

"I suppose we better hear it."

Sean nodded and began to read the article out loud. For the most part, it started off as I expected. Wendy covered my buying a building in a mid-range neighborhood and making the apartments blend in instead of making them high-end. She covered the legalities of why I could shield the apartment building in the first place.

"I'm not sure if that bit makes me sound protective or paranoid," I said as Sean reached the part where the three layers of shielding were described.

"I think she is going for both protective and making a point to the Commission since they don't always pay you to shield quite as thoroughly," Sean answered. "Especially considering this next bit. Listen, 'While this layered shielding, to many, seems unnecessary, reports show that attacks by the shadow creatures have risen by more than thirty percent in the last five years.' I didn't realize that."

"Me neither," I said frowning. "Although, it does explain why I'm now doing more than one shielding a month these days."

"Mmm," Sean said nodding, his eyes still on the screen. "Here's Bradford's bit," Sean said. He scanned the paragraph and chuckled. "Listen, 'When discussing the rise of attacks Bradford Addison called the rise abominable and expressed his distaste for the Ravenwood Arms Apartments claiming that Alice Appleton should work to shield those who truly needed protection rather than lining her own pockets. He went on to claim, "Many of the community's elite, even in her home town have no shielding on their apartments and she should be required to see to their safety before seeking her own profit." When this reporter pointed out the legal restrictions surrounding the shielding of residential properties, Bradford waved off such concerns claiming it was merely Appleton's lack of compassion that left these wealthy apartment renters shield-less.' Oh my, shame, shame Alice." Sean said shaking his head.

"I'll have to work on my compassion," I told him dryly.

"It gets better," Sean said. "She asked James about this as well. James confirmed that legally you couldn't shield those apartments as per regulation, that you rarely turned down a commission and if you did so it was due only to scheduling conflicts," Sean said paraphrasing the article. "In addition, he pointed out that the jobs you turned down were often undertaken by you at a later date when your schedule allowed it."

Sean smiled. "Bradford is not going to be happy about this part," Sean added. "She asked him about you too. 'When asked about Addison's claim that Appleton lacked compassion, Rutherford dismissed such claims. In her defense he cited her recent shielding of several schools claiming that so the shielding would be more affordable to these institutions she waived her fee, essentially donating her time and talents for the protection of the people.' Well, aren't you fabulous?"

"Yeah, I don't let monsters snack on little kids," I told him, somewhat uncomfortable with the praise. Keeping children safe was just something you did, not something that needed to be pointed out as extra. Sean laughed at me and continued through the article. Unsurprisingly, Wendy covered the trip she went on with me and the attack by the shadow creature while I worked. I came off looking calm and steady in the face of danger, so I was pleased she didn't notice my fear. The contractor on the site, Greg Timmons also received praise. Malak did not come off looking so well.

"Its official," Sean declared after reading the section. "It's no longer just my opinion, it is in the paper. I want to print out the article just so I can clip this part out and put it on the fridge." Sean looked back at the passage he just read aloud, reading it again with a grin on his face. "Malak is a 'surly, uncommunicative driver who instead of providing protection to Appleton while she works spends his time in the rented vehicle listening to audio books until she is finished with the task at hand. Of the eight Commission licensed contractors I spoke to who worked with Appleton on the properties she shields, three believed him to be only a driver and often wondered why the Commission would send her to the site without someone to watch out for her as she worked, given that her job by nature, requires making herself vulnerable to the shadow creatures. The other five could think of nothing complementary to say with regards to Malak. Their comments ranged from annoyed to nearly hostile.' I'm betting there were several four letter words in there as well." Sean added.

"As he tends to talk down to all of the construction crews when he deigns to talk to them at all, that would be a pretty safe bet."

"Do you think James will replace Malak?" Sean asked curiously. "I mean, I would in general, because if you are working on darkened construction sites you should have someone responsible to watch your back. Politically speaking though it could be interesting."

"You mean they would replace Malak claiming ignorance of the audio books and so they could say see, we aren't putting her in harm's way?"

"Something like that," Sean said nodding. "Of course we don't know why Malak was assigned to you in the first place, so they might have to keep him."

"Hmm," I said. A knock sounded at the door and I went to answer it as I thought about Malak's potential reassignment. I wondered if the new person would dog my footsteps, being over eager instead of grumpily distant. I wondered how Malak would respond if left to continue after reading the article. I opened the door and smiled as I saw Davis. "Well, don't you clean up nicely," I said as I let him in. Davis was wearing pressed dress pants, a buttoned down shirt, sport coat and necktie. His hair was neatly combed and he smelled vaguely of aftershave.

"I could say the same for you," he replied looking me over. "Although I believe the restaurant requires shoes on its patrons."

"Ah yes, I've heard of these fancy places and their obsessive shoe requirement," I told him as he stepped inside. I moved over to my shoes and slipped them on my feet. Sean and Davis shook hands and said hello as I picked up my coat from the back of the couch. Not wanting to fight with the closet in front of Davis, I excavated my dressier coat from its confines earlier.

"We're just going over the article," Sean told Davis.

"I take it you didn't see it earlier either?" Davis asked.

"Nope, by the time I found out, we were so buried in e-mails and phone calls I couldn't get to it. It will be interesting to see how this plays out."

"It certainly will," Davis agreed. "Ready to go?" Davis asked turning towards me.

"I am," I replied, slipping on my coat and double checking that my keys were in my clutch purse.

"You two have fun," Sean called, his eyes already turned back towards the screen to read the rest of the article. Davis and I left the apartment and went down to where he had parked. As he walked me around to the passenger's seat and opened my door I looked at his truck. "Did you wash your truck?" I asked noticing the lack of splashed mud and dirt from sanded roads.

"Drove it through a car wash," Davis said, smiling at me. He closed the door as I took my seat and walked around the vehicle to take his own place behind the wheel. "I didn't want to risk getting dirt on my one nice pair of pants." He told me with a wink.

"Well my dress appreciates it too," I replied, returning his smile. Davis started the engine and pulled away from the curb. "So where are we off to?" I asked wondering if we would be visiting a place closer to his side of town or mine.

"The Winery," he replied. "It's a bit of a drive, but not too bad. Good food, nice atmosphere."

"A bit of a drive? So neither your side of town or mine?"

Davis chuckled. "I would have to check the odometer, but I believe it is just as far away from you as it is from me making it neutral territory."

"An adventure for us both," I said.

"Because I have to ask," Davis said. "Why don't we get it out of the way in the car ride over, Sean said you guys got slammed?"

"Ah, the office. Yeah, remember how I was worried about not finding renters?"

"I remember."

"That's not going to be a problem. Both Sean and Gina, his assistant's, phones were ringing off the hook by the time I got to the office and Sean had over five thousand e-mails asking for more information. Apparently many of the calls came with heart wrenching stories." I shook my head. "I knew shielded apartments were hard to come by, but I didn't think it was that bad."

Davis shook his head. "You didn't get to the end of the article did you?"

"No," I replied. "Why?" I narrowed my eyes. "What don't I know?"

"Well according to Wendy's article there are less than three dozen people world-wide capable of shielding in any capacity, yourself included. At least twenty of them are retired, or nearing retirement and rarely shield anything outside of their own families. Of those that left, you are not only the strongest, but the only one even in your category. And to top it off, you are the only one who agreed to shield schools."

"What?" I replied frowning. "That can't be right."

Davis nodded. "Apparently the others cited scheduling conflicts when told the sum would be less than their usual fee. It's the reason the Commission changed the wording giving those who shield scholarship credits for their family members to the private schools. It's to encourage them to take the lower paid shielding jobs."

I shook my head and sighed.

"There's more."

"More," I asked.

"Only a little more," Davis assured me. "The reason the number of jobs sent your way has increased is not only due to the fact that the attacks have increased, but due to the fact that others turn more down, so they get offered to you," Davis told her.

"And since I only turn down for scheduling conflicts, often rescheduling the jobs for a later date even if I can't take them then, I do all the jobs others don't want to do." I finished.

"Apparently so. Also you seem to be the only one who has taken advantage of the loophole allowing you to buy an apartment building. Wendy couldn't find a single apartment building owned by anyone else who can shield."

"None?" I asked.

"Nope, not a single one."

"That's probably because they turn down jobs," I told him after taking a minute to process the information. "I used the extra money from those jobs to buy the building and pay for the renovation. Clearly since they don't take the jobs, they don't have the extra funds."

"Or they spend it on trips to Rio instead," Davis suggested.

"Maybe that's why I never seem to run into them," I returned, shaking away the dark thoughts the conversation caused to rise to the surface of my mind. "They're all in Rio. Perhaps I'll see them my next trip out."

Davis laughed. "When was the last time you went on vacation?"

"I go on vacations," I replied.

"Uh huh, you have 'classic workaholic' practically stamped across your forehead."

I sighed. "On occasion when I have to travel far afield for a shielding job I tack on a few extra days as vacation time. I'll have you know, about six months ago I spent almost a week in Prague."

"I'm sure Malak loved that," Davis said with a laugh.

"He grimaced at the schedule and didn't stay with me," I told him. "I have no idea what he did. On the final day of my vacation, James called and told me I was needed in Bucharest. I agreed to take that job for two extra days in Romania since I had never been there. He agreed and made the arrangements. Malak picked me up a little while later and once in Romania and the shielding job complete, he refused to leave his hotel room until our flight departed. He even took his meals inside. Maybe he thought vampires would get him. Or maybe gypsies. Personally I can't see either wanting to carry him off, but it sounds better than saying he was sulking because I threw off his schedule."

"Maybe he ran out of audio books," Davis suggested, a glint of amusement in his eyes. "So you wandered around Romania alone?" He asked.

"No, the contractor for the site I was sent to shield and his wife, Helena, showed me around since the shielding was actually the last thing needed on that project and there was a lag between it and his next one. I got to eat with them a few times. Helena made this fantastic soup. I wanted to smuggle a cauldron of it home with me. Trust me, I did not miss Malak."

"I can see that," Davis said nodding.

"So see, I take vacations," I replied. "Sort of. So what about you? When was your last vacation?"

"Around New Year's last year," Davis replied. "I went to Paris."

"For New Years? Sounds like fun," I told him. We shifted the details of the apartment building as well as the various issues it raised aside and passed the rest of the drive discussing trips, both business and pleasure as well as some of the fun and often times frantic happening's around them. By the time we pulled into the restaurant parking lot we were both laughing and in a good mood.

We entered the restaurant and were shown to our table. True to the name, the decor featured wine barrels and offered a large selection of locally produced vintages. The floor was made to resemble old cobblestone, the tables were covered in white cloth and low candles were arranged in the center of the tables. The table's elegance contrasted pleasantly with the designed rusticity of the rest of the room. The menu featured items where wine was often one of the components of the dish. We placed our orders and the menus were whisked away by an efficient waiter in black.

"So did they ever find your luggage," I asked, resuming our earlier conversation.

"Well they found a piece of luggage," Davis said with a grin. "And admittedly on the outside it resembled my bag, inside however was a different story. They were clothes designed for what had to be a very thin, rather short man. The airline rep insisted it was my bag, so I held up the pants, which only came to mid-calf."

"What did he say?" I asked.

"The clerk told me that he had heard that capri length pants for men were being touted by designers and complemented me on being fashion forward."

I laughed and shook my head.

"So figuring if the actual owner of the suitcase was found I could easily reimburse him for the dress shirt if nothing else, I slipped it on to prove my point."

"Oh no, it was a hulk-a-rific moment wasn't it?"

"All that was missing was the green skin," Davis said nodding. "Buttons went flying, seams pretty much exploded." Davis flexed for me as the waiter brought our wine. "It was quite something."

"And what did the clerk say to that?" I asked after the waiter left again.

"He informed me that sudden weight gain was cause to see my doctor," Davis responded with a laugh. "And when I got home I purchased a very lovely set of neon green luggage, which I decorated with personalized decals to ensure my bags looked like no other." We both laughed.

"My, doesn't this look cozy," a bored voice drawled from my left. Startled from our conversation, both of us looked to see Bradford Augustus Addison the fourth walking up to our table.

Chapter 18

While Bradford may not have been the last person in the world I wanted to run into tonight. He wasn't high on my list either. From the look on Davis' face, he wasn't entirely thrilled by the unexpected arrival either.

"Ms. Appleton," Bradford said with a slight, mocking incline to his head. His eyes hardened as they shifted to Davis. "Davis," he said, fairly biting the name off.

"Addison," Davis replied, his voice hard and flat.

"I expect you two are out celebrating the successful completion of your…little project together. I suppose congratulations are in order. I don't think I've seen you so clean since University, Davis. You must have soaked for hours."

"Surface dirt only takes moments to wipe away, Addison," Davis replied calmly, his voice edged with ice. "Of course, I doubt you would know that as you are only accustomed to the ingrained, soul-deep kind of filth that never actually leaves you."

Bradford smiled, the look resembling more of a bearing of teeth than a sign of amusement. I looked from one man to the other, feeling as though I was irrelevant. Clearly there was some history I was missing.

"Yes, well enjoy your moment in the spotlight while it lasts," Bradford said before turning around and walking off, nearly knocking over our waiter as he brought our meals.

"Well, wasn't that pleasant," I said. Our dinner plates arrived safe and sound and I put my napkin on my lap. "I take it you two have a history?"

"Yes," Davis said appearing to shake off his suddenly bad mood. "When you were…tested, you met others with your sort of …skills?" he asked, his words tempered for public ears.

"Yes, I did. One was tested with me and eight or nine others congratulated us after." I replied. "They were miffed that my young age made the celebration punch and cookies instead of one featuring adult beverages."

Davis smiled. "Well, Addison and I have the same category of skills and were tested together. He made a big deal about his bloodline and the reputations of his forbearers. And then I, the son of a mere builder, wiped the floor with him. He took it as a deliberate insult."

"Which it wasn't?" I asked taking a sip of my wine.

"Not then," Davis said shaking his head. "Later, it was of course. He started doing little things to me, my brothers, my cousins; annoying and irritating at first, kind of like Jimmy Lucas, but swiftly building to dangerous and painful as he was much stronger than Jimmy. I retaliated. He retaliated for my retaliation, which caused me to retaliate against his retaliation. And so on. Both of us flew under the radar, not getting caught. Barely."

"I'm sensing a point of no return situation? Something along the lines of mutually assured destruction?" I asked.

Davis smiled and shook his head. "It was heading that way by the time graduation rolled around. We were attending the same University. Luckily, we no longer had to see each other on a regular basis and with distance I was able to see just how badly our little feud could have gone. I've managed to reign in my temper ever since. Admittedly, it is helpful if I don't spend any time around him."

"So Bradford was born to be an object lesson," I said. "I always knew he had some purpose in life. I just didn't think that was it. You know he actually made me feel bad about not shielding his friend's apartment?" As we ate I told him of my run in with Bradford after the Fausti job.

"And that's when you became the imperialist's dupe?" Davis asked.

"I'm sure if asked he would tell you I became so much earlier and he just then pointed it out," I replied. "Then of course when I pointed out that to change things he probably ought to talk to the Commission rather than James as James only enforces the rules the Commission sets, I became an ignorant fool." I shrugged. "Of course, he probably thinks I was that earlier as well."

"If it helps, he said much nastier things about me," Davis told me. "None of which should be repeated at the dinner table."

"I don't think any talk of Bradford should be repeated at the dinner table," I said. "It promotes indigestion. Although I do wonder at the coincidence of running into him here. Tonight of all nights."

"It does seem rather coincidental doesn't it," Davis replied. "This place doesn't require reservations, but I booked one just in case, as it seemed a waste to drive out here and not get a table. That was after we made plans yesterday though. Not much time to figure out where we were going. Or me I suppose as I just made the reservation under my name."

"Which means if it isn't a coincidence, he was here for you and just was lucky I was here. Of course, he didn't have much to say to me. His snarky comments seemed aimed at you so my presence didn't really matter one way or the other." I said, thoughts spinning out into a web of intrigue. "Maybe he has your phone bugged and is determined to ruin your evenings out. Does he routinely cruise by your tables when you eat in restaurants?"

233

"Not normally," Davis said with a smile. "But after reading through the booklet of rules and regulations the other night, I did request an application for a permit to work with you," Davis said. "I wanted to see the exact details of what might be required if I did submit it on behalf of Davis Construction before I talked details with you."

"Sounds reasonable," I said nodding as I tried to corral some peas with my fork.

"I'm sure someone logged my request. After the article came out, it wouldn't take a genius to see why I might be interested in securing a permit. For all he knows I lured you out to dinner not only to celebrate the completion of the Ravenwood, but to convince you to work with Davis Construction on a more permanent basis." Davis blinked coquettishly at me.

"Oh my, you mean this is a permitting ruse instead of a celebration," I said with mock dismay. "Such deceit." I laughed. "Of course," I said in a more normal tone. "Bradford wouldn't know about that. Or he shouldn't anyway. Permit requests would be logged into the main Commission office, wouldn't they? So unless someone there told him you put in a request, he wouldn't know."

"You're right," Davis replied. "I thought the request would go to James, but it didn't go to the regional office, it went to the main one."

"I think it is supposed to prevent favoritism in the regions," I said vaguely recalling a conversation. "I remember Jeffrey was upset once because someone he didn't like passed some sort of inspection when he would have kept the man from passing."

"Well since James would probably deny me a permit if I do apply, I suppose it is just as well. Of course that also gets around Bradford as he is from our region as well."

"This is true," I replied.

"Who is Jeffrey?"

"Jeffrey Dobson," I said. He had James' job before James."

"Ah," Davis said nodding. His eyes slid past me and he lifted an eyebrow in surprise. "And speaking of James," He said softly.

"No," I answered resisting the urge to turn around and look. I might be willing to believe Bradford was a coincidence, but both Bradford and James stretched coincidence a little too far for me to believe. Davis nodded slightly.

"Mr. Davis," James said from behind me. "And Ms. Appleton, how lovely to see you both. I hear your project is complete so congratulations are in order, I expect. I see you are marking the occasion appropriately. I won't keep you of course. However, I was asked to pass on a message to you both. Tomorrow afternoon your presence is required in my office, two pm. Ms. Appleton knows the way if you need directions, Mr. Davis. A Commission representative will be there to meet with you both. I believe Ms. Watts' article will be the topic of choice. I will see you both there."

Without waiting for a response, James turned and left us. "Nothing like getting marching orders," I said.

Davis cocked his head to the side. "I don't think the Commission gave him any details."

"He did seem rather put out by the meeting," I replied. "However my last few conversations in his presence have been in the exact same tone. Actually usually Malak gives the reports so with the exception of the phone conversation when he ordered me out with Wendy; I don't really add anything to the conversations so I'm not certain you could call them conversations."

"And if him showing up he was pure coincidence, I'll eat that candle," Davis said.

"I think the candle is safe from tooth marks," I replied with a smile. "I would like to know how they knew we were here though."

Davis looked down at out plates. Both of us had managed to finish most of our meals. "How do you feel about desert to go?"

"I think that might be the smartest idea," I replied. "God only knows who will show up next at this rate."

Davis managed to flag down our waiter and in a short while we were on our way out of the door, chocolate cake filled clamshell box in hand. We reached Davis truck and at the edge of the parking lot we could see James and Bradford in conversation, their words puffing white around them like cartoon comic bubbles. Davis sighed.

"You know I'm tired of people thinking this is just a general celebration," He told me. He set the cake down on the hood of his truck as James and Bradford noticed us near the vehicle. Davis slipped his arms around me and looked down at me as I tilted my face up to him. "This is a date." He bent down and kissed me. This was not the chaste kiss from the other night but log, passionate kiss that sizzled the blood. I was surprised I didn't burst into flames where we stood. When we broke apart, Davis pulled back slowly as though reluctant to let go.

He took a shaky breath that sounded like I felt. He took a step back and picked up the boxed desert. Davis opened the door for me and handed me the box before walking around to his side of the vehicle. I fastened my seat belt as he got in, settled himself and turned the key in the ignition.

"So was that just for show," I asked noticing that Bradford and James were staring somewhat slack jawed at the truck as Davis pulled out of his parking space and headed towards the exit.

"The audience was just a side benefit," He said with a smile. "Or an excuse to do what I wanted to do anyway."

"I see."

"I'm also glad I don't have a roommate," he told me.

"Are you, and why is that?" I said in a half teasing tone.

"So we don't have to share the chocolate cake of course," He said as he turned out of the lot and onto the street. "And because chocolate cake is best when eaten naked."

"Is it?" I said with a laugh.

"Of course, it's a proven scientific fact," Davis replied. "You can't argue with science."

Chapter 19

The next day I knew I wasn't going to get anything done in the workshop and dressed in wool slacks and a nice sweater so I wouldn't look out of place in either Sean's office or later when meeting with James. Since I knew the location and Davis had the vehicle, he was swinging by to pick me up so that we could go together. Even though I knew the day was likely to be filled to the brim with insanity, I smiled on my way to work thinking of the night before and the science of eating chocolate cake.

Knowing it would leave a kink in Sammy's schedule, but seeing no way to avoid it, I left a note for the manager. I left it next to his calendar, since that is where he would first look, and hoped for the best. Then I went to join Sean in his office. While Gina was staring at her phone as though daring it to ring, nothing else seemed amiss. It was almost as if the explosion from the day before had not occurred.

"Good morning," I said almost making the greeting a question. Gina looked up from the phone and smiled.

"Good morning," she returned looking less frazzled than the day before. "He's expecting you so go on in."

"Thanks," I replied, glad things looked relatively normal on the surface. I walked past her and into Sean's office. Sean was seated at his desk, the phone already in his ear.

"Yes, I will pass the message along," Sean informed whoever was on the other end. He scrawled something on a note pad. "No I am not certain of the timeline yet, but I will let you know. Thank you. Yes. You have a good day as well." Sean hung up the phone. He looked up at me. "How do you feel about Chicago, or Sacramento, or Montreal for that matter?"

"Thinking about running away?" I asked.

"No just fielding questions from real estate agents," Sean said tapping his pen on the notepad.

"Real estate agents?"

"Yup, wanna buy a second apartment building?" Sean asked. "I now know several people looking to sell and it's not even nine am."

"Got anything in the easy commute range," I asked half-jokingly.

"Several," he answered.

I blinked in surprise, my smile disappearing. "Really?"

"Really," Sean flipped the page in his notebook and handed me a list of several names and numbers. "They all want to know when you plan to buy your next building, after all it is a property group."

I lifted an eyebrow at him. "Yes," he said waving away my unspoken comment. "I take full blame for the name. I just didn't think people would expect expansion so soon."

"Maybe they'll be satisfied if we add another one," I told him not really able to muster the anger for an argument as I was the one who got us into the whole mess in the first place.

"Two more at least," Sean replied. "A couple is two. You need three or more to be a group I think."

"Well the one or two more will have to wait until after my two o'clock meeting. Or I suppose I should say our, as Davis was summoned as well."

"Summoned?"

I quickly filled Sean in on both James and Bradford crashing my date the night before.

"Yeah, there is no way that is a coincidence," Sean said. "Although James really could have called for that instead of ruining your date."

"I wouldn't say ruined," I replied with a grin. "But yeah, I'm not buying the whole coincidence thing either."

"Uh huh, I thought you got in pretty late. And while I desperately want to needle you about it, that will have to wait."

"Definitely," I agreed. "Although building the real estate empire will have to wait too, at least until after two and the fallout from the Commission is dealt with, we do have quite a list."

"First on the list is sorting through tenants. I've been printing out the applications and I've begun to rank them." We talked about the possible tenants and all of the details involved with choosing between the reams of applicants.

"I think we need to get you into your apartment as fast as possible though," I told him. "Not only because I think you should be settled before we even think about actually becoming a group, but because someone should be in the building."

"In case we get whatchacalit…squatters," Sean said nodding. Stories from the landlord website I pulled up at the beginning of this project swam through my head in a sickening wave. The thought that any squatters my building would attract would have likely come with magical abilities of their own did not bear thinking about.

"And in case the Commission comes up with some sort of issue," I told him worried about what my meeting would entail. "Even if they tell me they are horrified by the idea of the apartment building, I can at least tell them I already have someone moving in so we are moving forward on occupancy rather than just letting it sit empty, even if they forbid me to do another one."

"I'm taking off early today to start my move," Sean said. "I know I was planning for Saturday but I figured a day early couldn't hurt. Or half a day anyway."

"I'm surprised you didn't take all of today off to get it done this morning," I replied.

"I just couldn't take the whole day today without knowing what the office was going to be like," Sean replied. "I couldn't just leave Gina here on her own."

"That's probably why Gina has never plotted to sneak into our apartment and kill you in your sleep," I told him.

"Probably," Sean said with a smile. "Now about Winston." We discussed dealing with the dog during the move and then shifted back into sorting through the applications, Sean periodically pausing to take calls. The first two categories were simple. While a lot of the applications were from those in town or who were planning to relocate to our fair city in the near future for a job or the University, others lived elsewhere. Those from elsewhere who hadn't been planning to relocate before the apartment building became available claimed to be willing to relocate should they get one of the apartments. Deciding we were not planning to start a migration Sean and I eliminated those applicants shifting them to a separate pile.

I felt oddly guilty as we began to cull the stack down to something manageable. I had to constantly remind myself that while attacks were on the rise, a set of stout locks usually kept the shadow creatures outside. Apartments above the first floor even kept them from looking in the windows as I had never heard of any instance where the shadow creatures could climb.

"*Admittedly until recently I hadn't heard of any attacking power cords,*" I thought to myself feeling another stab of guilt. "*Maybe they are evolving.*" The thought was not a pleasant one.

"I wonder where they come from in the first place," I said aloud, half to myself.

"Who?" Sean asked looking up from his stack of applications.

"The shadow creatures," I told him. "I mean they have to come from somewhere don't they? I mean there aren't just a finite amount of them in the world. There can't be," I thought an idea occurring to me for the first time. Usually I concentrated on not thinking about the shadow creatures at all. "I've seen them disintegrate into ash, so unless the ash blows away and then reforms into another shadow creature when no one is looking, they can die."

"You saw one turn to ash?" Sean asked sounding curious. "Who did that?

"Davis," I told him remembering I didn't tell him of the shadow creatures attack in front of our building. "It was on the morning I shielded his brother's house." I left off the location, letting Sean think the attack occurred elsewhere. "It was kind of cool actually. Not the terrifying attack part, but the turn to ash part."

"I'd kind of like to see that," Sean said. "Well as much as I'd like to see any shadow creature. So maybe I'd like to see that from a distance with binoculars. Or maybe on film. I don't suppose Davis has ever been attacked while carrying a video camera?"

"Not to my knowledge, but I'll ask," I told him, still thinking about where the shadow creatures came from. "People other than Davis have to be able to kill them," I said. "Yet we aren't running out of them, so they must reproduce somehow."

"That's a disturbing thought," Sean replied.

"Well the article did say that attacks were on the rise," I said. "That would mean that either there are more of them than there were before or like other formerly wild areas humans are encroaching on their territory."

"They could have breeding grounds," Sean said. "Wouldn't that be a nightmare to stumble on," He shivered and we both realized the conversation was scaring us both, like a horror story told around a campfire. Not that I had ever sat around a campfire before. The closest I came was roasting marshmallows over the fire in the living room fireplace.

"That is enough of that," Sean declared. "Otherwise I'll have nightmares for weeks." He tapped the stack of papers. "To the tenants or possible tenants." The two of us went through the applications until noon, slowly whittling down the pile. At noon, we each grabbed a quick sandwich and headed back to the apartment. Winston was overjoyed to see us and when Sean's friends started arriving to assist with the move, he thought it was a party just for him and greeted each new arrival with over the top enthusiasm. His happiness lasted until they started taking boxes out of the apartment and into the van downstairs.

My job was to keep Winston under control. I clipped his leash on to his collar and we made a nearly continuous circuit between the apartment and the moving van as Winston watched Sean's things being loaded up. When everything was loaded, I walked Winston over to the Ravenwood Arms and we watched the process in reverse as Sean's belongings were ferried out of the van and into the new apartment. While I was on my date the night before, Sean and Jake stripped out the staging items, taking them back to the store. As we approached two o'clock and the time for my meeting in James' office drew near, I was forced to leave Winston in Sean's new place since he refused to go back to the apartment.

Wondering how events would play out, I walked over to the furniture store, arriving as Davis was pulling up. After a quick check with Sammy, I climbed into the truck and we headed out.

Like me, Davis opted for mid-range sprucing in his attire for the meeting. He was wearing dress slacks and a buttoned down shirt, but no tie or sport coat.

"You look worried," Davis said as he drove.

"More for Winston than the Commission," I told him with a smile. "The Commission will either yell at me for doing something that is completely legal or tell me not to do it again even though it was legal. Winston however is not exactly thrilled with Sean's move."

"I thought he wasn't moving until tomorrow?"

"That was the plan, but having someone already living in the building when the Commission was concerned about the building sounded like a good idea"

"That way it looks like it's already getting settled and the uproar is dying down," Davis said with a nod. "Nice. The uproar is dying down?"

"Mostly, especially now that the website is up. People are filling out the applications and sending them in rather than blowing up the phone lines." I shook my head thinking about how desperate some of the callers had been. "I don't suppose you know where the shadow creatures come from do you?"

"Not a clue," Davis replied. "I do know someone who might know, but I also know that once she started looking into it she fell into the Commissions bad graces."

"The Commission didn't want her to look into it?" I asked puzzled. "Why?"

"I don't know and truth be told I'm not sure if that's what got her in their bad graces to begin with, the timing might just be coincidental as I'm sure at the time she was probably doing several other things they weren't too happy with."

"Oh," I replied.

"Today might not be the best day to go asking the Commission about the origin of shadow creatures," He advised.

"Probably not," I agreed. "In all fairness though, I wasn't really planning on asking them anything. When in James' office I tend not to talk much at all."

"That does tend to be the smartest course of action where the Commission is concerned."

We arrived at the airport and Davis parked. It felt strange to arrive without luggage, but I shrugged it off as the two of us went inside and walked down the corridor to the office. Without the sound of the wheels on the luggage, our walk was ominously quiet. We entered the office and I was surprised to see Bradford paging through a magazine while seated in the waiting area. He looked up as we entered, eyes narrowed in annoyance. He turned the page of his magazine so fiercely the page almost tore, but he didn't say a word as he turned his eyes back to the magazine.

"They are expecting you," Marcie said politely to us. Her eyes darted nervously to Bradford before returning to us. "You may go right in."

I nodded and Davis followed me as we walked into the inner office. I half expected Bradford to rise and follow, but he stayed seated. I wondered why he bothered to come to the office at all as Davis pulled the door shut behind us. There were already two people in the office, James was of course one of them. He sat behind his desk looking extra banker-ly in his three piece pin striped suit; glasses already perched on the end of his nose. Today he had even added a pocket watch and the silver chain glinted as he stood to greet us. I found my eyes oddly drawn to the silver chain, thinking it a strange addition.

"So glad the two of you could make it," James said, his tone more pleasant than any turned my way in the past few months. "Alice Appleton, William Davis, I would like you to meet the Commission Representative, Michael Townsend. Mr. Townsend," James continued. "This is the owner for the apartment building and the contractor in charge of construction."

"Pleasure to meet you both and thank you for agreeing to this meeting on such short notice," Townsend said, not bothering to stand. James gestured to the two empty chairs and resumed his seat behind the desk. I took one of the chairs and Davis took the other.

"I see no reason to beat about the bush in this matter, if you do not mind some directness?" He asked. I nodded but he was already proceeding, the question more for formalities sake rather than because he wanted our agreement. In fact he didn't really seem to be looking at us, instead gazing at the middle ground between us. I fought the urge to frown at him, keeping my face a neutral mask of polite attention.

"While everything you have done is perfectly legal and beyond reproach, admirable even," he continued, his tone slightly grudging. "It has caused the Commission some concern." His lips twitched as though he wanted to smile, but wasn't accustomed to the sensation and couldn't complete the act. "Wealthy people can become quite difficult to deal with when they feel they have been slighted."

Townsend looked at Davis instead of the empty space between. "Mr. Davis, your application for a permit to work with Ms. Appleton to create shielded properties has been approved." He gestured towards James who picked up a file and leaned forward to hand it to Davis. Davis took the file and looked at Townsend.

"I haven't filled out the application yet," Davis said with a slight frown. "Let alone sent it in for review."

Townsend ignored his statement and turned to me. "Ms. Appleton, while you will no doubt be kept busy with both the projects James arranges and the projects you collaborate on with Davis Construction, I expect you will be working on more apartment buildings in the area. After all, the paperwork your lawyer filed labeled you as a property group. One property does not a group make. To settle things a bit we ask that one out of every three buildings your…group shields be scaled to the more affluent members of our community. That way you have two buildings for whatever economic scale you wish and one that will allow us some reprieve. We have taken the liberty of drawing up a press release to be sent to <u>The Whisper</u>." He gestured to James, who picked up a piece of paper and held it out. As Davis was closer he took it from James and handed it to me.

I scanned the page. Even though it was a fairly simple statement, I found my temper building as I read it. I bought the Ravenwood Arms by accident and, making the best of my mistake, I paid to have it renovated so it could be rented out. Now the Commission was issuing a press release essentially pledging me to purchase at least two more apartment buildings in the next six months.

While I knew I had the savings to do so, depending of course on the buildings, and thinking of all of the applications Sean and I were going to have to turn down once the seven available apartments were filled I was fairly certain I would work on another building. I just hadn't thought about doing so before actually having Ravenwood rented. Any vague thoughts I had involved giving the apartment building I currently owned a year or two while I learned what was needed to be a landlord and recouped the funds I put into the building before moving ahead. The Commission apparently wasn't planning on waiting a year or two for me to purchase my next building.

I looked up from the page to find Townsend studying me as though actually awaiting my response. "I'll have my lawyer look it over and get back to you," I replied before I could stop myself. James blinked in surprise and Townsend lifted his eyebrow in reaction.

"Alice," James said a note of rebuke in his voice.

"Of course," Townsend replied, startling James. "If you could have him contact us no later than close of business Monday it would be appreciated. He took a business card from his pocket, stood, took two steps in my direction and held the card out to me. "Any changes he makes to the statement can be e-mailed to the address on the card. If there are any questions he, or you have, please do not hesitate to call." I took the card, glancing at the info it contained before looking up. "Mr. Malak will, for the moment, continue to accompany you on the Commission projects. He has however been rebuked and his behavior corrected. I hope you bear him no ill will. A pleasure meeting you Ms. Appleton, Mr. Davis," he said.

Apparently this signaled the end of the meeting as he turned and walked to the door. James stood as he turned the doorknob and let himself out. Davis and I stood and turned towards the door.

"I trust you will be sensible Alice," James said. I frowned allowing my irritation to show.

"Aren't I always?" I replied. I walked to the door, Davis following, attempting to hide his smile. Bradford was still in the waiting room and he looked up as we left the inner office, an expectant look on his face. Whatever he saw on our faces didn't thrill him and his expression soured.

"You may go in now Mr. Addison," Marcie told him as we reached the door. Davis opened the door and we left as Bradford walked in to meet with James.

"How much do you want to bet that he arrived thinking he could sit in on our meeting and was told by Townsend that he had to wait outside?" I asked as we walked away.

"That would be a sucker bet," Davis said with a smile. "As would be betting that Addison expected us to be chastised severely."

"Yeah, he was clearly expecting us to be yelled at," I replied nodding as we exited the building and walked to the truck.

"Speaking of yelling, I wonder how Malak's rebuke went," Davis said. We got into the vehicle and after fastening seatbelts, he piloted us towards my side of town.

"I'm more concerned with his post rebuke reaction," I replied. "He's already quite surly, I'm sure this won't help any."

"True," Davis agreed. "I have to say though, this is the first time I've ever had an application approved before I've even filled it out. Of course I hadn't actually decided if I was going to fill it out. I was supposed to meet with our board on Monday to go over the paperwork and reach a decision."

"This isn't going to cause you any trouble is it?"

"It shouldn't," Davis replied. "After all, just because we have the permit doesn't mean we have to use it."

"This is true," I replied.

"Besides you are going to be very busy in the near future and not only with those two buildings you are supposed to purchase. I'm betting the number of people who call the Commission for shields is soon to go up."

"Probably," I said resigned. I had the feeling I would be pulled more and more away from the furniture store in the near future. I also had the feeling a conversation with couple of my part time employees about more full time employment might be in my near future.

"Just promise me one thing," Davis said.

"What's that?"

"Before you buy your next building, let me take a look at it so we can get a scope of work *before* you purchase it. That way we can actually set a proper construction schedule."

"Deal," I replied. "As long as you give me fair warning before you accept jobs involving my shielding so Sammy doesn't explode from scheduling trauma."

"Deal," he replied. "Now let's do something important and make sure Winston isn't traumatized. After all, Miss Sensibility, you need to have your lawyer go over your press release."

"That sounds like an excellent idea," I replied smiling at him.

Follow Alice's continuing adventures in

The Gilded Lily

Coming in 2016

www.valeriegaumont.weebly.com

Printed in Germany
by Amazon Distribution
GmbH, Leipzig